An Invisible Nemesis

Mal Foster

AN INVISIBLE NEMESIS

Copyright © 2019 Mal Foster

First published in 2019 by Frigsake Publishing

This book or any portion thereof may not be reproduced or used in any manner whatsoever without the express written permission of the author or his publisher except for the use of brief quotations in a book review. The right of Mal Foster to be identified as the author of this work has been asserted by him in accordance with Section 77 of the Copyright, Designs and Patents Act 1988.

This book is a work of fiction. Names, characters and incidents are used fictitiously and are products of the author's imagination. Any resemblance to actual people, living or dead is entirely coincidental.

Cover Design by Oliver Bennett at More Visual Limited

'Suzanne' by Leonard Cohen lyric excerpt Courtesy: Sony/ATV Music Publishing PLC

ISBN: 978-0-244-79113-1

All rights reserved.

To someone who is still very precious...

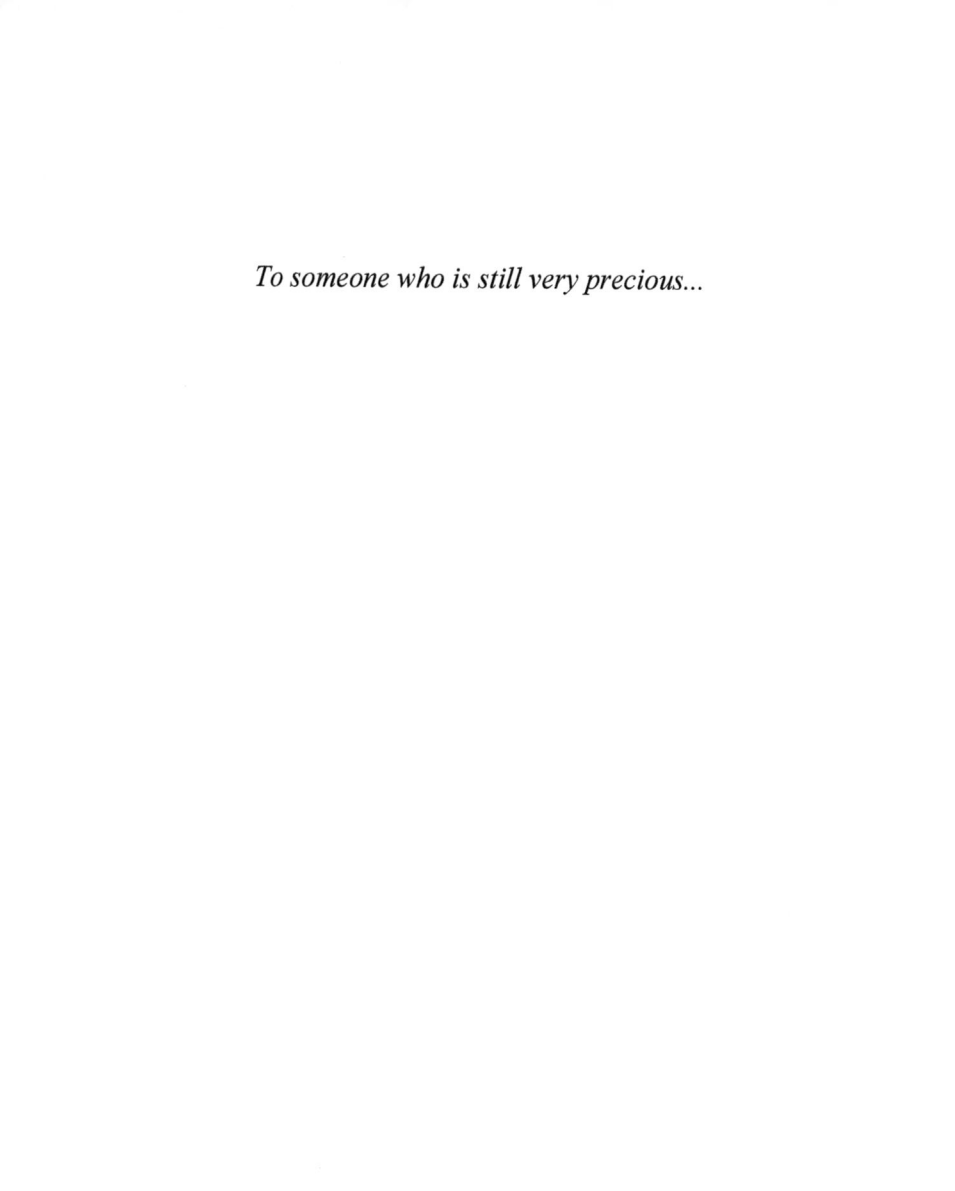

"There are crooks everywhere you look now.
The situation is desperate."

Daphne Caruana Galizia
[1964-2017]

ACKNOWLEDGEMENTS

Very special thanks to Michelle Emerson and Alessandra Maio.

Thanks also to Andrew 'Frankie' Franklyn and Rachel Saker.

AUTHOR'S NOTE

I've been visiting Malta, particularly its smaller sister island, Gozo on a regular basis since 1988. The archipelago with its unique landscape of volcanic rock, salt pans, sun-blanched countryside and 17th century coastal watchtowers is steeped in history and is set in the beautiful Mediterranean Sea just a short distance south of Sicily (Italy). Its people are always welcoming and friendly and to me, it feels like a second home. Sadly though, all is not well in my personal paradise.

Since it gained independence from the United Kingdom in 1964, Malta has developed a dark under-belly. It has been alternatively governed by the conservative Nationalist and the social-democratic Labour parties. Both parties have very close ties to the country's most powerful families, including some with very strong mafia connections.

The lines between police, justice and business are often blurred. Malta's economic success, especially since it joined the European Union in 2004, has been largely based on tourism, financial services, tax avoidance schemes, shell companies and online gambling.

Corruption is rife throughout, and even Malta's prime-minister, Joseph Muscat was forced to call a snap general election in 2017 in an attempt to clear himself and his wife of any wrong doing. Almost inevitably, the corruption goes on and the unjustified killings and harassment of those who attempt to expose the truth continue.

Thank you for taking an interest in my writing.

1

'JACK... call me back as soon as you get this, mate!'

It was a rude awakening, a frantic message left in my voicemail box. It was my old colleague, Rick Storey, calling from Malta. The news was devastating. It usually is bad news when he phones me but this was the worst news ever. Suzanne Camilleri, my good friend and kindred spirit, was dead. Murdered!

I worked with Suzanne at the *Sunday Herald* in London until we got fired in the wake of the phone-hacking scandal in 2011. Fortunately, neither of us was implicated, but all the same, it was extremely disappointing and, to say the least, very annoying. After that, Suzanne went back to her native Malta to work as an investigative reporter for both television and the press. Rick later went to work in Malta as well. As for me, I eventually managed to find myself a niche as a freelance journalist, working from home and sporadically submitting articles and features to a number of broadsheet newspapers and magazines as well as some bits for the local press.

Suzanne had been a great friend of mine since the late 1990s, but because she was married we could never be as close to each other as I would have liked. I last saw her two months ago when I was on holiday in Gozo where she lived. She came to the Grand Hotel in Għajnsielem and we enjoyed a few glasses of red wine on the patio which overlooks the picturesque harbour at Mġarr. She told me she was slightly concerned that her continuing investigations into a cold case we had once both worked on might have some serious impact and cause her some very unwelcome problems. She was also convinced that someone had been following her. I told her not to worry. But I guess the naiveté of my well-intended advice didn't really help.

The cold case we had been working on when we were together at the *Herald* unfortunately lacked any hard evidence, which prevented us from netting the scoop that we had been hoping for. The eventual shutdown of the paper scuppered everything. Despite this, Suzanne recently said that she was determined to follow up a new lead involving the Sicilian mafia when she could find the time. The facts behind the story, if proven, could be an international revelation and would certainly cause major wholesale embarrassment to the UK government, the royal household and the UK security services as well as the Government of Malta. It could also be the one of the biggest stories reported internationally for years.

Suzanne was a tall slender woman with long brown hair, deep brown eyes and an electric smile, always accentuated with her trademark red lipstick. She was a loving person and had time for anyone. In contrast, professionally, she didn't take any prisoners and harboured a direct, no-nonsense reporting style. Most people respected her for that, but she did have her enemies. I needed to make some sense of it all, find out why she had been killed so mercilessly. I needed to know why someone actually wanted her dead. I felt that I needed to bring some justice, and hopefully some closure, to her family.

I've met her husband Peter a couple of times. He's wheelchair-bound these days, so doesn't get about as much as he used to. They have a son and a daughter: Adam, who is in his early twenties, and Lorca, who has just turned 17. I had to get to Gozo as soon as I could but needed to speak to Rick again and gather as much information as possible before I travelled.

Rick emailed me his latest report which was included in today's *Malta Telegraph;* it makes for some disturbing reading:

Maltese Journalist Suzanne Camilleri Murdered

> *The award-winning journalist, who once led an investigation which implicated the Government of Malta and the UK government with corruption between them and the Sicilian mafia, was killed on Tuesday by a car bomb on the road to Ramla Bay in Gozo.*

Suzanne Camilleri died just after 11.30am when her car, a white Toyota Starlet, was destroyed by a powerful explosive device which blew the vehicle into several pieces and threw the debris down into the valley on a bend close to the new cemetery at Triq Ghajn Qasab, Nadur.

In the wake of the car bomb attack, no group or individual has yet accepted responsibility.

Former president Marie-Louise Coleiro Preca called for calm and said, "Once again, in these moments when the country is shocked by such a vicious attack, I urge everyone to think about their words very carefully, to not pass judgment and to show solidarity."

This was a repeat of a message made by Coleiro Preca, following a similar attack on another journalist, Valerie Farrugia, on mainland Malta in 2017.

Commentators, since the last General Election, have been fearing a return to the political violence that rocked the country during the 1980s. In a statement, Prime Minister Joseph Muscat, condemned the 'sheer evil of the attack', saying he had asked senior officers in the police to reach out to other countries' security services for help in identifying the perpetrators.

"Everyone knows that Suzanne Camilleri, like others before her, was a harsh and aggressive critic of mine and our government," added Muscat at a hastily convened press conference, "but nobody can justify such a barbaric act on any individual in this way."

Muscat announced later in parliament that FBI officers were already preparing to travel to Malta to assist with the investigation, following his request for outside help from the US government and others.

A Nationalist Party representative, Jonathan Melia, once himself the subject of alleged negative stories by Camilleri, claimed the killing may be linked to her somewhat colourful style of reporting. He said in a statement, "She takes no prisoners, what happened today is not an ordinary killing. It is a consequence of the total collapse of the rule of law which has been happening in Malta for the past six or seven years and is *heavily influenced by the will of the Sicilians and by some from beyond, even some in Britain and America."*

The journalist had submitted her final story to the Telegraph only the day before her death.

Officers stated she could not yet be formally identified as forensic scientists were still combing the fields down in the valley for body parts, although her torso had been retrieved soon after the explosion.

Mario Xuereb who owns the Ramla Bay beach café a mile from the scene, told the Telegraph, "We heard the explosion from down here, there wasn't a cloud in the sky so we knew it couldn't be thunder. The shooting range up on the cliffs is closed this week and the bang was too loud to have come from there anyway. I was told the road back up to Nadur was closed for over five hours and people had to take the long route round to get back to Mgarr for their ferry," he added.

Camilleri, who always claimed not to have any political affiliations, was best known in media circles to have been close to revealing some kind of cover-up while investigating the death of Diana, Princess of Wales, in 1997. It was a potential conspiracy she had been chasing ever since her time with the Milan News Agency and later with the Sunday Herald in London. She was once named as a 'person of interest' by a senior officer at the Ministry for Home Affairs and National Security, solely because of her so-called obsession with the British royal family. Many thought it was just a matter of time before she exposed one of the biggest ever international cover-ups, fully implicating the UK government and others closer to home.

There have been several assassinations targeting journalists in Malta and elsewhere during recent years and the perpetrators have never been fully identified. All potential suspects had been released without charge. Police on this occasion are keeping an open mind, but the question remains, why was Suzanne Camilleri killed so brutally and what, if anything, did she actually know?

Suzanne Camilleri was 52 and leaves a husband, son and daughter.

The report is quite comprehensive and it must have been very difficult writing something up when you actually know the victim so well. As a journalist myself, I know you can't always print everything, so I thought I'd give Rick a quick ring to find out what else, if anything, he knew.

'Rick, hello, it's Jack.'

'Jack, so sorry to bring you that news, my old mate, it wasn't easy but I had to tell you as soon as I could. I know how close you and Suzanne were.'

'Yes, it's been a great shock and I still can't comprehend what's happened. Is there anything else you know that wasn't in your report?'

'Well there is since I filed the item: a witness has told the police she saw a black car with British number plates driving up the hill from Ramla Bay and stopping by the monument shortly before she heard the blast. It could be a red herring, but officers now believe the car bomb was set by a remote device and are linking the vehicle to their enquiries. They have a number of officers down at the ferry port at Mġarr and they're scouring the island for a car of that description. A four-door saloon, an Audi or Mercedes they seem to think.'

'That's very interesting. Are you going to do any follow up reports?'

'I would, but this is my last week in Malta, I've been here since the end of 2011. I travel back to England at the weekend to take up a new post with the *Saltash Chronicle*.'

'*Saltash Chronicle*?'

'Yes, in Cornwall. I've got a job as a sub-editor there. It's close to where my old mum lives. She was diagnosed with the big "C" a few months ago and doctors don't expect her to last that long, a year or two perhaps.'

'I'm so sorry to hear that.'

'You might remember, my sister Hannah died with it some years ago.'

'I do. I'm really sorry your mum has ended up with it as well.'

'It is a worry. Anyway, one more thing you need to know is that last week Suzanne received some new information on the missing woman story she'd been following. I didn't report it as it would have been more trouble than it was worth. Someone phoned her out of the blue. When I spoke to her she was very excited but hadn't had time to *something big and now she has been silenced, simply for doing her job. My finger points firmly at the government!"*

He also shared his father's concerns about the investigation, which he said, "appears to be focusing only on supposition rather than examining more important evidence that could and should be available to them. They don't seem to have the intelligence or the will to look in all the right places."

He also suggested corruption from within the Pulizija itself could intimidate potential informants.

"My mother had her finger in a lot of criminals' pies and rattled their cages. One of those criminals jumped out of the pie and then decided to kill her."

The most significant investigation by the murdered journalist was that she was known to have been following up a bizarre conspiracy theory, following the death of Diana, Princess of Wales, during her time with the Milan News Agency and the Sunday Herald in London but nothing was ever published. The Government of Malta has said they are now offering a €1m reward for information related to the killing.

A top Italian prosecutor, Maria Allegranza, has said she believes the murder could be linked to an investigation she was leading when she was a police detective, involving the disappearance of a UK national in Venice, in 1997. "I remember I met with Mrs Camilleri a couple of times while making my enquiries," she said.

Stephan Di Canio, a senior Italian politician and judge who was a prosecutor in Italy's anti-corruption Mani Pulite trials in the 1990s, said he believed Mrs Camilleri's murder had all the hallmarks of a mafia-style killing but said he was trying to keep an open mind on this occasion. When interviewed yesterday, he told the Telegraph, "The Government of Malta had to be involved, and for them to offer a €1m reward implicates them in the killing very much. Once again, I think they're mediating between the dark forces of something quite sinister and have probably been paid quite handsomely for their troubles. It's 'guilt money' and €1m is just a drop in the ocean to them. It was a professional and classic mafia-style homicide. The target was not only Suzanne Camilleri, but all those around her because it was a clear warning: be careful or you'll suffer the same fate."

Di Canio's words echo the sentiment of Peter Camilleri where he states the killer's intent was, perhaps, an indirect declaration of war on our freedom of speech, and even, our democracy.

The investigation continues...

I'd also been online to see what else I could find. Some of it made for interesting reading. A Malta-based blogger called "Herman the German" suggested the investigation was not as solid as it should be because it lacked a motive and an accessory before the fact. The three suspects had all been arrested on the basis of word of mouth and local gossip. There was certainly no hard evidence against them.

Most reports suggested police detectives were following up leads from two very different sources, 'two-pronged' as they called it; stories which, whatever Suzanne had access to, could be the reason behind her death.

She did mention her concerns when I last saw her but she was always very protective when it came to sharing information. Someone must have known what she was on to, however, and I think they were responsible for arranging the car bombing... but who?

I found some other news reports. They confirmed Suzanne's white Toyota Starlet was blown off the road to Ramla Bay by a remotely triggered device. She loved that little car and refused to change it, even though she could have afforded a top of the range Porsche or BMW. 'If I had a posh car, I would only crash it, and what a waste of money and a load of hassle that would be!' I remember her telling me.

A police report confirmed the bomb was made up of a TNT component and detonated by text from a hi-tech smart phone. Officers are investigating further. It was also confirmed the explosion happened on Tuesday at 11.32am. Suzanne would have been on her almost daily trip to Ramla for her usual coffee at Mario's beach café and a swim.

'Whoever killed her knew her movements pretty well,' a police inspector said. That statement worried me. Someone must have been following her movements for quite a while. She was a creature of habit, even back in our *Sunday Herald* days.

Another piece of information gained from her family reveals how the police were already aware of an attempt on Suzanne's life. She had contacted them a week before, fearing she was being followed. She saw this as a potential threat to her life but officers didn't take her seriously and refused to follow up her claims.

On the Nadur Council website, Giovanni Mifsud, the Mayor of Nadur, stated...

> *'I am completely shocked by the incident. We have seen record numbers of tourists visiting Malta, particularly Gozo, in recent years. Vast improvements to the country's infrastructure enabled this and we can now boast one of the most reliable transport systems in Europe. That wasn't the case as little as ten years ago. Everything was a mess and the island was still quite isolated. The killing of Mrs Camilleri is particularly devastating news for us as a village community. Of course my thoughts are with all her family.'*

3

The flight from Gatwick was completely full as usual. I sat next to a couple of expats who had emigrated from England to Malta in the late 1980s. They were on their way back after visiting their daughter, Heather, who apparently lives near me, so it all made for a reasonable and light-hearted conversation and the flight seemed to go quite quickly.

On arrival, it took longer than usual going through customs. An elderly Scottish guy in the queue quipped it had something to do with Britain not wanting to be in the European Union, or the Common Market, as he called it.

It was still quite early, 7.15am, so I had nearly an hour to wait at the airport before the next bus to the ferry port at Ċirkewwa. Whilst waiting, I sat in the bar and treated myself to a bottle of the local lager. It gave me time to open up my laptop and read through some of my notes.

I had planned to stop off at the Mater Dei Hospital at Msida after pre-arranging an early meeting with Dr George Borg. He is the Head of Pathological Studies at the university which is based at the hospital. I was hoping he would let me view Suzanne's body, or at least tell me what kind of condition it was in. I wanted some form of closure, and as macabre as it sounds, I needed this. I suppose all I really wanted was to say a personal goodbye to an amazing lady. I knew it would be difficult.

I arrived at the hospital just before 10am. It was a large, intimidating building. Beige bricks, a regimented window design and a very tall cylindrical chimney. A woman in a light blue uniform pointed out where I needed to go for the pathology department, although a hearse parked outside gave the area away. When I entered, I introduced myself to a smart, young receptionist who spoke excellent English. She told me she had lived and studied in London during her teens and early twenties.

'I'm thirty-three now,' she said rather proudly.

Eventually Dr Borg emerged and guided me through to his office.

'So you're Jack Compton. Your visit here intrigues me,' he said.

I smiled. 'I suppose it does, but I have a number of reasons for being here and I need some answers. Suzanne Camilleri was a good friend. Very good, in fact, and I need some definite closure.'

'Were you lovers?'

'No nothing like that. There were too many things in the way, and besides I never really knew what kind of feelings she had for me, if any. I was always too scared to ask, and apart from that I had to respect the fact she was married. I know her husband.'

'You should never be scared, you only have one life and you should live it. Now, tell me why you're really here.'

'I was hoping to be able to view Suzanne's body before it is given over for your scientific research.'

'Impossible. The cadaver was only released to us very recently and it's not all in one piece. There is nothing to see.'

'Cadaver?'

'Yes, cadaver. It's the medical term given to a human body that has been donated for scientific research. This lady's cadaver is unique to us. It's the first time the university has ever received one in such a condition. It will be preserved in its current state. We will be able to teach students what happens to the human body when it is traumatised by an explosion such as the one which killed your friend.'

'Traumatised? That's a rather understated way of putting it!'

'Just medical jargon, a term we frequently use here at the university,' he said.

'Do you get many bodies being left here for scientific research?'

'Yes, quite a few, and did you know that 65% of those are British? It's a desperate gift.'

'What do you mean by "desperate"?'

'Many claim to be non-religious. To ease the burden on their families, many foreigners choose to donate their bodies to us. It is a very simple process and only needs one form to be signed with two signatures. One is that of the eventual donor and the other, a witness.'

'So what do you do with all the bodies?'

'The bodies are used for learning purposes and to also provide research opportunities. We receive on average, fifteen cadavers a year. Like I said, many are British and come to us straight from the morgue. There is no formal service, although sometimes a memorial without a body may be held at one of the local churches.'

'So, do you use them to show students how to perform post-mortems?'

'Autopsies, yes, but we also use them for dissection so that our students can study all parts of the human anatomy. We also use cryogenics in collaboration with other universities in the United States.'

'Are you saying that one day you will be able to bring someone back to life?'

'Yes, one day. As research continues I believe it will be possible, but probably not in my lifetime.'

As we walked back to the corridor I thanked Dr Borg for his time. I had told him I was here to find out why Suzanne was murdered and he wished me luck with my investigation.

'Ah, just one more thing before I forget,' he said as he reached into the right hand pocket of his white coat and pulled out a small translucent surgical bag.

'Take this, I found it secreted in the lady's private parts. It was obviously missed by police forensic officers. Please don't say where you got it from.'

I was intrigued and as I left the building I could see the bag contained a small black and red USB stick. This could hold all the information I've been looking for and may explain why Suzanne had been killed. She must have known something was going to happen to her quite imminently which is why she'd hidden it where she did.

I caught the next bus down to Ċirkewwa for the ferry over to Gozo. It gave me time to think and plan my next move. Work out who to see and what questions to ask.

There is always something magical about arriving on Gozo and it's just a short walk up the hill to the Grand Hotel from Mġarr Harbour. Just before I entered, I glanced across to the patio where I last met with Suzanne. It all felt very poignant and I could feel a huge lump in my throat.

'Room 566, that's the one you had before with the nice view, isn't it Mr Compton?'

'Ah, yes, thank you, you have a very good memory.'

It was young Rita, the receptionist. She'd apparently worked at the hotel for a couple of years and immediately seemed to remember me from my last visit a couple of months ago, which I felt was strange. I think she's related to Joseph, who owns a popular wine bar somewhere in Victoria. Suzanne, I believe, used to know him quite well.

When I got to my room I hurriedly opened my laptop and plugged in the USB stick. It took quite a while for everything to kick in. I could see there were several files but they were all encrypted in a programme called VeraCrypt which I didn't have. I couldn't break the codes so it all became quite frustrating. The original version of VeraCrypt is an old piece of software dating back to the 1990s which was quite popular with journalists for storing their work securely.

It was a dilemma. I didn't want to tell anyone I was in possession of possible evidence that could lead to solving who was behind Suzanne's murder. Well, not yet anyway. I decided to do a Google search to see if I could find anything. It helped a bit. I found a useful item which confirmed I may only need one password to access all the files but I still needed access to the appropriate software.

I reminded myself that I still had to visit Suzanne's husband, Peter, in Nadur and offer my condolences. It was going to be a very difficult conversation but one that had to happen, even if only for my own peace of mind. I was hoping he might be able to throw some extra light on what had happened, especially as I didn't speak to him the other day when I phoned. Perhaps he could tell me a little more than what he's already told the Maltese press and more importantly, the police.

4

After breakfast I decided to walk up to Suzanne's home in Imnarja Street, Nadur. When I got to the house, Peter seemed quite happy to see me as I leant forward to shake his hand.

'Come, come inside, it's good to see you,' he said as his daughter, Lorca, also came to the door.

From the outside, like most Maltese farmhouses, the front facade looked quite drab. Inside though, it resembled a palace, extremely plush, with lovingly polished marble and stone. I could see Suzanne's influence with the soft furnishings. The house definitely had her mark all over it.

'I'm very sorry for your loss, Peter. Suzanne was a great friend and someone I always enjoyed working with. I learned a lot from her when we worked together at the *Sunday Herald*.'

'Yes, she spoke of you often, towards the end, even more so. She had uncovered some new information on a case you were both working on many years ago. She told me she had attracted some unwanted attention. She was fearful someone had been following her but couldn't prove it. The police weren't interested when we contacted them and now my poor wife is dead.'

'The case we were working on was loosely linked to the death of Princess Diana. That was back in the late 1990s. I know she had uncovered some recent new information. You don't think her death was anything to do with that, do you?'

'Anything is possible and it's the one thing she mostly spoke about over the last few months. Over the last couple of years, she had been reporting on alleged corruption between the Sicilian mafia and the Government of Malta; but her interest waned as other journalists competed for reports. She had a desire to follow up on something more unique and the Diana story was something she couldn't leave alone.'

'Is it true that a car with British plates was seen just before the bomb went off?'

'Yes, Adam and I had seen it a few times but we thought no more of it. One thing, though, the driver didn't look British. I seem to remember he was always looking down at something, probably a mobile phone.'

'Did you tell the police?'

'Of course, but they were dismissive. They accused Suzanne and me of being paranoid and told us not to worry. How fucking wrong they were!'

'Didn't the police eliminate the car from their enquiries when they found out it was being driven by British tourists?'

'I heard that, but it probably wasn't the same car that we had seen. So, Jack, why are you here?'

'I'm here to try and find out why your wife has been killed. The Diana aspect of what she was investigating is something we had in common. It goes back to our *Sunday Herald* days. I believe she now had some new information and I think she was definitely on to something. She was convinced, as time went by, there was some kind of conspiracy involving the UK government.'

'Only the night before she was killed, Suzanne had pulled out her original article on the death of Princess Diana in Paris from when she worked at the news agency in Milan. Here, take a look, it's dated 1st September 1997. It was wired to newspaper offices all over the world.'

Peter then handed me a copy of the original press communiqué...

Princess Diana Killed in High Speed Car Accident

<u>From: Suzanne Camilleri, MINA (Milan International News Agency)</u>

Diana, the Princess of Wales, was killed shortly after midnight in a car accident in a tunnel by the Seine in Paris, France. The accident also killed Emad Mohammed Al Fayed, the Harrods heir, and their chauffeur, Henri Paul.

Diana's death was formally announced by the Interior Minister of France, Jean-Pierre Chevènement. The Princess died shortly after being hospitalised in intensive care at the Pitié-Salpêtrière Hospital in south east Paris. The emergency ambulance was stopped en-route while attempts were made to resuscitate her, but all efforts by medical staff later proved to be unsuccessful.

The bodyguard to the Princess, Trevor Rees-Jones, a German-born former British paratrooper, was seriously injured. A police spokesman at the scene stated, "The vehicle was being chased by photographers on motorcycles commonly known in media circles as 'Paparazzi', which we have reason to believe is the likely cause of the accident," while a spokesman for the Prefecture of Police added, "Several motorcyclists were detained for questioning after the crash."

The Princess, who turned thirty-six on 1st July, was divorced from Prince Charles, the Prince of Wales and heir to the British throne, last year. She had been on holiday with Mr Al Fayed, 41, the son of the controversial Harrods's owner, Mohammed Al Fayed, on the French Riviera earlier this month and had been expected to return to London yesterday to be with her two young sons, the Princes William and Harry.

French radio stations reported that a spokesman for the British Royal Family in London expressed anger and said the accident was predictable because photographers relentlessly pursued the Princess wherever she went. Another report suggests the visit was brought forward a week to avoid such harassment by the press. The move had apparently caught the British and French governments on the hop, as not all usual security measures could be put in place in time.

The accident happened at around 00.35hrs in the Alma Tunnel, on the right bank of the Seine under the Pont de l'Alma. The chauffer, Henri Paul, was hired from the Ritz Hotel in Paris. The Princess and Mr Al Fayed had been pursued from the Ritz Hotel, where they were believed to be staying after spending time together on the Riviera.

Police in Paris have said the Interior Minister, Jean-Pierre Chevènement, and the Prefect of Police, Philippe Massoni, had accompanied the British Ambassador in Paris to the hospital where the Princess was treated.

Witnesses have said the car is a total write-off. The force of the impact caused the car's radiator to be hurled on to the front passenger seat. The Princess was travelling in the back seat of the hired vehicle.

The site of the accident, in the Eighth Arrondissement, is on a high-speed road along the Seine with a divided roadway as it passes under the Pont de l'Alma to the Place de la Concorde.

On August 21st, Diana and Mr Al Fayed, who is of Egyptian extraction and is more commonly known as 'Dodi', flew to the French Mediterranean resort of St. Tropez for their third holiday together in just five weeks of courting. Mr Al Fayed's father told the Associated Press only last week that Diana and Dodi "were simply two young people getting to know each other."

Diana first met Mr Al Fayed almost ten years ago when he and Prince Charles played polo on opposing teams. Films he had produced or co-produced included the 1981 Oscar-winning Chariots of Fire, The World According to Garp, F/X and Hook.

A well-known multimillionaire, Mr Al Fayed had homes in London, New York, Los Angeles and Switzerland. He also maintained a garage full of luxury vintage and modern cars. He was divorced after a marriage that lasted just eight months in 1994.

Diana was elevated into the public eye at nineteen-years-old in 1981, when it was announced she was engaged to Prince Charles, twelve years her senior. The couple were married on 29th July that year in London in what was dubbed a fairy tale wedding, watched by millions on television.

Diana became a mother to Prince William in June 1982, but by the birth of her second son, Harry, in September 1984, her biographer Andrew Morton wrote in Diana: Her True Story, that she was already suffering from bulimia and had allegedly attempted suicide five times.

From 1986, the first press stories began appearing of cracks in the marriage, and Mr Morton later wrote that Charles had resumed his relationship with a married friend, Camilla Parker Bowles, at that time.

'The thing she spoke about most was that the ambulance had stopped for a short time on its route to the hospital. This has always been the trigger for her interest in the incident and Suzanne just wouldn't leave it alone,' said Peter.

'I remember her mentioning that to me when she joined us at the *Sunday Herald* a year later. I was never sure of the relevance. I saw TV images of the ambulance but nothing looked out of place.'

'She was adamant that if a conspiracy had taken place, the ambulance was a key part of it. She spent hours and hours looking into it. Just recently, I think she stumbled on something. I think she may have opened a whole new Pandora's Box of nasty surprises.'

I could sense a mixture of rage and emotion and perhaps some nervousness in Peter's voice and became concerned, so I called Lorca over.

'Don't worry. He's been like this ever since Mother was killed. He's angry and grieving and it's not easy, is it, Papa?' she said.

I then realised there was no sign of Adam.

'He's gone to Valletta to see if he can identify any of the three suspects the police have in custody. He's not holding out much hope and they will probably all be released if he doesn't recognise them,' said Lorca.

At this point I decided to make my excuses and leave.

'Look, thank you for coming to see us, Jack, it means a lot. Suzanne thought a lot of you. She was very fond of you. She was always very loyal to me, particularly since my diving accident. As I'm paralysed from the waist down, I wouldn't have blamed her if she had strayed. She had an incredible sexual appetite. The last ten years must have been very difficult for her.'

It was an odd comment, particularly as it came from Peter. I wasn't sure if he was just fishing to see if anything had happened between me and Suzanne so I decided not to respond.

'Thank you for your time, Peter. I'm sorry it's taken your loss for us to be able to get together again for a proper chat. If I find anything out, I promise you will be the first to know.'

He smiled and wheeled himself through to the back room of the house while Lorca showed me to the door.

'Jack, like Papa says, my mother always thought a lot of you. She told me once she had the greatest respect for you. Papa was always cruel to her but had to rely on her so much after his accident. She always wanted to take me and Adam to live in England but it was never to be. She felt she had to stay here and look after Papa,' she whispered.

What Lorca had said affected me and I felt somewhat numb. I had to find a bar and quick. I needed a drink. Fortunately the Gebuba wine bar in Nadur Square, just around the corner was open.

I sat outside with a bottle of beer watching the people and the traffic. I looked up at the sky. I needed to think, and re-examine everything that had just been said.

5

After what Lorca had told me, I found it very difficult to sleep last night. There had been a religious festival, a "feast" as they're called, on another part of the island. People were coming back to the hotel as late as three in the morning, which is about the time I must have drifted off.

    I remember having a recurring dream. It was Suzanne. She was sitting on a rock at Dwejra by the sea, near where the Azure Window used to be. She was smiling and waving and shouting something but because of the sound of the waves lashing against the rocks I couldn't hear her words. As I moved closer, she moved further away. Suddenly a big wave came and she was gone. I saw the sun move slowly across the sky until it became an orange glow... and then the sea became calmer. Suzanne came back. It looked as if she had grown a serpent's tail. This time I could hear her clearly. 'Lorca' she was saying. 'Lorca'. 'LORCA!' And then she was gone again just as a seagull landed on a rock beside me.

    I couldn't make much sense of the dream. I had never been to Dwejra with her and wondered why she was calling out her daughter's name. I must have gone over the same dream sequence three or four times before first light flickered through the window, and the sound of workmen shouting and laughing down in the street below woke me up.

    It was my last full day on Gozo. I remembered Suzanne had a good friend called Rosie, 'my confidante', as she used to call her. Rosie runs the drinks kiosk down at Hondoq Bay which overlooks the smaller island of Comino. I decided to take the scenic route from Mġarr

Harbour along the coast. The cliff tops were crumbling away, so parts of the walk were quite treacherous.

When I reached Hondoq, no-one was in the water. There was a red flag. I looked closer and not for the first time, I could see the sea was full of jellyfish. Because of this, the kiosk was quite busy. I had seen Rosie a few times before and remembered her as being a short rotund woman with swept back chestnut coloured hair and a squint. I wondered if she would remember me. When the time was right, I approached.

'Hello. Please could I have a bottle of Cisk?'

'Two Euros, please.'

'Excuse me, you're Rosie, aren't you?'

'Yes I am. I'm Rosie, have we met?'

'We've spoken before. Last time I was here, there was a thunderstorm and I sheltered here for about an hour. We were talking about how the weather can change so quickly here in Gozo.'

'Ah yes, I remember now, you're the English newspaper reporter. Are you enjoying your holiday?'

'Well, sort of. I'm here because of the murder of my friend, Suzanne. I believe you knew each other.'

'Yes, we went to school together, we've known each other since we were both babies. Our mothers were also very good friends. I was so deeply shocked by what happened. I had to close the kiosk for a few days and only opened up again recently.'

'Do you think she may have known who was after her?'

'Suzanne used to tell me everything. She was very worried someone had been following her, but wasn't sure why.'

'I'm currently looking at a British connection, something to do with the death of Princess Diana in 1997.'

'Oh that, I think she had been besotted with what had happened to Diana that night in Paris for as long as I can remember. She was working for a news agency in Milan at the time. I remember her phoning me and saying there was something not quite right and that she was following up some leads.'

'Was there a recent development concerning the case, do you think?'

'She told me another journalist, who I also know, had recently contacted her about a missing person. Some new evidence was supposed to have emerged about a woman in her mid-thirties, but I'm not sure what, Suzanne never said, probably because she wasn't too sure herself. A British woman had apparently gone missing in Venice. It was a few weeks before Diana was killed. Suzanne believed there could be a connection. I do know she was supposed to be a Diana look-a-like. Suzanne later came across a picture of the woman in Italy and immediately made a comparison, although no-one else did at the time.'

'This is all very interesting...'

Just then, I realised there was a long queue developing behind me. I thanked Rosie for her time and stated I may be back on the island again quite soon.

'Goodbye, and good luck,' she said with a little smile as I stepped away.

The walk up towards Qala was a steep one. At the top of the long and winding road there was a church, the Church of Immaculate Conception of Our Lady. I paused for a rest, which gave me another chance to admire the view. My arthritic left knee was almost killing me, even though I was wearing a surgical support. As I was walking along, I stopped to speak to an old man in a heavily stained white vest who was polishing one of the old Gozo buses which had been taken out of service a few years ago.

'This is my pride and joy. I drove it all around the place for over thirty years. My nephew is driving it to England for me next week. I just sold it to a collector there for 20,000 Euros.'

I had always loved the old buses ever since my first visit to Malta as far back as 1988. It was a shame to see them replaced by a more modern fleet.

I carried on with my walk to Nadur and couldn't help thinking how friendly everyone was. My plan now was to spend a few hours at the Gebuba wine bar and the Rabokk pizzeria mixing with the locals to see what else I could find out about Suzanne. She was very popular in Nadur and used to be a member of the Nadur Council.

In Nadur Square, a stage and mic stands were set up ready for an evening of entertainment. A well-known Maltese band, "The Buckskin Boys" were due to perform and some local musicians were providing the support. At the wine bar, there were a few familiar faces I remembered from my previous visit.

'Hey, Jack,' shouted a voice.

It was Rita from the hotel.

'This is Joseph, Joseph Buttiġieġ, my uncle,' she said.

'Hello, Joseph, yes, I remember you, how are you?'

'I'm all good, very good, well, I think so anyway. I'm still in shock about Mrs Camilleri. We don't expect that sort of thing to happen here in Gozo, certainly not to such a lovely lady,' he said almost apologetically.

Throughout the evening, Suzanne's name was mentioned quite a few times but no-one came up with anything I didn't already know. By now it was dark and the music was in full swing. There was a long queue for the hog roast and people were coming out of the Rabokk clutching their pizzas.

After the music had finished, I decided to walk down the road to the hotel at Għajnsielem. The buses were being diverted away from the square because of the concert. It was a pleasant evening and the stars were all quite prominent. I kept looking up, thinking of Suzanne. I was serenaded by the sound of what seemed like a million cicadas humming in complete unison as I passed by the farmland overlooking the sea.

When I got to the hotel, I stopped at the bar.

'Cisk?' asked the waiter with a smile.

'Ha, ha, you know me too well, but not on this occasion,' I replied.

'Then what can I interest you in?' he asked as he offered me the drinks menu.

'Victoria Heights.'

'Red or white?'

'Red, most definitely red. Just the whole bottle and a glass, oh, and please charge it to me, Room 566.'

I ventured outside on to the patio at the front of the hotel and found the table where I had sat with Suzanne just a few short months ago. I needed some quality time to reflect. She was such a beautiful person. I had always felt there was a strong sense of something between us but circumstances would never allow anything to happen. I had always wondered if Suzanne felt more, but now I will never know.

6

This morning I felt quite sombre. I sat in the window of the breakfast room at the hotel. I could barely eat, but my hunger got the better of me. Scrambled eggs, sausages, hash browns and baked beans. The view over the harbour was magnificent as usual, bright sunshine, blue sky and the sea was a colourful mosaic of activity, fishermen returning with their catch, tourist vessels and other daily commerce. I was absorbing the moment just as a young blonde guy in a purple polo-shirt and lime green shorts asked if he could join me. All the other tables were taken.

'Are you a regular here?' he asked.

'Yes, sort of, I come here as often as I can. I love Malta, particularly Gozo.'

'I've been working here for a holiday firm for the last few months. I find it okay but the money isn't great. I'm planning to go back to Australia soon,' he said.

'So that would explain your accent then.'

He laughed. 'Yeah, that's right, mate. By the way, have you noticed there are very few seagulls in Malta?'

I guessed that he was just trying to make polite conversation.

'No, I can't say I have. I've never really noticed. I wonder why that is.'

'I was speaking to a Canadian tourist yesterday. He's some kind of ornithologist. He reckons that because the Maltese have a reputation for shooting any bird in sight, including protected species, the seagulls have got wise to the fact and stay away from the islands.'

'This is all very interesting. I'm flying back to Gatwick later, and now you've told me all this, I'll probably spend most of my time on the bus to the airport looking out for seagulls.'

He grinned. 'Well, have a safe journey, mate, and thanks again for letting me share your table.'

'No problem.'

Just as I got up to leave, I noticed the logo on his top, Acrol Holidays Limited. I was drawn to it for some reason, but couldn't figure out why.

When I went to check out of the hotel, Rita was at the reception desk.

'Hello, Jack, have you enjoyed your stay?'

'Yes thank you, well as much as I could, given the circumstances.'

'Are you coming back?'

'Yes, soon I hope, very soon.'

'It'll be nice to see you again. Have a safe journey home.'

'I will, you take care as well. Please say goodbye to Joseph for me.'

She smiled. 'Of course I will.'

There is something special about Rita, she is always very friendly when I see her and seems to have a good memory. She appears to have taken an interest in me for some reason. Perhaps she's just intrigued by what I do. Maybe she knows something about Suzanne, I should have asked. Too late, I was on the ferry.

The trip across the Gozo Channel was brief. About twenty minutes. I spent the whole time at the back of the ferry watching the dome of the church up in Nadur fade into the distance. It always feels quite sad when leaving the island. I was also looking out for seagulls.

On the plane I kept thinking about what could be on the USB stick Dr Borg had given me. I was becoming itchy and nervous. Not knowing the password was frustrating. I knew I needed to crack it and soon, and I needed to somehow download the VeraCrypt programme from somewhere as well.

About an hour into the flight all eyes were on the air hostess as she came through with the trolley. I bought a couple of small bottles of red wine with my last remaining Euros. The plane was somewhere over Northern Italy and I began to think about what Rosie had said about Suzanne investigating the disappearance of a woman in Venice in 1997. I also remembered Rick's second news report where he said an Italian prosecutor claimed she had 'crossed paths' with Suzanne around the same time. I was trying to make the connection when something suddenly dawned on me.

LORCA... the password had to be Lorca! Unfortunately my laptop was in the hold of the aeroplane with my other luggage. I now thought about the signs, Suzanne in my dream, she had turned into a mermaid and was calling Lorca's name. The Australian guy at breakfast in the hotel, the logo on his shirt, Acrol Holidays Limited, Acrol is Lorca backwards! Now I had to wait until I was reunited with my bag before I could find out for sure. Patience is certainly not one of my strong points and now the suspense was almost unbearable.

I eventually got through customs at Gatwick and found myself a quiet table in the coffee shop in the arrivals lounge. I opened my laptop. Fortunately there was still some battery charge left. I inserted the USB stick which I had kept safely in my wallet. Eventually the screen came alive, a complicated page of moving text, gobble-de-gook and a box which said 'Enter Code' at the top. I entered 'LORCA' but it was declined. I paused and then guessed that the password could be case sensitive. I entered 'Lorca' again, no luck. I felt myself becoming quite agitated and angry. I then looked at the foot of the page and noticed that the code had to be a minimum of ten characters. I took a sip of my coffee and took some extra time to think. I don't know why but I then entered it as L.O.R.C.A. An hourglass icon came into view and seemed to take an age, as if it was churning through data... and then a message. 'Hello! Welcome Back Suzanne.' I felt a chill and then clicked on the 'Next' button. Suddenly there they were. Seventeen files, some looked historical and others quite recent but they all needed decrypting. I knew I just needed to get access to VeraCrypt.

7

With all the new information unravelling quite quickly I realised I would need an office base to work from. Working from home would not be sufficient and I most certainly needed access to the appropriate software so that I could run and download Suzanne's files properly. I had tried converting everything through Excel but the files became even more distorted. Access to the international news database would also be useful. I needed a cable connection and I could only do that from a news office. I decided to phone one of my former colleagues from way back, Lisa Luscombe, now editor at the *Woking Tribune*.

'Lisa, it's Jack.'

'Jack who?'

I laughed. 'Jack Compton, that's who!'

'Bloody hell!'

I laughed again... 'No need to swear,' I said as Lisa chuckled down the phone.

'So what have I done to deserve this pleasure, it's been a while?'

'I need a favour, a massive favour. I was wondering if you had room for me to work from your office over the next few weeks. I'm on to a big story and I need to cross-check some sensitive files by using your software.'

'Of course you can, we are very, very busy, so I will need to clear it with our MD but it should be okay. You could sit at your old desk. No-one's using it at the moment.'

'That's great, when's the best time to stop by?'

'Anytime, I'm not always here but I'll let the others know what's going on so they can expect you.'

'Brilliant, thank you, silly question, I am right in assuming you use the PA platform to access the international news database?'

'Yes of course, we use others too, since the new legislation came in we can even use computer robots to glean all the information we need to verify our local stories. It's all mod cons now you know, much different to when you worked here before.'

'Most importantly, have you still got the original version of a programme called VeraCrypt installed on any of your computers? I need it to access and open all the files I have on a USB stick I'm trying to make sense of.'

'Yes, I think we do, it's been replaced by a more updated programme. We don't actually use VeraCrypt anymore. I'm sure we still have it here somewhere though.'

'That's great, thank you, exactly what I need. I'll see you early tomorrow.'

'Okay, I look forward to it. By the way, remind me, what does USB stand for?'

'Err, you've got me now. Universal Serial Bus, I think, but I'm not one hundred per cent sure on that.'

'Ah, okay, I'll trust you,' said Lisa as she put the phone down.

I wondered how much had really changed over the last twenty or so years since I left the *Tribune*. Lisa was just an office girl and a fledgling journalist when I worked there and I don't think anyone else is left.

I remember going to my old colleague, Geoff Bridger's, funeral a few years ago. He was a fine journalist but at the same time, a right old bigot and that often got him into trouble. There was only a few of us who turned up for the ceremony in Southampton. I travelled in the limousine with his widow, Doreen, and their two daughters. It was teeming with rain that day and as the cortege turned into the drive of the crematorium I remember Doreen looking at her watch. 'Dead on time,' she said. We all laughed. It was only when we got out of the car I realised three of the pallbearers were black guys. I could almost hear Geoff banging on the coffin lid in rage as they carried him in. It was funny. I must ask Lisa what happened to all of the others I used to work with.

In some ways I've missed the humdrum of local reporting so I'll be glad to see how it all works these days. Everyone in the newspaper industry is under scrutiny and some, even close colleagues, are out to stab you in the back, metaphorically speaking anyway... and yes, talking from my experience at the *Sunday Herald*, they most certainly do. Perhaps that's why I prefer my current role as a freelancer although the pay is a little hit and miss, well, quite shit really.

8

Walking up the steps to the office made me feel quite nostalgic. I had been back a few times just to visit, but this was the first time for quite a while and I wondered what everyone would be like. I opened the door and poked my head around the corner. No-one saw me. I walked in, still no-one noticed. I slung my jacket onto a chair and entered the main office.

'Good morning!' I shouted.

Immediately they turned around in synchronised shock.

'Hello, I'm Jack, Jack Compton,' I said quite assertively.

There were three of them, none of whom I recognised, two men and a woman, all slightly younger than myself.

'We've heard a lot about you, Jack,' said the woman as she reached out to shake my hand.

'I'm Helen, by the way, Helen Ricmeyer. You already know our editor, Lisa, of course. I'm her PA and secretarial support colleague. I write the LGBT column and also deal with the classifieds and other everyday stuff.'

'Wow, oh yes, Lisa, how is she?'

'She's fine, she'll be in shortly. She's always spoken very highly of you. You should be very proud.'

'I'm not sure if proud is the right word, but I'll take that. Now, who are these two fine young gentlemen?'

'This is Stuart Janner. He's our roving reporter. Stuart acts as our editor when Lisa is away. He's also our court correspondent. Stuart's been very busy covering the Rodney Frazier story recently, you know, the guy who strangled his twin brother, Richard, to death for allegedly having an affair with his wife. The wife denies it. It's all very sordid and it has become quite a high profile case. We don't get many murders to report on these days. Hopefully the red tops will buy into it and that could bring us some much needed additional revenue. The short-ass behind him is Jon Moseley. Jon deals with all the local sport and helps us out on deadline day. Deadline is now Tuesday. Did you know we moved our weekly publication day from Friday back to Thursday a couple of years ago?'

'No, actually I didn't, so where are all the others?'

'There are no others, this is it.'

'What?'

'Believe me, this is it. There are a couple of freelancers who submit material but their submissions are quite sporadic and we never see them. I think Lisa only keeps them on board to help try and give the paper a higher profile.'

'So who owns the paper now? I heard Roger Hackett, the previous owner had passed away.'

'Yes, only quite recently. He died in prison following a cardiac arrest. He was convicted of fraud and embezzlement around six months ago, something to do with our pension scheme. The paper is now owned by the Infinity Group, they're based in Reading. We come under their umbrella and Lisa works quite closely with Nancy Salem who is one of their non-executive directors. Anyway, let me show you to your desk.'

'Nancy Salem, ouch! Now that's a name from the past I didn't expect to hear. She was the editor when I worked here. She's got to be in her seventies now.'

'Yes, she must be,' said Helen pointing at the internal door.

As we walked through the office I noticed not too much had changed. The walls had received a lick of pale yellow paint and there were different pictures hanging up. Pictures of Woking as I remember it, before they knocked it down the second time.

'Here you are,' said Helen, 'I believe this is where you used to sit, isn't it?'

'Yes, indeed it is. It's the very same oak desk with the same old scars. I guess it's seen much better times.'

'Well it can tell a few stories if you pardon the pun, but make the most of it, the whole office is being refurnished soon and it will be all mod-cons,' said Stuart as he joined the conversation.

'Anyone for coffee?' shouted Jon.

Now I really did feel like I was back at the *Tribune*. In the old days, coffee was always our mainstay. None of us could function until the second cup had come around.

'Helen, while I'm waiting for Lisa, could I use one of your computers? I need to download the VeraCrypt programme onto my laptop via a USB stick. It's something I agreed with Lisa over the phone yesterday. It will help immensely with a story I'm investigating.'

'Yes, use mine. I nearly wiped it off, no-one's really used it for a couple of years, you're lucky we still have it. Make yourself comfortable, I imagine you and Lisa will have a lot to talk about when she gets in.'

'Thank you.'

It didn't take long to download the VeraCrypt software onto my laptop and I could see all the files jumping into life and at last making some kind of sense. I made sure I didn't leave anything incriminating on Helen's computer and then closed it down.

Whilst waiting for Lisa I took some time to look through a few back copies of the *Tribune* to see what had been going on but also to study the format and examine the style of writing. Not a lot had changed, but in a way, I felt it needed to. Everything looked too safe. In these days of modern technology and social media, the paper could get left behind. It all looked too tame as well as disjointed. The paper had also shrunk in size, from broadsheet to tabloid and only thirty-two pages in length. It was sad to see.

It got to eleven o' clock and there was still no sign of Lisa. Helen started to become quite anxious.

'She'd better be here soon. We're all waiting for our weekly brief and we haven't even discussed this week's helicopter sheet yet,' she said.

'Helicopter sheet?'

'It's the paper plan, we look at the overview and discuss which stories need to be followed up and then used for this week's edition. We also need to work out where they'd fit as we have to leave part of the front page and immediate inside pages open in case anything happens at the last minute. Last week there was a car accident on Anchor Hill. A black Corsa hit a telegraph pole and smashed into a house. The woman driver from St John's was arrested for drunk driving. It happened on Tuesday evening just before we sent everything off to the printers in Leamington Spa. We had to change everything at very short notice. Lisa, Stuart and I didn't get away from here until two in the morning. The good thing is, we get every Wednesday off, so we had time to recuperate.'

As Helen was speaking I heard a car pull up outside.

'Hello, hello, good morning peeps,' screamed a voice as the office door swung open.

It was Lisa with an armful of box files.

'Sorry I'm late, I got caught up in traffic, then there was a queue in the post office, and Sainsbury's was jam packed and then I couldn't find anywhere to park the old jalopy, so I've dumped it out the front for now.'

Lisa had certainly changed since I last saw her. We have communicated quite a few times since by email. She's a friend on Facebook but I don't go on there too much these days.

'Jack, sorry, how are you, old boy? So nice to see you after all this time, we must go into my office and catch up, we no doubt have a lot of stories to share.'

I couldn't help thinking Lisa had become rather frumpy in some ways. She'd definitely put on a lot of weight. I remember her being slim and quite pretty; unfortunately her face was still quite badly scarred down one side following her near fatal car crash in 1994. Now, she just seemed different.

'Where's Stuart and Jon?' she asked.

'They waited until just before eleven but had to go, both had stories to cover which were time sensitive, they should be back by three, though,' said Helen.

'Okay, okay that's fine. Helen, make the coffees, there's a darling,' she said. 'I've got some catching up to do with Jack, haven't I, old boy?' she chuckled.

Helen smiled and then left the room. Lisa's new way of talking had really surprised me, it all seemed very pretentious.

'Come on, Jack, let's get cosy. Tell me what you've been up to all these years. I will be intrigued to hear everything, and my, have I got a few things to tell you. Oh, and by the way, don't think Helen fancies you. I saw her smile at you, but she bats for the other side, if you get my drift.'

The door opened. There was a pause in the conversation as Helen brought the coffees in. After she left the room Lisa banged her teaspoon on the cup. I laughed.

'Why are you laughing?' she asked.

'The coffee, it's awful. What happened to the good old Nescafé we used to have in the old days?'

'Well Helen brings the coffee in each month, speak to her!'

'Don't worry, I will.'

'So, Jack, tell me about life with the nationals, what were the highlights?'

'Highlights? There weren't that many but my time at the *Sunday Herald,* was interesting to say the least; that is until we were all sacked when it got shut down.'

'Oh yes, the phone hacking scandal, I remember all that, you weren't one of the naughty boys, were you?'

'To be honest I wish I was. I was working on a very sensitive story with my colleague, Suzanne. If proven it could have rocked the government to its foundations and still might if even a smidgeon of what we were investigating is found to be true.'

'Sounds interesting, so what was it all about?'

'There was a so-called conspiracy theory going about that the Princess of Wales could still be alive and her death was actually a cover up by the government and security services in the wake of the Dodi Fayed scandal. The initial information myself and Suzanne had received was quite plausible but there wasn't a shred of evidence anywhere to support what we had been given.'

'Surely that's all nonsense, though, isn't it?' said Lisa inquisitively.

'Yes, perhaps, but I've decided to keep an open mind, we both had. Suzanne kept the case open and was recently murdered by a car bomb in Malta, I think there could be a connection, something to do with a woman who went missing in Venice in August 1997, and I'm looking for answers. I don't think it has anything to do directly with the death of Diana, but I'm certain something else was going on which got quite messy. I think that's how Suzanne managed to get herself killed.'

'I'm sorry about your colleague.'

'Thank you. She became a very close friend. Look, I'm very grateful for the use of the office facilities. I may need to go off gallivanting in different directions, particularly if any more information comes to light. If the story comes to fruition it could earn me a tidy fortune.' I said, grimacing. 'Losing Suzanne, though, is my main incentive, she was a highly respected journalist and her loss has affected me quite a lot.'

Lisa smiled. 'Well, with respect, just make sure you don't waste all your time chasing shadows. It's not worth it.'

I smiled back but knew I could be on to something; the answer just had to be on the USB stick, or at least some information that could lead me in the right direction.

'Anyway, back to wonderful Woking and the local stuff, not much has been happening recently apart from the Frazier case,' Lisa said with a look of concern. 'While you're here, I was wondering if you could give me some helpful advice on how to regenerate the paper, freshen it up, make it appeal more to a wider readership, so any ideas you may have will be greatly appreciated,' she pleaded.

'Well, obviously the quality of news is important as well as the style of journalism which reports it. I've already taken the liberty to look through a few back copies. Some of the headlines come over as slightly boring if not, naive. They lack imagination even before you start to read the story in depth. It doesn't need to be sensationalist but it does have to be eye-catching and it simply isn't. I don't think it's your fault, but in fact, the *Tribune* was always more ambitious in the old days, it had to be; now it looks like the paper has lost its competitive edge.'

'Exactly,' said Lisa. 'That's exactly why I needed to ask. Your expertise will be invaluable in helping me to turn things round.'

'Well, I don't know about that. Local reporting has changed a lot since I was last here but I'll do my best. Big question, though, why hasn't this happened already?'

'We've not had the right people on board for some time now, mainly because of the tight budget. We simply cannot afford to pay salaries of over £20k and we've not really had a quality reporter since Alfie Nubeebuckus left.'

'Alfie Nubeebuckus, now there's another name I remember. He was always creeping around Nancy to get his stories on the front page. He was a complete ass, whatever happened to him?'

'I married him,' said Lisa with a frown.

'Oops, sorry, but that isn't your surname now, though, is it?'

'No, I got shot of the bastard when I found out he was having an affair with a bunny boiler called Sally who used to work behind the bar at the Hen and Chickens in Bisley. He stayed here in England for a few months afterwards but it became quite awkward.'

'So where is he now?'

'He eventually buggered off back to Mauritius. I actually enjoyed putting the flags out to mark the grand occasion!'

Despite her attempt at humour, I detected an air of bitterness in Lisa's voice which was unusual, but then I hadn't seen her for so long. She never ever used to swear, she seems to have changed quite a lot.

'So your surname now, I assume you married again after Alfie?'

'Yes, I'm called Lisa Arrowsmith now. I married a guy called Jamie, one of my friend Trudy's cousins but it didn't work out. He was a wanker really but even now I still have a soft spot for him. We lasted about three months but then we had only been seeing each other for a few weeks before deciding to get married. It was a whirlwind thing. I'm changing my name back to Luscombe shortly, in memory of my poor father. He died last year and I miss him so much. I also need to restore some self-esteem, and that will help.'

'So sorry, Lisa, I remember talking to your father on the phone years ago, around the time of your car accident. He sounded like a really nice man.'

'Yes he was, he was a lovely man, my rock,' said Lisa tearfully.

I moved around the desk to console her. She grabbed my hand.

'Thank you, thank you,' she said.

At that moment I decided to back off. Now was the time to change the subject, I thought.

'I've only ever known you as Lisa Luscombe. I didn't know you had been married, certainly not twice. Look, if you don't mind, can we continue this conversation when I come back tomorrow? I need to get back home and have a closer look at what's on this USB stick now I've downloaded the software.'

As I left her office, Lisa started sobbing about her father again but I felt it best not to say any more. I was wondering if she was using it as an excuse to get close to me, which I was not prepared for. Then again, I shouldn't have moved around her desk. It all felt quite awkward.

9

The way Suzanne had arranged her files was very comprehensive and methodical...

    SCDiana-11.97
    SCRosalinda-11.97
    SCFiona-04.98
    SCFrankie-04.98 and so on...

The first two files went back to November 1997. The information had been scanned in from an exchange of faxes, photographs and other data. There were also copies of a number of receipts from companies scattered across the world. I remembered her talking about this when we were at the *Sunday Herald* and was now beginning to see why she thought she may be on to something.

The first file, SC-Diana11.97 was a scan which contained a diagram of an ambulance with part of its floor replaced by what looked like a metal sliding door. There was also a receipt from a garage owner confirming the work had been carried out at a workshop in Toulouse, France. Suzanne had always been suspicious about why the ambulance had stopped on its way to the hospital the night Diana was killed. There was also a close-up photograph of that stretch of road. I could see what looks like a manhole cover. Something written in Suzanne's handwriting asks, 'Is this a water main or sewerage tunnel? Could people walk through?' I couldn't find much more about the ambulance itself until I found a copy of an unsigned fax which had been sent to *Le Monde*, the French newspaper. It claimed the ambulance did not belong to the hospital. Suzanne had written question marks all over it. A clipping from *Le Monde,* dated 27 November 1997, which Suzanne had translated, suggests the claim was just a hoax, but doesn't rule it out altogether. It also states there had been a number of other claims received from the same source suggesting there could have been a body switch while the ambulance had remained briefly stationary. The report, in conclusion, dismisses all the claims as absurd. Suzanne herself had written the word 'bollocks' at the end of it. It looked like she was trying to trace the source but then everything seemed to run dry.

The second file, also dated November 1997, contained copies of a letter sent to the Milan International News Agency via its London office from a Rosalinda Rochos who worked for Madame Tussauds in Marylebone Road, the letter states...

> *'I need to tell someone that in March, Madame Tussauds was privately commissioned to produce a wax model of Princess Diana. This was a new model which was to include her most up-to-date features including slight wrinkles and hairstyle. The curator was very guarded about it and on at least two occasions men in dark suits came to inspect the work. It was eventually taken away and those of us involved in the project were sworn to secrecy. I have always been suspicious about this as everything was being done outside our normal code of ethics. When I heard Princess Diana was killed in the accident in Paris I could not help thinking there could be some kind of connection.'* The letter ends, *'Please forgive me if I am wrong. Yours, Rosalinda Rochos.'*

Suzanne had tried to contact Rosalinda but she refused to speak any further. A short transcript of a telephone conversation between Suzanne and the curator of Madame Tussauds confirms the waxworks company blatantly denied such a commission had taken place. Again, Suzanne had written question marks all over the document, which was one of her little habits.

Several pages didn't really make any sense at all. Suzanne had just collated all the information she had received as best she could, placing asterisks on the ones she thought might be useful. Eventually I found something else which caught my eye. A newspaper cutting from the *Washington Post...*

US Sex Doll Manufacturer Caught in Diana Scandal

A company which manufacturers latex dolls to order for the global sex market has been caught up in the latest revelations surrounding the death of Diana, Princess of Wales in Paris... writes Frankie Fletcher.

Rumours that UK government agents commissioned such a doll with a remit for it to resemble the dead Princess are rife throughout the multimillion dollar industry. The purchase was allegedly made some six months before the fatal crash that killed the Princess. It was then shipped to a rented address in Pimlico, London. The revelation has been raising eyebrows amid growing speculation there may have been a bid to have the Princess 'taken out of the equation' after forming a close relationship with the Egyptian polo player and film-maker, Dodi Al Fayed, the Muslim son of Harrod's owner, Mohamed Al Fayed, who also died in the crash.

The latex dolls, which have a durable metal 'skeleton', are designed to recreate the appearance, texture, and weight of the human female (or male) form. Their primary function is to serve as sex partners. Some medical experts (and cynics) say they are also used as a cure for necrophilia. This activity can be accompanied by certain preparations such as dressing them up in lingerie, a nurse, schoolgirl or other outfits, changing their wigs or even makeup. This is believed to be the first time the maker of the dolls, Dreamlife, in Houston, Tx, had been asked to come up with a look-a-like creation.

Jez Bywater, owner of the Dreamlife factory, has confirmed a transaction did take place but was not aware it was instigated by any UK government official. "We do not ask too many personal questions about our customers, as discretion is one of our watchwords, simply because of what we do," he said.

A spokesperson at the UK government's press office in London, England stated, "We have heard about a number of unwarranted allegations connected to the death of Diana,

Princess of Wales, and take every report very seriously. However, there have also been a number of ludicrous suggestions we are not prepared to follow up, although such allegations have been passed on to the police as a matter of course."

All this made for some interesting reading and I was beginning to understand even more why Suzanne believed she may have uncovered one of the biggest ever conspiracies. The report was filed by Frankie Fletcher in April 1998. His name came up recently when I spoke to Rick. Suzanne refers to him as Frankie 'Fourfingers' Fletcher. I decided to do a Google search and found his personal profile. He was born in 1947, served in the Royal Navy and the Special Boat Squadron and then became a journalist in 1980. He was covering the Falklands War in 1982 as a freelance correspondent for the British press and lost part of his left hand when he was onboard a Royal Fleet Auxiliary vessel, the Sir Galahad, which was attacked by Argentine forces. He was lucky. Forty-eight soldiers and crew lost their lives during the attack. Indeed, from a recent photograph I could see he's a portly silver-haired gentleman. The thumb of his left hand is missing. A short quote on his LinkedIn page states: 'I've seen more action as a journalist than I ever did in the Royal Navy.' Rather ironic, I thought.

The obvious question I had to ask myself? Did Suzanne really believe both Madame Tussauds and Dreamlife created Diana look-a-like figures as part of a conspiracy? She used to mention little snippets but was always quite guarded. 'You'll only think I've gone off my trolley,' she used to say, I think that was around the time when I really started to get interested in the investigation myself.

Was there a plan to switch the real Diana with a dummy when the ambulance stopped on its route to the hospital? Perhaps it was possible, but why? It all seemed far too elaborate and farfetched. I was beginning to realise I may have only scratched the surface of what was contained within Suzanne's files. I felt there was more, much more to come and needed to keep digging.

A press cutting in another file, this time from the *South London Journal*, dated 4 January 1998, reports that a group of children had discovered a large black sack containing a headless body on the bank of the Thames near Southwark. Police confirmed it was only a mannequin but did say they were surprised it appeared to be made from wax. Madame Tussauds denied they had any involvement.

I wondered why the "body" had been found headless. I could now see why the letter from Rosalinda Rochos to the news agency was so important to Suzanne. Also, what happened to the latex sex doll that had been imported from America? Did that suffer a similar fate or was it used for something more sinister?

Disturbingly, one of Suzanne's later files, SCEnemy-10.18, contained over 250 Twitter and avatar names of people who she thought were out to get her.

10

The most intriguing file however, was SCFiona-04.98 which contained an Italian report about a woman who went missing in Venice on Saturday 9 August 1997 after a night out with a "friend". She had been staying at the Hotel Kette on San Marco. The alarm was raised by hotel staff when she failed to check out as expected. All her possessions, including her passport, were discovered in her 1st floor room.

Suzanne had somehow procured a document which had been sent to her office in Milan. The document was a profile of Fiona Meredith, 35, from Oakley near Basingstoke in Hampshire. She had travelled alone to Venice for a long weekend and was the only child of Arthur and Linda Meredith. Attached was a news report from an Italian newspaper dated Wednesday 13 August 1997, which Suzanne had had translated and then sent to Frankie Fletcher. His name keeps cropping up, I thought.

British Woman Goes Missing in Venice

Police are becoming increasingly concerned for the welfare of a lone British traveller who has been missing in Venice since Saturday 9 August. Fiona Meredith, 35, from Oakley, a rural village near Basingstoke in England, was last seen leaving the Hotel Kette at around 7.30pm.

Staff called the police when they realised Miss Meredith had not checked out by midday on Sunday. They later found all her possessions, including her passport, in the hotel room.

The manager of the hotel, Luigi Larusso, said, 'I called the police at around 7pm on Sunday to say what had happened. I had a feeling in my gut something was not quite right. It is unusual for anyone to just leave and forget their belongings. I remember the guest as being very polite, I had also complimented the lady on her fluent speaking of the Italian language although she did speak it with a Roma accent.'

The police have described the woman as 'well-heeled, of wealthy English stock, around 1.70m tall, blonde with blue eyes.' They believe she had received some unwelcome attention during her stay from a suited gentleman in the foyer at the hotel who likened her to Diana, Princess of Wales. The police would very much like to speak with this man.

It is believed Miss Meredith may have arranged to meet the man later that evening at Harry's Bar; a brief walk from the hotel towards the ferry stage. Police have examined CCTV footage from the hotel's foyer but have said the images are "too grainy", preventing them from clearly identifying their main suspect, and have appealed to the public for more help. Further images taken from cameras at Harry's Bar are inconclusive; indeed, there is no evidence to suggest Miss Meredith had visited the bar, which is popular with wealthy tourists.

Inspector Maria Allegranza said, 'This is a very unusual disappearance. The lady is well-educated, of mature stature and would not have simply gone off with a complete stranger unless she thought it was absolutely safe to do so. She would not have left all her things in the hotel room. It is obvious she intended to go back. Yes, we are very concerned.'

Fiona Meredith is a music teacher with a fondness of the violin. Her parents say she is a great admirer of Niccolò Paganini (1782-1840) and it was his music that first attracted her to Italian arts and culture; it was this which had inspired her to visit Venice.

Inspector Allegranza added, "We are now widening our search and Interpol have been informed. We are keeping an open mind and of course we hope Miss Meredith will be found very soon. However, we cannot rule out the possibility she may have been abducted and taken somewhere against her will. We are asking anyone with information to come forward as a matter of extreme urgency."

I noticed the report contained the name of Maria Allegranza who is now an Italian prosecutor. Indeed, there was a mobile telephone number for her in a directory amongst Suzanne's files. I thought, perhaps, I should give her a ring. It was clear I should also speak to Frankie Fletcher as it was obvious he also had a keen interest in this case.

'Good morning, is that Maria Allegranza?'

'Yes, who's that?'

'My name is Jack Compton, I'm a reporter from England, I believe you were acquainted with Suzanne Camilleri, the journalist from Malta who was recently killed in a car bomb attack.'

'Yes, I remember her, I had met her only once and that was a long time ago when I was still a police officer.'

'Yes, I know, I have seen some documents.'

'So what do you want?'

'I believe Suzanne's killing may be linked to a missing person's case you were working on in 1997, shortly before Princess Diana was killed. Do you think there was a link?'

'Listen, Jack, I suggest you stop there. I do not want to talk about this on the telephone.'

'Well then, can we meet? I can come to Italy.'

'No need, I'm already in London. I can meet you in the city somewhere. There's a pub near the office I'm working from in The Strand. Meet me there. I'm free tomorrow for lunch. Say twelve or just after? I will be in the room upstairs. The pub is called The Coal Hole. It's quaint and we can have a discreet conversation there.'

'So, how will I know who you are?'

'White hair, but you English call it grey, emerald nail varnish, but none on my little fingers... and what about you?'

'I'm in my fifties, grey suit.'

'Boring...'

'Sorry?'

'Boring... bring a rolled up copy of the *Metro* with you. Oh, and some money, you can buy me dinner.'

'Dinner?'

'Yes, dinner...'

She paused then laughed. After I put the phone down I couldn't help thinking about what I might be getting myself into. I was going to try and contact Frankie Fletcher but then decided to wait until after I had met with Maria. Reading between the lines, it did feel like she was eager and had something important to tell me. I was surprised that I had managed to arrange a meeting with her so easily.

11

The walk along The Strand towards The Coal Hole was all hustle and bustle as I meandered my way through the stampede of lunchtime shoppers. I had been to the pub before but still found it difficult finding my bearings. Eventually, I found it further down the road on the right. It's an oldie-worldy sort of place set between buildings of a more imposing nature. I walked in. It was much quieter than I thought it would be. Eventually, I got served. I think the barmaid was from the Czech Republic as far as I could make out, very polite and very thorough with the change as she pressed the coins firmly into my hand. I found my way to the foot of the stairs which led to a room overlooking the downstairs bar. I guessed it was where I was supposed to meet Maria. I then realised I had forgotten my rolled-up copy of the *Metro*. I was about to turn away when a voice shouted,

'Mr Compton?'

'Err yes,' I said. 'I was just about to go and get a paper.'

'No need, no need. I know who you are, I recognise you from a picture I found in an old news file. I'm Maria Allegranza, by the way.'

'Yes, I can tell by the accent and green nail varnish,' I said rather nervously as she shook my hand.

After arranging an Irish coffee and a couple of menus we sat down out of the way where everything seemed quiet.

'So, Maria, may I call you Maria? What brings you to London?'

'Oh yes, of course. I'm here working on a boring extradition case; "run of the mill" I think you call it in England. I'm here quite often. I always enjoy my little trips to London. I find the shops are very cheap, even the Italian fashions cost less than they do back home in Venice or Milan. Anyway, did you know Mrs Camilleri well?' she asked.

'Yes, pretty well. We worked at the *Sunday Herald* together and remained good friends after it closed. We always stayed in touch.'

'Were you ever lovers?'

'No, and you're not the first person to ask me that. She was a married woman and I always respected that. If things had been different, then who knows?'

'So, Jack, you're interested in the Fiona Meredith story. Why?'

'Yes, it seems Suzanne had found a link between Fiona's disappearance in Venice in 1997 and the death of Diana, Princess of Wales.'

Just then there was a pause and Maria looked me in the eye.

'I think I can trust you, Jack. Be careful what you print. It is a very delicate matter. I met with Mrs Camilleri when I was an inspector in the police. She came to the station in Venice. I was quite abrupt with her at first as I thought she was talking complete nonsense. That was until she showed me a number of photographs.'

'Photographs?'

'Yes, there were four photographs. They all displayed that Miss Meredith bore a striking resemblance to the late Princess.'

'That's very interesting. I have actually seen one of the pictures Suzanne had stored on file.'

'Stored on file? What do you mean?'

I explained to Maria how I had obtained the USB stick and how I worked out the password code and then had to find somewhere that still used the old software which supported the files. I think she was quite impressed.

'Do you think Suzanne could have come across some new information which may have led to her death?' I asked.

'It's very possible. Another reporter was actively pursuing the case, although for slightly different reasons. He had found a connection between the UK government and the Sicilian mafia. He believed the Government of Malta were acting as mediators. Indeed, we in the Italian prosecutor's office believe that too, which is why I wanted to speak to you privately. There have already been a number of deaths, mostly without motive or unexplained. I firmly believe sensitive data is being leaked to the mafia and they are always one step ahead of the game.'

'So, do you think it was the mafia who murdered Suzanne?'

'It's possible but they would not have done it of their own accord. Someone else would have ordered the killing,' she said.

'Who?'

'More than likely the UK government or, more accurately, the Secret Intelligence Service - MI6 as they're better known.'

'That's incredible. I find it hard to believe all this would still be going on well over twenty years after Princess Diana was killed.'

'Believe me, it is. It's all about the UK government and the royal family saving face. A lot of people have got their hands very dirty. Here in England, in Malta and back home in Italy. It all stinks.'

The conversation paused for a while as we ate our meals and ordered more drinks. Gradually the room began to fill up with more people and it became difficult to talk, almost impossible to hear each other without shouting.

'Come on, let's go for a quick walk, I've still got a little time but I have to be back at the office for a 3pm video conference,' Maria said.

We ended up walking along by the Thames. The sky was full of seagulls and I had a little chuckle to myself as I remembered Malta, where there weren't any.

'When do you fly back to Italy?'

'I fly home on Saturday. I have a string of court cases coming up. One actually involves the Sicilian mafia, but fortunately that's not connected to what we've been talking about. I must spend my weekend getting up to speed with all the relevant documents.'

'So what does an Italian prosecutor actually do?'

'Prosecute,' she laughed. 'Seriously, it's a risky business. We secure convictions. Many times I've put someone away for over twenty-five years and sometimes that means life. Many are members of the mafia. The mafia, though, often fights amongst itself, usually over territory. I've even received a letter of thanks from a mafia boss who was happy I put someone away.'

'You mentioned earlier another reporter was actively pursuing the so-called Princess Diana conspiracy case. I don't suppose you would happen to know who that was, by any chance?'

Maria hesitated, almost as if she didn't want to tell me. 'Actually, you probably already know him, or at least, know of him. I'd be shocked if you didn't.'

'Who then?'

'Frankie Fletcher, he's an undercover reporter but has also been working on and off for the secret security services in the UK. I've met with him many times. He has an agreement that anything he discovers, he gives to them. You will not find any recent reports anywhere from Frankie. He's effectively been silenced. Everything he writes lately is censored and remains unpublished. He is also known to be on a mafia hit list, but then so am I.'

'Frankie Fletcher? That's weird. By pure co-incidence I was going to contact him next!'

'Well if you're lucky enough to get hold of him he may be economical with the facts. Be very careful. Frankie is an ex-military man. He is known to have links with MI5 and MI6. I suspect he may have been gleaning information which has seen him compromised and I think this may have resulted in him becoming what you might call, a person of interest, both with the goodies and the baddies. I know he's holed up in a safe house somewhere, probably here in London. My advice to you right now would be to leave him alone. Well alone! Where he sits, is on very dangerous ground. Believe me, it's well out of your depth,' she said with a look of concern. 'By the way, I have some information to suggest Fiona Meredith is still alive,' she added. 'Frankie communicated that just a few weeks ago. I believe he exchanged some sensitive information with your deceased friend, Mrs Camilleri. I will contact you if I find out any more.'

That news came as one hell of a parting shot. Quite a revelation and probably exactly what Maria thought I may be after. I thanked her for her time before she quickly vanished into the bustling crowd. I then decided to return to The Coal Hole for a couple more pints before walking back over Hungerford Bridge towards Waterloo Station to catch my train back down to Woking. I needed some time to think, even more time, probably, to figure out my next moves.

12

Back in the *Tribune* office this morning Helen was becoming curious about my activities.

'What are you actually doing, it must be important?'

'Yes, quite important. Important to me, anyway,' I replied.

Jon joined the conversation. 'What was it like working for the *Sunday Herald*?'

'To be honest I didn't enjoy working there at all. It was far too cut-throat and most of my time was spent sorting out fantasy from reality. Sometimes the line was so blurred it was difficult to tell the two things apart.'

'What were the other journalists like?'

'Most were complete assholes. They had a total lack of respect, particularly for each other. No respect for the public. No respect for protocol, nothing. Too many people were pretending to be something they weren't. My colleague, Suzanne, felt very uncomfortable with that and I agreed with her. Actually, it was a blessing in disguise when the paper was eventually forced to cease publication.'

'What did you do after that?' asked Helen.

'I retrained as an investigative journalist and became a freelance reporter, but ended up working mainly for a couple of local rags in London. The problem with that, though, was I couldn't put my training into practice because the stories were always too safe and mundane.'

'What do you mean by that?' asked Jon.

'You know, basic stuff, school plays, cake sales and the odd shoplifting case - utterly boring in other words.'

'A bit like working here,' shouted Lisa as she entered the room.

'Have you got a minute, Jack?' she asked, beckoning me into her office.

'How can I help you?' I chuckled.

'I see the others are giving you grief, is that bothering you?'

'No, not at all, they were just asking me about my time at the *Herald* and what I've been doing since. I think they're curious about what I'm really doing here.'

'So am I. I know it's about your friend's murder, where are you going with it? Are you writing a story for a paper?'

'Do you know, I haven't thought about that yet, I just want to find out the truth about why Suzanne was killed, I need to know if there was any substance behind the information she had been receiving before her death. I also need to follow up some information an Italian prosecutor called Maria Allegranza gave me. A chat with Frankie Fletcher would also help, but Maria warned me against that. I guess talking to him could open up a whole new can of worms.'

'Well, be brave. Open a can of worms. You might just get your story and find everything you're looking for.'

'I've thought about it. I'm not sure if that's being brave or just plain stupid. There's a whole raft of possibilities out there. I'm not sure if I'm investigating something that is actually true or something that is only a conspiracy theory. I need to be absolutely sure before I go stomping around and putting my big foot in it.'

Lisa laughed. 'Actually, I don't blame you,' she said.

I was just about to get up and leave when Lisa asked me about Paris.

'Have you ever been to the crash site, you know, the road tunnel where Princess Diana was killed?'

'No, I've researched everything I need to know online. I've reached a conclusion that the tunnel in Paris is just another red herring. What happened there happened. It's as simple as that. I don't think the actual death of Diana has anything to do directly with what I'm looking for.'

'Call yourself an investigative journalist, do you? Look, how about I take you there next weekend? We can go on the Eurostar, it's quite cheap these days. We can have a look at the crash site; get a taxi through the tunnel. You can experience everything first hand and get a real feel for the place, and then you can buy me lunch,' she said with a smile.

'It's a nice gesture, thank you, but you don't need to be wasting your money on me. We won't find anything there and anyway, it would just be a waste of time. We'd be chasing shadows that don't exist.'

'Well Jack, old boy, I won't be wasting my money. I've never been to Paris; I've always wanted to visit Notre-Dame and the Eiffel Tower. Anyway, we're both adults aren't we, what's the harm in that?'

'None, I suppose.'

'Well at least think about it. Give me an answer by tomorrow and I'll book the tickets.'

'Okay, thank you.'

When I got home I kept mulling over everything. The conversation the other day with Maria was particularly bugging me and I still wasn't sure whether to contact Frankie Fletcher or not. I needed some time to collect my thoughts. Perhaps a weekend in Paris with Lisa might be just the tonic but I need to be careful on so many fronts and watch where things with her might end up... that's one particular mess I wouldn't want to get into.

I must spend some time tomorrow going through the rest of Suzanne's files. There are so many. I've only just scratched the surface and I'm actually becoming quite anxious about what I might find. Some of the latter entries contain references with a question mark, PC? What does the "PC?" mean? And, why is it always endorsed or circled in red? What if I do actually find something that is of particular interest to the authorities, the mafia or any others who may be out there?

13

It was my first trip to Paris since 1985. Back then there was no Eurostar. It was a train to Dover Priory and then a ferry to Dunkirk. In those days it was a slow overnight train journey, arriving at Gare du Nord just after sunrise. This was different, slick and fast. Lisa had purchased first-class tickets so we were well looked after by the on-train stewards all the way. Lisa told me she had only booked one room at the hotel.

'Don't worry, it has single beds,' she said, but I was still quite suspicious.

On arrival at the station we stopped off for a quick coffee and some croissants before hiring a cab to take us through the tunnel where Princess Diana was killed. It all seemed slightly weird, and even the taxi driver who picked us up and drove us there looked rather bewildered by it all. We asked him to drive slowly so we could observe the crash site as much as possible. There was hardly anything to see, just a bouquet of flowers, and a chilly eeriness about it all and that was that.

'There, Jack, you've done it now, you've experienced the place, you can write your piece with a true sense of purpose now,' said Lisa as she leant forward to pay the driver. Personally, I felt it was all unnecessary but chose not to tell Lisa what I was thinking.

We then found ourselves in a restaurant near the River Seine, quite close to Notre-Dame. I could see the Eiffel Tower in the distance. I had been up there before with Nadine; the French girl I visited here in 1985. Lisa was looking forward to going up there after dinner, after deciding to add Sacré-Coeur to her to-do list as well.

'It makes sense, it's close to our hotel,' she kept saying.

The whole day just seemed to be a sightseeing trip to suit Lisa's cravings for being in tourist mode. I was admiring the sights too, but spent most of my time putting the context of the tunnel in line with all the other information I had been gathering without coming to any conclusions.

Eventually, we reached the hotel. It was the Hotel Mercure; a plush four-star hotel in Boulevard de Clichy; just a stone's throw from the Moulin Rouge.

'Look, it's English speaking,' said Lisa as she pointed to a sign in the main front window.

We checked in and a bell boy took us to our room on the 2nd floor. Fortunately, there were two single beds but they had been conveniently pushed together. Lisa just smiled and that in itself was making me feel very nervous about the whole situation.

'Don't worry, this is not intentional, I didn't arrange it,' she said as she reached for the complimentary bottle of champagne that had been left on a small table by the en-suite shower room.

While Lisa elected to go for a quick shower, I looked out of the window and could see the neon lights of the Moulin Rouge. Prostitutes were milling around in the doorway of a closed up old cinema opposite. Men were stopping, negotiating, some shaking their heads and walking off. I saw at least one, a young guy in his twenties, stop and then disappear up a side doorway with a leggy red-haired woman in a black mackintosh and fishnet stockings. She must have been in her forties at least. I then began thinking about all the moral issues just as Lisa came out from her shower.

'Are you okay?' she asked.

'Yes, fine, just looking at all the sights.'

'Oh down below, the prozzies,' she laughed. 'Have you ever been with a prostitute?'

'No, I have not!'

'Liar, liar, pants on fire, all men have, they just don't admit to it.'

I just grinned and tried to change the subject. Eventually she backed off and suggested we went down to the bar for a late drink.

Lisa confirmed our train back to St Pancras was at 10.43 in the morning. A rather odd departure time, I thought. After about an hour, and three drinks later, came the time I had been dreading.

'Come on, time to go up,' Lisa said.

Apart from a glass of champagne in the room, she had only been drinking lime and soda water, so she was still quite alert, even though she admitted being very tired.

'All that marching around Paris has done me in,' she said as we entered the room.

'But we got the metro to most places.'

'It's still tiring. Anyway, I need to get ready for some well-earned sleep,' she said as she took her washbag into the bathroom.

I sat on the end of one of the beds waiting for my turn to use the facilities, conscious I would need to keep my wits about me. I had only brought a spare pair of boxers and a T-shirt to sleep in.

Eventually, Lisa re-emerged with just a large pink bathroom robe wrapped around her.

'Don't worry, Jack, I don't bite. The choice is yours. You can either have me now or we can call it quits and we can just go to sleep for the rest of the night. I know you're in love with Suzanne but she's gone now and I know you miss her, you've made that so bloody obvious. You have memories and I know you will always cherish those. Look, I'm here. I'm your friend. We've known each other for donkey's years. This may be our only chance to get it together?'

Just then she dropped the robe to the floor and there she was, completely naked.

'So, Jack, what do you think?'

'Think of what?'

'What you see before you, silly!'

'Err, very nice.'

'You look like you've never seen a woman naked before.'

'Well it's been a while, a couple of years I guess.'

She stepped forward and pressed herself against me.

'Can you feel my boobies against your chest?'

'Err, yes, err, thank you.'

I was in a position where I didn't know what to say, let alone know what to do. I could feel my heart racing.

'So Jack, what's it like being in a bedroom scene with a gorgeous beauty like me?' she asked.

'Err, surreal at least, very surreal.'

'So, do you want to take me or not?' she said, stroking her hand through my hair.

'Well, like I said it's been a while, too long in fact.'

'Relax, you're too tense,' she whispered as she took me by the hand.

Eventually we lay astride across the bed. She slowly positioned herself on top and started kissing my neck, strategically moving towards my lower regions and then removing my clothes. She reached her hand up towards my face and covered my eyes, placing her fingers in my mouth, and then I felt it, I was getting harder all the time and then it happened. After a couple of minutes, she shot up and looked me in the eyes.

'There, how was that?'

'Err, wow, sorry it was so quick, I don't know what to say.'

'Don't say anything, just make love to me all night long, make me happy, it's your turn to make me come,' she said, directing my hand towards her kinky-spot as she called it.

The whole scenario lasted the best part of a couple of hours until at last I detected she was asleep.

14

It was the morning after the night before. Lisa was very quiet. I pretended to still be asleep while she got up and zig-zagged her way into the shower room. The street outside was very noisy and early morning sunlight was beginning to filter into the room through the shutters.

'Come on, get up, we have a train to catch,' she shouted as she emerged fully clothed and ready for the trip home.

I hurriedly got washed and dressed and packed my things. We then went downstairs for breakfast and waited for the taxi to take us back to Gare du Nord.

On the train, Lisa remained very quiet.

'Are you alright?' I kept asking.

'Yes, now shut up,' she replied.

I wasn't too sure what to think, so I just gazed at the greenery of the French countryside rushing by the window as the train gathered speed. Eventually, we entered the Channel Tunnel and the mood changed. Lisa grabbed my hand.

'What do you think?' she asked.

'Think about what?'

'Us, silly. Us!'

'Are you talking about what happened last night?'

'Yes and no. Will it happen again? Will you be my new boyfriend?'

'Ah, well I suppose I will have to be now we've already consummated the relationship,' I joked. 'Look, let's give it a go and see what happens.'

'How about you spoil me? Take me for dinner on Friday. There's a really nice menu at the Worplesdon Place Hotel. I always enjoy it there. Anyway, it's your turn to pay, old boy.'

'Okay, I will. I look forward to it. And thanks for this weekend. I've really enjoyed it.'

'I enjoyed it too, and I'm not just talking about the sex,' she said with what looked like a false smile.

Eventually, I got home. I had a long look at myself in the mirror and then sat down with a glass of Jameson's. I needed something strong to drink and most certainly needed to think things through. I was beginning to feel very guilty about what I had just done in the wake of Suzanne's murder. Now I was wondering if, perhaps, I did have feelings for Lisa. I knew I had to be honest with myself before I could really be honest with her.

15

When I got to the office I set my mind to finding out more about Frankie Fletcher. I was still contemplating whether I should contact him despite being warned against it by Maria. There were so many questions to ask, and so much that remained unanswered. It was all getting very complicated. Too much of the information, though, was pure speculation. I really needed the facts.

Eventually, I plucked up the courage and punched out his mobile number. It rang and rang and then eventually cut out without even going to voicemail. I sifted through Suzanne's files to see if I could find any other contact details but there was nothing current, just an old number from his *Washington Post* days in 1997. I tried that, but the number no longer existed. I had drawn a blank.

I decided to read through some press cuttings which Suzanne had scanned and stored in one of her files. Frankie's reports all seemed to have a controversial edge whatever he was writing about. Each article looked like it had the potential to unlock something or upset someone. That is probably the reason why he's apparently gone into hiding, I surmised, underlining everything Maria had told me.

Just as I was thinking that any hope of contacting Frankie had diminished, my phone rang. It was a withheld number.

'Hello, who's that?'

'Frankie.'

'What, Frankie Fletcher?'

'Yes mate, now, who the fuck are you?'

'Err, Jack, Jack Compton.'

'Compton, where have I heard that name before?'

'I'm a friend of Suzanne Camilleri, the journalist who was killed in Malta.'

'Yeah, she was a fucking good reporter. I've known her for years. So, Compton, what the fuck do you want?'

'It's just that your name has come up quite a few times, particularly in some of Suzanne's files and I was wondering if you may be able to shed any light on why she was killed.'

'Look, I don't know you, mate, you could be anybody, there's loads of fucking nutjobs out there. How do I know you're not one of them?'

'I'm sorry, but you don't.'

'Well, I ain't gonna say anything over the phone. It's probably bugged like my other numbers. I'm gagged from saying anything anyway. The SIU have placed me in a safe house and banned me from saying anything. They say it's something to do with the Sicilian mafia, but I reckon it's closer to home. MI5 or MI6, or even the CIA.'

'Why do you think that?'

'Look, cunt, I just told you, I ain't gonna talk over the phone. I've said too much already, and I only did that for their benefit to let them know I know they're listening.'

'Yes, yes, I get that,' I said.

'Look, dick for brains, this is crazy, I ain't enjoying myself. Every time I go out there's some cunt in a blue denim jacket and sunglasses following me. If I venture over a mile radius my tag sets an alarm off and the men in suits pile in to take me back to the house. It ain't fucking pleasant.'

'I'm sorry.'

'Right, dickhead, Jack, or whatever your name is. I'm not sure what you're really after but you seem quite bright, and any mate of Suzanne's is a mate of mine. Don't say anything. I will only say this word once and I don't want you to reply, got it!'

'Err yes, thank you, got it!'

'Buttiġieġ.'

After Frankie said the name, he immediately extinguished the call. I then realised Lisa was sitting on the desk just behind me.

'Are you alright?' she asked.

'Yes, I think so.'

'That was Frankie Fletcher, wasn't it? You seem a little shaken.'

'Yeah, well he was abrupt and swore a lot. He also called me a See You Next Tuesday.'

'Oh, you mean he called you a cunt. No, I don't like that word either. It's an awful word.' She laughed and then walked over and kissed the top of my head.

'Hello, hello, what's going on here?' said Helen, as she walked in with a couple of coffees.

'First you bugger off to Paris together and now you're cavorting around like a couple of sex-starved teenagers.'

'Oh, we're just being friendly. Jack has just spoken to one of the greats of international journalism and is overawed by it all, aren't you, Jack?'

'Yes, I suppose I am, well sort of, anyway.'

Afterwards, I kept thinking about what Frankie had said. Why did he mention Buttiġieġ? I guess he meant Joseph Buttiġieġ who I had met in Gozo and I was now actually beginning to wonder why his niece, Rita, was always so friendly. In fact, looking back, she was always over-friendly and very keen to know everything about what I was doing. I think my next trip to Malta will now be sooner rather than later.

On my way home, I decided to pop into one of my local pubs, the Garibaldi in Knaphill, for a quick drink. An old friend and retired national journalist, Stan Clement, is part of the furniture in there these days and I thought I would take the opportunity to have a chat. I hoped he would be gracing the place with his usual presence.

'Guinness, is it?' asked Charlene, one of the barmaids as soon as I walked up to the bar.

'Err, yes please. You have a good memory, I haven't been in for a few weeks, I've missed your jolly fine service.'

'Aw bless you, been slumming it somewhere else, have we?' she said with a smile.

'No, not really, just been busy.'

'Still a reporter? Still telling those stories, are we?'

'Well that's one way of putting it. Talking of which, you haven't seen Stan this evening, have you?'

'Yes, he's outside on the veranda trying out one of those electronic fandangos, he reckons it's going to help him quit smoking.'

'Smoking and vaping, that's the same thing, isn't it?'

'I don't think so. Anyway, ask Stan, I'm sure he'll tell you.'

'Thank you, I will.'

When I went outside there was a huge plume of smoke and everyone was laughing. Apparently electronic cigarettes have a number of settings and Stan had put his on the highest level. One of the other regulars amongst a group of builders likened him to a steam engine.

'Choo, choo,' he shouted.

While another burst into song... *'Choo, choo to boogie, choo, choo.'*

I laughed and could see that I had just joined the conversation on the back end of the joke. When everything had settled down, Stan realised I was sat at an adjacent table and came over to speak.

'Jack, how you doing. I haven't seen you for a while, are you okay?'

'Err, yes thanks, fine, thank you.'

'I saw what happened to your friend in Malta, it was on the news.'

'Yes, I've been out there and met up with her family. I'm now trying to find out who and what was behind it all.'

'Well it's an opportunity for you to put your investigative reporter's hat on at last and put your training to the test. You haven't had a chance to do that since leaving the *Herald*, have you?'

'No, not properly, I've spent too much time working with the local rags and doing other stuff.'

'There's no money in working for the locals these days, they just pay peanuts.'

'Yeah, tell me about it. Anyway, I was hoping to bump into you. In your time at *The Sun*, did you ever come across a guy called Frankie Fletcher?'

'Blimey, old Frankie Fourfingers, he was always stirring up the cuckoo's nest, he was. He's been gagged lately, I believe. I heard he got sent back from Malta.'

'Yes, I know. You don't happen to know why, do you?'

'No, I've only heard rumours. I don't think it's related but I do know he'd hacked into some coded GCHQ data a few months ago and got hold of some sensitive information. His antics did eventually get reported across the board but that's when he seemed to disappear off the face of the earth. He is alright, though, isn't he?'

'Yes, I only spoke to him on the phone his afternoon. His name kept coming up while I was looking into what was behind Suzanne's murder. I was warned not to speak to him as it could cause problems, but I decided to bite the bullet and give him a call.'

'Well, be very careful. What he's into is well out of your league, it was certainly out of mine. Did you get anything off him?'

'Frankie didn't like the idea of me contacting him and he was certainly very abrupt when I spoke to him on the phone but he gave me a name. That of a Maltese guy who I met out in Gozo. I think it's a crucial lead and one I didn't expect.'

'What? Frankie being abrupt? He hasn't changed then, that's how I seem to remember him, a real character and a bit of a ladies' man but no manners and he always led with his chin. He had a certain knack of attracting enemies and spent his whole career ducking and diving and dodging one problem after another, and they were all usually of his own making, that's why no-one would ever properly employ him. Always controversial was our Frankie!'

'Thanks, it's useful to know more about his background. I knew you would be the best person to ask.'

'Ha, just a fluke, but he is one of those knob-jockeys that always stood out. Now, do you fancy another drink?'

'Why not? Thanks Stan, and then I'd better go.'

'Not before you've bought me one back, I hope.'

'Ha, ha, no I haven't forgotten pub protocol.'

In the end I stayed until about 10pm and four pints of Guinness later. I tried to exchange numbers with Charlene but she declined my kind offer, politely reminding me she was a good friend of Lisa's and knew all about our 'sordid little trip to Paris' as she put it.

'Best go home before you get in to any more trouble,' Stan quipped.

I think he was right.

16

When I woke up this morning, I noticed a missed call on my mobile from a number I didn't recognise. It was timed at 7.24 which was quite early for someone to be calling me. The number had a 356 prefix, which is the international dialling code for Malta. I was intrigued, but also a little concerned about who might be trying to get hold of me. I decided to dial the number from another phone just in case it was something malicious. The phone rang for a while and then a female voice answered.

'Hello, hello, who's that?'
'Err, hello, I'm a newspaper reporter calling from England.'
'Is that Jack?'
'Yes, that's right, Jack, Jack Compton. Who am I speaking to please?'
'This is Rosie.'
'Rosie?'
'Yes Rosie from the Cisk kiosk at Hondoq Bay.'
'Ah, Rosie, how are you?'
'I'm alright.'
'How did you get my number?'
'I had been talking to Lorca, Suzanne's daughter, the other day. She let me have it.'
'Why?'
'When you last came to Gozo, I was too busy to talk to you properly and I couldn't be sure who was listening so I did not tell you everything. I've since found out a little more.'
'About what?'
'About Suzanne and why she may have been killed.'

'I thought you had already told me quite a lot.'

'I did, but like I just said, there's more.'

'Like what?'

'Two days before she was killed a man called Frankie Fourfingers phoned from London telling her to watch her back as he had grave concerns about her safety.'

'Frankie Fourfingers Fletcher?'

'Yes. He had previously given her information about the missing British woman from 1997.'

'Fiona Meredith?'

'Yes. He had information she was living here in Malta, right here in Gozo to be precise. He had given Suzanne all the details but I don't think she had time to record anything. Last time Frankie was here was about three months ago. He was arrested but no-one knew why, and he was taken to the British Embassy in Valletta.'

'Three months ago?'

'Yes. Fortunately Suzanne had a conversation with Lorca the day before she was killed. She told Lorca everything she knew. She confided that things were becoming increasingly desperate. She was absolutely convinced someone was out to harm her.'

'So what does Lorca actually know?'

'Lorca told me that when the British woman was kidnapped in Venice, they were going to use her body as a decoy to replace Princess Diana. It was a plan by the UK intelligence services to save the British monarchy. There were concerns because of Diana's relationship with Dodi Al Fayed. They were going to kill him and fake the death of Diana.'

'This all sounds ridiculous.'

'It does, but wait, there's more. The whole thing was seriously flawed. They hadn't taken into consideration that the British woman had never borne any children. Diana had two. There was also a three-inch height difference. DNA had just started to be used as evidence in British courts as well, so it was decided to abort the plan. On top of all that, they couldn't even get the date right. Diana and Dodi visited Paris a week before their little plan was supposed to happen.'

'This is all supposition though, isn't it?'

'Possibly, but like I just said, Diana and Dodi went to Paris a week earlier than first planned. We all know what happened to them, that event was real. It was just an accident probably caused by the chauffeur who had been drinking as everyone has suggested.'

'So, what about Fiona Meredith?'

'She was kidnapped by members of the Sicilian mafia who were being paid by the UK government via someone here in Malta. It used to happen quite a lot. The mafia are often contracted to work on behalf of various governments and regimes. It's a shame, but Malta is frequently used as their playground. There have been six or seven car bombs over recent years and I fear Suzanne won't be the last to die this way.'

'So where, if she is still alive, has Fiona been all this time?'

'I think the mafia originally intended to kill her. Frankie Fourfingers had told Suzanne she had been kept alive because she fell in love with her captor and he protected her from almost certain death. The woman was always kept behind closed doors because of her resemblance to Princess Diana and the threat of unwanted media interest. Frankie and Suzanne were really the only two journalists who had still been chasing the story.'

'Rosie, if you don't mind me asking, you seem quite in tune with all this for someone who just works in a confectionary kiosk.'

'Don't underestimate me, Jack. I have three separate degrees, one in law, one in English and one in politics.'

'Sorry, I obviously had the wrong perception of you.'

'Don't be sorry, I prefer it that way. It helps me to keep my head down.'

'Anyway, do you think we are close to finding Fiona?'

'Yes, I'm sure she's here on Gozo, quite possibly in Qala. There has also been an unconfirmed sighting of her in Victoria. She was allegedly seen with a young lady called Rita.'

'Rita? Do you mean the same Rita who works at the Grand Hotel in Għajnsielem, the blonde girl who always wears her hair in a ponytail?'

'Yes, that's her.'

'That may explain why she's taken an unusual interest in me during my last couple of visits. I have even met her uncle, Joseph Buttiġieġ.'

'Well you must be very wary of him. Everyone knows he's on the mafia payroll. Qala also has an historical link with the surname Buttiġieġ and it would make sense if that's where Fiona may now be living. There seems to have been a lot of secrecy around the place in recent months. I think something is happening. Remember, she would be in her fifties now and will have changed a lot since she first went missing all those years ago.

'Yes, I'm aware of that. Actually, I'm planning to come over to Gozo again very soon, can we meet?'

'No, no. I've told you all this because I don't want Suzanne's death to have been in vain. The truth must come out but I will not be the person seen to reveal it. I have too much to lose. That, Jack, my reporter friend, is for you to do. I've told you everything and I must go now. Bye!'

Rosie hung up quite suddenly and left me with no time to continue the conversation. She had, though, helped answer a few questions. I spent the rest of the day searching the internet for more clues based on what she had told me. I also thought about calling Frankie Fletcher again but decided against it. He is a marked man and to put it quite simply, I knew I didn't want to end up in the same boat as him.

17

Lisa's eyes looked very bleary this morning. It had been the first time I'd seen her for a couple of weeks.

'Oh, Jack, come into my office, I need a word,' she said as soon as I arrived.

'Jack, I have some bad news, unfortunately I need your desk space back. HQ has given me orders. I've been asked to take on a couple of graduate trainees. One will work with Stuart on the reporting side, while the other will be trained up to help out with our new advertising campaign.'

Actually, the news didn't hurt at all. I had already made good use of the facilities and transferred all the necessary data to new software on my laptop. I had all Suzanne's files to hand and everything else I needed to know had come from other sources. I decided to thank Lisa for allowing me to use the office and told her it was great to see the old place again after all those years. I was reaching for my jacket but sensed she wasn't quite finished with me yet.

'Jack, what about us? Do we have a future, can we build on what happened in Paris?'

'I'm not sure, to be honest. Our time in Paris was great and I loved being with you. I still need to get my head around things, you know, be sure of what I really want without hurting anyone in the process. Of course it would be good to go out again.'

'That would be very nice, thank you.'

'Okay, I'll see if I can come up with something and let you know.'

'By the way, do ever hear from your ex-wife, Kazkia these days?'

'No, she died.'

'What, as in dead?'

'Yes, dead. She was found lying on the bathroom floor in her apartment near Guildford. She apparently had a seizure and then choked on her own vomit.'

'Oh how awful! Was she with anyone at the time?'

'Sort of, some bloke who worked in a bar, his name was Tony but he disappeared off the face of the earth just after her body was found. I was told he was a pot-smoking crackhead. Apparently, that was the kind of people she had been mixing with for the last few months, right up until she died.'

'When did all this happen?'

'A few years ago, it was towards the end of October 2015 to be precise. I got a call from Surrey Police. A policewoman had found my number on her phone. Kazkia still had me on her contact list as "hubby", which I thought was quite bizarre. We had been divorced for nearly twenty years and I always avoided communicating with her because of what she had put me through.'

'Yes, I remember all that. You seem a different person now, and of course appear much better for it.'

'Well, as you know, there is nothing good about depression. I have an old friend called Jooltz. We've known each other since school. She's a slightly crazy lady but was someone I trusted and could always talk to. I knew I could tell her everything. She was the one person who listened to me and understood where I was coming from. She probably saved my life.'

'How?'

'Well, with just very good advice. She always spelt things out quite graphically, and even once explained the word "sad" to me... S = Stress. A = Anxiety. D = Depression. S.A.D. really means Seasonal Affective Disorder, that's what I was eventually diagnosed with when I had my problems in the 1990s. Stress, anxiety and depression are not good things to have, particularly if you suffer from them all at the same time. She once told me to look in the rear view mirror and leave everything behind. "Never look back," she said.'

'But you don't drive!'

'I'm speaking metaphorically.'

'Yes, I know,' Lisa laughed. 'I'm joking. I'm not that young dumb blonde custard puppy you used to know way back then,' she added.

I laughed. We both laughed. Afterwards I popped my head around the door, said my goodbyes to the others and grabbed my jacket but not before Lisa pulled me to one side and smothered both of my cheeks with bright pink lipstick.

'There, off you go, old boy, and don't forget to call me. I'm free this weekend and I'm already looking forward to another weekend away. Don't forget, right?'

'I won't,' I said as I left the office quite clumsily through the back door.

When I got home I decided to look up some flight times for my next trip to Malta. I knew it had to be imminent. I wasn't sure whether to stay at the Grand Hotel again because of Rita, but I couldn't think of any other reasonable alternatives. The Grand Hotel is in walking distance from Nadur and Qala, and also an easy bus ride to Victoria. It's just convenient, and besides, I love the view of the harbour and have made friends with a couple from England who run one of the quayside bars down in Mġarr. It would be good to see them again.

Before booking, I decided to sleep on it.

18

Today, I thought, was always going to be a "nothing" kind of day. I had booked my flight and hotel for Malta and that was it. I had nothing else planned apart from a little shopping in Woking and perhaps a bite to eat. The day was typically grey and overcast. The magpies on the back fence seemed quite boisterous and appeared to be intimidating the next door neighbour's cat.

Whilst walking towards town I noticed a white BMW convertible overtake me a couple of times. About half an hour later it came towards me again as I was waiting to cross the road near The Lightbox exhibition centre. I thought no more of it but then a little later I saw it parked up close to the Ogilvy pub where I was heading for. There was a guy with shoulder length grey hair wearing sunglasses and a blue denim jacket. He was leaning on the bonnet of the car and seemed intent just to stare at me. I started to feel rather paranoid as I walked past him to reach the entrance. Even the girl behind the bar, who I had never seen before, asked me if I was alright when I walked up to get served.

'Err, yes, I think so,' I stuttered.

As she served me I noticed the car drive off from outside. I felt some relief but wondered who was taking an unhealthy interest in me.

The pub was quite quiet so I found a table at the back and decided to phone Rick. I tried a couple of times but there was no answer. I think the incident with the man outside had unsettled me and I needed to talk to a friend, just to help calm my nerves. I opened my laptop and decided to have another look through Suzanne's files just to be sure nothing had been missed. I came across an internet link to a WordPress blog entitled 'Corruption in Malta and the Sicilian mafia'. It looked like some material had recently been deleted but when I scrolled down the page, I found a new item that had only been posted yesterday, and it made for uncomfortable reading...

Corruption in Malta and the Sicilian Mafia

It appears the Sicilian mafia is set to be a delicate issue for the UK government over the coming days, as a single remark made in a Covent Garden café which was overheard by two investigative journalists in 1997 has the potential to cause its biggest ever embarrassment, even after over twenty years.

One of the said journalists, Edward Etheridge, mysteriously died by his own hand some months later in 1998 after 'apparently' falling from a cliff into the sea near Mġarr ix-Xini. The other, Frankie Fletcher, a seasoned journalist and former Royal Navy seaman, allegedly continued to investigate a story which could amount to the biggest conspiracy in UK government history. But is it true?

Documents leaked to the international press community are vague, however, they do suggest there was a plan in place to eliminate the Egyptian businessman and playboy, Dodi Al Fayed, in the lead up to his eventual demise in that fatal crash with Diana, Princess of Wales in a Paris road tunnel on 31 August 1997.

Nothing was ever proven. "Nothing added up, so the investigation was shelved," reported Mr Fletcher at the time. It now appears other journalists have been discreetly following up Mr Fletcher's earlier work and could now be close to revealing the facts behind a possible collusion between the UK government, MI6 and the mafia.

Indeed one journalist who was hot on their trail was recently killed in a car bomb attack on Gozo. Suzanne Camilleri is believed to have received sensitive information from Frankie Fletcher whom she'd known for a number of years. In another twist, three months ago, Mr Fletcher was arrested in Valletta for no apparent crime and escorted back to England by agents from the UK security services. He is now believed to be under house arrest (for his own safety) at a location near Southwark in South London. Two other journalists known to have been investigating the case are Rick Storey, who recently moved from the Malta Telegraph to work for the Saltash Chronicle in Cornwall, and roving freelance reporter Jack Compton who once worked with Suzanne Camilleri at the Sunday Herald in London.

In reaction to the document leak, it is now believed backbenchers in the British parliament are about to give their Prime Minister a grilling over these revelations as they seek to gain some truth in the matter. MI6 has already publicly denied any involvement but some ex-government officials who were in office at the time of Diana, Princess of Wales and Dodi Al Fayed's death have been lying low. Suspiciously, none have been available for comment.

"Too many inconsistencies and mixed messages, and, certainly no denial," said Frankie Fletcher when questioned just before his arrest.

The arrest is said to have greatly embarrassed the Government of Malta who appear to have no jurisdiction in their own backyard. They have since openly expressed concerns that their country is increasingly being used as a killing field by the mafia and have promised to tighten up its existing security measures. The pulizija (police) and the AFM (Armed Forces of Malta) have apparently been fully briefed on the new arrangements. The Government of Malta, though, has previously been heavily criticised by the European Commission for not dealing with serious crime on the islands. They have also been accused of colluding with the mafia during previous scandals. Other journalists and individuals have been murdered in their quest to find out and expose the truth behind all the various allegations. It's already very well documented that corruption is rife on the islands.

One minister, on behalf of the Government of Malta, has stated that if you give strength and authority to the mafia, you risk increasing its already menacing presence in a once peaceful and safe environment. Whatever the implications are regarding the murder of Suzanne Camilleri in Gozo and her investigation into an alleged collaboration between the UK *government and the mafia, we must not let our country become the key location for their enterprise. In regard to the death of Suzanne Camilleri, he said, "Remember, these people are responsible for the death of one of our own citizens!" It has been noted however, that other Government of Malta ministers have remained silent over this issue, which in a way, tells its own story.*

Some political observers now suggest that very soon, the UK government's role in an alleged plan to murder Dodi Al Fayed and perhaps the Princess as well, will be exposed. To what extent MI6 and the mafia had been involved, remains to be seen. Watch this space!

What worried me is that the person behind the blog post is "Anon". He or she has implicated both myself and Rick in the continuing investigations. All this had left me very curious. I thought I knew everyone who was privy to what we were investigating. It now seems someone else has knowledge of what we have been doing; but who? I definitely needed to contact Rick.

Before I went home I decided to stop off at the Garibaldi for another couple of pints. I could feel an end of summer chill in the air but it was still a pleasant evening. I noticed an old friend who I hadn't seen for a few years, sitting outside on the patio, so decided to join him for a chat.

'Jack, been a while, how are you?'

'Good, I think, all good,' I replied, hastily trying to remember his name.

'Still working for the *Tribune*?' he asked.

'Blimey, is it that long ago since we last spoke properly?'

He laughed. 'No, it was a few years back, but I can't remember where you'd moved on to, was it the *Sunday Herald*?'

'Yeah, sore point, we all lost our jobs when the paper was shut down.'

'Yes, I remember that, so what are you doing now?'

I hesitated. 'Well this and that, really. I'm currently investigating the death of a former colleague of mine. She was killed in Gozo, Malta, in a car bomb attack. We used to work at the *Herald* together.'

'Oh, I think I read something about that a few months ago. It was all over the internet.'

'So what about you, what are you up to these days?' I asked, still frantically trying to remember his name.

'I was working as a techie for the Metropolitan Police in a civilian role until a few weeks ago but have decided to leave and set up my own business as an IT consultant. It's something I've always wanted to do. I would regret it if I didn't give it a bash. Look, here's my new business card.'

Russell Lancaster, IT Consultant. Well that's got me off the hook, I thought. For some reason I kept thinking his name was Mick. It had been so long since I'd spoken to him. I don't think I've ever known his surname. With a name like Lancaster, I certainly would have remembered that. I decided to tell him about the blog post from earlier and asked how I could trace a person who was hiding behind an alias or posting as "anonymous".

'It's possible. Long-winded but possible,' he said.

'How?'

'It's all to do with internet protocol. It's the method by which data is sent from one computer to another on the internet. Each computer - which is also known as a host - has at least one IP address that uniquely identifies it from all other computers on the internet. Tracing a user should be simple. For example, when someone signs up for a new email address through their web service provider, the IP address is automatically stored.'

'So how are people actually matched to an IP address?'

'When I was working for the police, we had to do this quite often, but had to get written consent from the Chief Constable or one of his understudies first. It was just a case of linking an IP address to a web service provider and then a person's Wi-Fi account. Some people use the computer facilities at libraries or internet cafés thinking they won't get traced. What they don't consider is if they've already signed up to a website or blog, their username is already on file. When they enter it remotely they can still be found. It's not really rocket science. Anyway, why are you asking me about this?'

'Like I said, the blog post has mentioned mine and a friend's name and I feel it has compromised us. Bearing in mind my friend Suzanne has already been killed, it's all quite worrying.'

I decided to get my laptop from my backpack, open it and show Russell the actual blog post.

'Ah, Malta,' he said enthusiastically. 'Been there loads of times, I owned a flat in Valletta once, stayed for a couple of years just before I came back here to work for the police.'

'That's interesting, small world and all that, did you like it there?'

'It was alright. Some people call it a Marmite country, you know, you either love it or hate it.'

'What about Gozo?'

'In all the time I lived in Malta, I never went there. I don't know why, I always intended to, but it just didn't happen. Anyway, back to this blog post. I actually think that whoever is behind this is Maltese, or certainly someone who has lived in Malta for a while.'

'Why?'

'They keep referring to the government as the "Government of Malta", me and you for instance, or anybody else would simply call it the "Maltese Government".'

'That's a good point, I didn't think about that.'

'Well, I can say my time working with the police has taught me that sometimes the obvious is staring you in the face. It looks like that's what's happening here.'

After another pint I decided to make a move. Russell had taken a call from his wife, telling him his dinner would be in the dog if he didn't get home soon. We said our goodbyes and I promised to give him a ring if I saw any business that could help him with his new venture.

When I got home, I began to wonder who in Malta might be behind the blog post. I had already ruled Rita out as I think she is actually involved somewhere else along the line. Rosie's name kept springing to mind. She had an interest because Suzanne was one of her best friends. She had also called me recently with more information. I was trying to figure out if there was a common thread between what she told me and what was in the blog. I tried to get hold of Rick again, but each time my call went straight through to voicemail.

19

My phone rang at 7am. It was Russell. I'd forgotten I had given him my number.

'Hello Jack, our conversation at the pub yesterday excited me so I decided to do some digging. I spoke to a friend of mine at the Met and we've been able to trace the owner of the blog post you showed me. It was a user called "Anon", wasn't it?'

'Yes, that's right!'

'In the end the trace was quite simple. The person had been regularly logging on to the blog site using their home pc and a work's computer. A simple search and a Wi-Fi information request linked the two IP addresses to one person. I've even got their full postal address.'

'Who is it then?'

'It's a British woman living in Victoria, Gozo. Her name is Julie Etheridge. Do you know her?'

'No, I don't but the name Etheridge rings a bell, I've seen it somewhere very recently.'

'Okay, mate, I hope the info is of use, I'll text you with all the other details shortly.'

I thanked Russell for the call and immediately went to my laptop. I realised the name Etheridge was mentioned at the beginning of the blog post we had been looking at. Edward Etheridge was the journalist who had killed himself, the same guy who had been working with Frankie Fletcher in 1997. Was Julie his wife or daughter? I decided to do a quick Google search to see what I could find. There wasn't much but I did find an old *Times of Malta* clip of an obituary relating to Edward dated 9 August 1998:

> *On 30th July 1998 in Nadur, Gozo, my beloved brother, Edward John Etheridge, died unexpectedly by his own hand at the age of 32, comforted by the rites of the Holy Church. He leaves to mourn his great loss, his mother Eileen, his sister, Julie, and her son, Michael, his cousins, other relatives and friends including his long-time partner and friend, Deborah Cutajar. The funeral cortège leaves the Etheridge family home in Victoria on Friday 14 August at 8am for the Basilica and Collegiate Parish Church of Saint George where Mass præsente cadavere will be said at 9am followed by internment at the Santa Maria Cemetery. No flowers by request but donations to the Malta Society for the Protection of Care of Animals will be appreciated. Lord, grant him eternal rest.*

Unfortunately, the obituary was all I could find. There was no other information except that Julie Etheridge is obviously his sister. I began to wonder if she was undertaking her own investigation into why Edward had killed himself. There is nothing which states how he died, both the blog post and the obituary cutting just says; "by his own hand". From what Russell has sent me, she lives in an apartment in Luigi Vella Street in Victoria, close to the Maldonado restaurant where I've eaten a couple of times. I think I will be having a very interesting conversation if she agrees to speak to me. I need to find out what her agenda really is and if there is anything sinister going on. On the other hand, she could be one of the missing links I am looking for in my search to find out who killed Suzanne.

20

Finally Rick has been in touch.

'Hey mate, sorry I missed your calls. I've had a few issues recently, in fact it's all been tough,' he said.

'What's happened?'

'We buried Mum last Friday, we thought she was going to pull through but she had a relapse and the cancer got her in the end. At least she died peacefully. My brothers and I were both at her side. It was important for all of us that we were together to share Mum's final moments.'

When I get drawn into a conversation like this I always find it hard to know what to say and it's difficult sometimes to respond. Fortunately, Rick decided to change the conversation quite quickly.

'How are you getting on with the Suzanne investigation?' he asked.

'I feel more like a policeman than a journalist at times, there seems to be so many twists and turns recently and there are quite a few different people emerging who could hold the clue about the missing woman. I think I'm close, but the whole thing is getting quite scary.'

'What do you mean, scary?'

'Only the other day I thought I was being followed. There was a guy driving around in a white BMW convertible. It had a black top which was down and he seemed to be taking quite an interest in my movements. We nearly brushed shoulders when I went to the Ogilvy pub in Woking; he was leaning against the bonnet of his car and seemed reluctant to move out of my way when I tried to pass.'

'What did he look like?'

'I would say he was a bit older than me, late fifties, even sixty perhaps. Shoulder length grey hair and sunglasses. He was wearing a blue denim jacket and what looked like beige cargo trousers.'

'That fits the description of a guy who turned up at Mum's funeral. He was standing at the entrance to the church in Redruth as we came away. Shoulder length grey hair, but wearing a long black coat. He drew our attention as we were all sweltering in 25 degree heat. It was bloody hot for the end of summer, in fact.'

'That's worrying, I wonder if it's the same guy. I guess we both just need to be careful. Have you been involving yourself in the Suzanne case since you moved down to Saltash?'

'No, no, definitely not, I've been too busy with the *Chronicle* and besides I had Mum to look after, it's taken all my time.'

I told Rick I was going back to Malta in a couple of days. I also mentioned the call I had from Rosie and told him my concerns about us both being named in a blog post. I told him I felt we could be compromised which was the reason I had been trying to get hold of him in the first place.

'Unfortunately for journalists, that's a position we often find ourselves in,' he said.

I agreed.

'Do you know who posted on the blog?'

'Yes, an old friend of mine who's a techie traced it through something called internet protocol the other night. The post was put up by someone called Julie Etheridge who he believes lives in Gozo.'

'I think I know who that is,' he replied.

'Who?'

'I remember hearing at the *Telegraph* that Julie Etheridge once had a fling with Frankie Fletcher. They met when Frankie was working with her brother, Edward. I believe Edward committed suicide around the late nineties. I think Suzanne was on to it.'

'That doesn't surprise me, and yes, I've seen a newspaper cutting of the obituary.'

'Julie had an illegitimate son by Frankie. He must be twenty-something now.'

'His name wasn't Michael, was it?'

'Yes, I think it was.'

'I thought so, there's a Michael, son of Julie, mentioned in the obituary. I only found it on the internet a day or two ago.'

'So what's Frankie up to now, do you know?'

'I've never ever physically met the man although I did speak to him on the phone a while ago. He was abrupt and swore at me a lot, but did end up giving me a name which I am still following up. The last I heard he was arrested by UK security services in Valletta, brought back to England and is now somewhere in South London, Southwark, I think. When I spoke to him on the phone, he told me he had been forced to wear a tag.'

'That all sounds bizarre.'

'Every time I talk to someone about Frankie, they all seem to have a story to tell. There is always a wry smile at the end of the conversation as well. I think people have mixed feelings about him.'

'Well I did meet him once, back in the day. He was always up his own ass. I can understand why the women always liked him, though, I suppose he had that big cuddly demeanour some women like, which is probably why Julie was attracted to him.'

'I'm hoping to meet with Julie when I get to Gozo. Amongst others, she's on my list of people to visit.'

'Well, enjoy your trip and let me know how you get on.'

'I will. Stay safe. Once again, I'm very sorry to hear about your mum, I'm sure she'll be looking down on you.'

'Yeah, thanks Jack, that's most appreciated.'

After the conversation ended I became even more concerned about the man in the blue denim jacket. I seemed to remember Frankie mentioning a man of that description the day we had the telephone conversation. I think I need to be very wary and not be too habitual with my movements. I hope Rick is thinking the same.

22

I had just finished an early breakfast when Lisa called.

'Jack, how the devil are you, old boy? Are you enjoying the weather out there?'

'Err, yes thank you,' I said, not expecting her call.

'I phoned about a couple of things, I hope you don't mind.'

'No, of course not, it's good to hear from you.'

'Firstly, do you remember our old boss, Nancy?'

'You know I do, we were only talking about her the other week. She still works at the *Tribune's* parent company in Reading, doesn't she?'

'Well I'm sorry to have to tell you I had a call from a friend last night saying that she had died a couple of days ago.'

'What? What from?'

'Natural causes, she was getting on a bit, I've been invited to her funeral in Canterbury next Friday. I was wondering if you would be able to come with me?'

'Obviously I would if I could, but I'll almost certainly still be here. Things are beginning to hot up. Strange things are happening. I'll let you know if anything changes.'

'Okay, right and now the second thing.'

'Ah sorry, I was meaning to contact you, you know, about going for a meal, maybe like going on another trip, I did enjoy Paris and the things that happened there, you know!'

'Yes, you're an asshole, we'll put that right as soon as we can, but that wasn't what I was going to talk to you about.'

'What then?'

'I noticed on the news yesterday your flight was delayed for a few hours at Gatwick. The airport was shut for a while. They arrested a man who was trying to board your flight, didn't they?'

'Yes, apparently someone was trying to smuggle a lethal nerve agent on board.'

'Well, I've just seen on the telly that he's been released without charge. The substance he was carrying was no more than saline solution. Police have commented that they acted on a tipoff which they now believe was malicious.'

'Did they say anything more about the man?'

'Just that his name was Reno something...'

'Yes, Reno Stavola. I've seen his picture and he is the same man that followed me around Woking the other day. He also turned up in Cornwall, at my friend Rick's mum's funeral. Something weird is going on and none of it is making much sense.'

'Well, you just be very careful. I wish I was there to look after you and help keep you safe. Take care, oh, and by the way, know this, I love you and can't wait for another fuck, darling.'

Lisa hung up. It was a strange ending to the call and I could sense a flicker of emotion in her voice at the end.

After a shower, I decided to pop down to the harbour for a coffee at one of the kiosks. Two men were discussing the front page article on today's local paper. It carried a picture of Reno Stavola. I heard them mention his name a couple of times. One of them kept laughing. 'Bastardo, Bastardo!' he kept saying. Their conversation then changed from English into Maltese and seemed to become more intense. I tried to eavesdrop without making it too obvious I was listening, even though I don't understand a word of the Maltese language. The other man then started making a slashing gesture across his throat and they both laughed. Their conversation then returned to English as they stood up and made their way to a small fishing boat that had been moored alongside the quay. I wasn't sure what to make of their conversation but they did seem to have a problem with Reno Stavola. I wasn't sure if that was good or bad!

Later, after a short bus ride, I found myself in Victoria. Before getting something to eat I decided to look for somewhere to get a haircut. Eventually, I found a small unisex salon called Blue Velvet in Main Gate Street just around the corner from the bus station. A very pretty lady around thirty-years-old with flame-red hair, tied back with a dark green bow was finishing a woman's perm. I asked if she could quickly fit me in as I noticed the salon was about to close for the rest of the afternoon.

'Ah, yes of course I can, sir, sit down there, I won't be two ticks.' After the woman left, the hairdresser who had a strong Irish accent asked me to move to the middle chair of three.

'How can I help you today?'

'Err, a grade one back and sides, square across the back with the top just trimmed and blended in.'

'No problem. I don't get too many Englishmen in here. You're a rarity.'

'Well, this is my first ever haircut in Malta. I meant to have it done before when I've been over but either just forgot, or didn't have time... so you're obviously from Ireland?'

'Oh yes, I've been here at the salon for a few years now. I bought it from an Italian lady. I always wanted my own business. I came to Gozo for the first time when I was around twenty and just fell in love with the place. I somehow knew this would be my destiny, so I did.'

'So do you get a lot of customers?'

'To be honest, it's usually just a trickle, but I make enough to pay the bills and buy nice things, so that keeps me happy.'

I couldn't help smiling at her accent and the way she spoke. It was a very raw southern Irish accent. I think she noticed I was quite amused.

'You have a fine head of hair for a gentleman of your age, so you have. Tell me, what brings you here to Gozo?'

'Well firstly, like you, I love the place. I find Gozo has that magnetic feel to it. It just draws you back. I like the people, the scenery, the food, oh and of course the wine and the beer.'

'Most people say that, so what do you do for a living?'

'I'm a newspaper reporter, freelance actually. I'm sort of here on what you would call a working holiday. It's all a bit sad really. I was good friends with a lady who was killed in a car bomb attack near Ramla a few months ago.'

'Ah, Suzanne, Suzanne Camilleri, I used to do her hair once a month, she used to sit in this very chair. She was a lovely lady and became a good friend of mine. It's terrible what happened to her. She did not deserve to die like that. No-one deserves to die like that.'

'Do you know any more about what happened?' I thought it prudent to ask.

'No, not really, but something strange happened here a few weeks before. Whilst I was in the process of cutting a woman's hair, the woman let it slip she had been living in a big house in Qala since the very late 1990s. It was a strange conversation. The woman told me it was nice to have her hair back to normal again even though it was dyed black and her grey roots were showing through. I asked her if she would like me to colour it for her but she declined, saying that she just wanted it all cut off with a grade one.'

'But surely, you must get customers like that all the time.'

'Yes, in a way but this was different. Just as I was finishing, a black Mercedes car parked outside and blocked the street for at least twenty minutes, it caused havoc. The car had a chauffeur and another man in a suit got out. He came into the salon, thrust a 50 Euro note into my hand, gently grabbed hold of my customer's wrist, took her to the car and whisked her away before I even had a chance to reach for the mirror and show her the back of her head, like we do.'

'That's very strange.'

'Well, just a couple of days later, your friend Suzanne came in for her monthly trim and I told her about the incident. She asked me who had made the booking. It was made by someone called Rita. Suzanne knew her, she worked at the Grand Hotel in Għajnsielem.'

'It's a small world. I've actually met Rita and her uncle at least a couple of times,' I said without saying too much else.

'I remember Suzanne being very curious about the whole episode although she never told me why. Later that day, two men came in and asked me questions about her visit and exactly what was said. I didn't give them anything, I just told them I did her hair like I normally do and that was it. They left empty handed and I never saw them again. The next thing I knew, Suzanne was dead.'

'Did you tell the police?'

'Oh, the police yes, of course, but I don't think they did anything. I didn't hear any more.'

'Well you've been very helpful, oh, and thanks for cutting my hair. I'm Jack by the way.'

'You're very welcome so you are, I'm Danielle O'Leary. I'm from County Cork in Ireland by the way. Two customers in a row talking about Suzanne, I didn't expect that today.'

'Two customers in a row?'

'Yes, the lady I was finishing when you arrived, Julie Etheridge, she was a great friend of Suzanne's. Thick as thieves, I believe they were. Julie lives here in Victoria, just along from the Maldonado restaurant near the statue. It's just a two or three-minute walk up the road from here.'

'What statue?'

'The statue of Luigi Vella, it's who the street's named after.'

'Oh, thanks, I'll definitely come back for a trim next time I'm over, bye.'

Danielle was a breath of fresh air. It was a good conversation and I've learnt more about Suzanne's movements in her final weeks. I can't believe the lady who was there when I arrived was actually Julie Etheridge. At least I already know what she looks like now. Who, though, was the woman from Qala, could it have been Fiona Meredith? Even after all these years, were the men in the car, her captors? I knew I had to be very careful about how to approach everything so decided to make my way back to the hotel to give myself time to think. I had even forgotten to eat which is really why I had gone to Victoria in the first place. I was famished. I needed some food, and quick.

When I got back to the hotel, the restaurant was still open and I was able to order some local fish from the specials menu. Lampuki, a favourite dish of mine, was well in season now and I wasn't disappointed. Afterwards, I needed to use the toilet and noticed some interesting photographs of hotel staff and other Gozitans up on the wall in the corridor. I recognised a few of the people even though some of the pictures were quite old. There was one with a man standing by a bus; it was the same man I saw last time I was here who was selling his bus to someone in England. The picture that really caught my eye, though, was the one in the middle. It was of four men sitting on a wall down at the harbour, mending a long fishing net. Two of them were the same men I had seen talking down at the quay earlier today. The others were Joseph Buttiġieġ and, unbelievably, Reno Stavola. This proved they were all connected. Just then I sensed someone standing behind me, it was one of the hotel's kitchen staff.

'*Inti tidher interessat ħafna fir-ritratti,*' he said.

'Err sorry. I don't understand, I can't speak Maltese,' I replied.

'Sorry, my English is not very good. I will try and translate... you seem very interested in the photographs.'

'Yes, I recognise quite a few of the people in them, especially this one taken of four fishermen.'

'Ah, it was taken five or six years ago down at the harbour. Those two are Luis Micallef and Sam Sultana. When they're not out in their boat, they both work in the kitchen here. That's Reno Stavola, he used to be a waiter and the other is my Uncle Joseph.'

'Joseph Buttiġieġ.'

'Yes, forgive me, how do you know?'

'I've met him a couple of times, I also know your sister, Rita, she used to work here as a receptionist.'

'Rita is not my sister, she is my cousin. She's from another part of the family. There were once seven brothers. Joseph is the only one still alive but he is very ill with lung cancer, it's come to him quite quick. It was only, how you say, diagnosed a month or two ago. Rita is looking after him now.'

After saying goodbye and thanking him for the chat I decided to go back to my room and make a few notes. I should have asked his name but I was so interested in what he was saying, I forgot. I did notice Reno Stavola had the word 'Mafioso' printed on his T-shirt in the photograph and wondered what that really meant. Was it enough confirmation that he was a member of the mafia? I also decided to revisit some of Suzanne's files on my laptop, there was so much information. I had to decipher and decide what was relevant. The last file was a jpeg, a photograph. It was of Suzanne in a restaurant sitting with Rosie and another woman who I now recognise to be Julie Etheridge. In the background there was a waiter. When I looked closer, I could identify him as Reno Stavola. The photo had a caption, "Antony's, Nadur 2009". I remembered there used to be a restaurant called Antony's in a small square behind the church in Nadur but it closed a few years ago. It must have been shortly after the photograph was taken. Now I wondered what, if any part, Reno may have had in Suzanne's murder.

23

The last couple of days have been really hot. I spent my time sitting outside and re-examining everything I had done so far whilst enjoying the Gozo sunshine. It was all getting a little frustrating and I felt today had to be the day I needed to get the ball rolling in my quest for answers. Time was running out and I needed to get my story done and then pitch it to the highest bidder, if I could find one. Money was also an issue, so things were beginning to get a little fraught.

I decided to take myself back up to Victoria and see if I could find Julie Etheridge, I had a rough idea of where she lived. I probably only needed to ask at the Maldonado restaurant, which is on the same street. Someone there would almost certainly know her and be able to confirm her exact address details. Fortunately, when I reached the restaurant there was a woman with a very wrinkly face and tightly permed white hair sitting at a table down the steps just inside. She was stroking a small pug dog. It was the same woman I had seen at the hair salon the other day, the one Danielle told me was Julie.

'Good afternoon, you're Mrs Etheridge, aren't you?' I asked.

'Yes, I am. You must be that English reporter I've been told about. Jack, isn't it?'

'Yes, Jack Compton, how do you know?'

'Let's just say a little bird told me. Remember, this is Gozo, nothing much goes unnoticed around here, you know. I know quite a lot about you.'

'I thought you might. Sorry, do you mind if I join you? Would you like another coffee?'

'Dear, of course you can join me but I would like something a little stronger if you don't mind. I was just about to order myself a large cherry brandy. I also have a friend joining me shortly so if you don't mind, I would prefer to move further inside to a larger table. I guess, because you are a reporter you'd also like to ask me some questions, am I right?'

It was a response I wasn't expecting.

'Yes, if you don't mind.'

Shortly after we settled inside there was a pause whilst Julie rifled through her bag. Eventually, she pulled out a large plain brown envelope and inside was a photograph.

'Here, look, he's a handsome chap, isn't he?'

'Err yes, that looks like it was taken a while ago.'

'Yes, right back in the nineties, he's not with us anymore; this is my brother, Edward. They say he took his own life but I never believed it. None of us did. They found his body floating in the sea off Mġarr ix-Xini. They said he had fallen from a clifftop, but there was an unexplained wound at the base of his neck. One young policeman told me it was not consistent with a fall. He suggested Edward had been struck by an object such as a machete before being thrown into the sea but his superiors told him off for being overzealous. They did nothing, except announce his death as a suicide. It's not true. He was murdered.'

'If you don't mind me asking, who do you think killed him?'

'Some people say it was the mafia. I don't think so. It was the UK government. MI5 or MI6 maybe! They were trying to cover up a conspiracy. Edward and Frankie were on to it.'

'Frankie. Frankie Fletcher?'

'Yes, of course, you would know. He was very good to me in the aftermath. He comforted me.' Julie reached for her bag again. 'Look here, this is my son,' she said, proudly showing me another photograph.

'I see. He looks very handsome. How old is he?'

'He's twenty-one now but this was taken a few years ago at Xlendi Bay. Around 2012, I think. Frankie is his father.'

I already knew, so decided not to respond. Just as Julie was putting everything back in her bag, a silhouette of a woman appeared at the doorway. The sun was so strong I could only see her outline at first, until she came over to where we were sitting.'

'Jack, meet my friend, this is Rosie.'

I immediately recognised her. It was Rosie from the kiosk at Hondoq.

'Hello, Rosie, we're already acquainted, aren't we?'

'We are. Nice to see you again, it's Jack, isn't it?'

'Yes, sorry. I didn't realise you two knew each other.'

'Oh yes, we've known one another since Edward died. Suzanne, as you know, was a good friend of mine. Both me and Julie knew Suzanne very well.'

'So Rosie, how did you know I was back on the island?'

'Julie told me. Her hairdresser phoned her and said an English reporter had been asking questions. I guessed it was you.'

'Ah, Danielle!'

'That's right. Like I said, nothing goes unnoticed here on Gozo,' said Julie.

I smiled, realising the error of my ways. I had been trying to keep a low profile but still managed to give myself away. It would have been difficult not to, though, I thought.

'Julie, I must ask about your blog post, you call yourself "Anon", I believe?'

'How do you know that?'

'When I saw the post I was unsettled because obviously my name was mentioned. I have a friend who is an IT and internet geek, he was able to trace you through your IP address and Wi-Fi account.'

'Oh my God, I didn't realise that was possible. If a reporter could find that out, then so could the police,' said Julie looking quite horrified.

'So what do you know? Have you found out any more about Suzanne since our telephone conversation the other week?' asked Rosie changing the subject quickly on Julie's behalf.

Just as she asked we were interrupted by the waiter brandishing a menu.

'Fish of the day, lampuki, it was freshly caught this morning.'

'Later, later,' said Julie, shooing him away.

'Drinks, though, more drinks please,' shouted Rosie as she gesticulated towards the bar.

Eventually the drinks arrived, my pint of Cisk and their two large cherry brandies, both with an ice-cream float.

'Right, Rosie, you were asking me about Suzanne,' I said.

'Yes, what more do you know?'

'I know that I was being followed near my home in Woking a couple of weeks ago. An old colleague of mine, Rick Storey, was being watched, almost certainly by the same man, down in Cornwall. The man who followed us was later arrested at Gatwick airport the other day trying to board the same flight I was on. I recognised him when I saw his picture on a news bulletin. I think he may have even been booked to sit next to me. A friend of mine, Lisa, has since phoned and told me he was later released without charge. His name is Reno Stavola.'

'Yes, I know him, I saw it all on the news,' said Julie. 'We think he does some work for the mafia now, he may even be a member. I know he used to also work for the government in the UK. Wait a minute.' Julie rummaged through her bag again. 'Look, this is him. This is Reno Stavola.'

It was a 1991 newspaper cutting from the *Daily Mirror*. The picture showed Princess Diana and Prince Charles boarding the royal train at Hampton Court railway station. Stavola is standing in the background. The caption underneath the photo says "The royal couple with their equerry".

'Equerry?'

'He was never that, he was never a member of the royal household, that's just the tabloids getting it wrong as usual,' said Julie quite angrily.

'So what more do you know about him?' I asked.

'He's already back here on Gozo, he came back yesterday. There was a kerfuffle down at Mġarr Harbour with the press when he got off the ferry. We think he's in hiding now, probably in Qala.'

'Why Qala?'

'He has close links with the Buttiġieġ family. They all come from the village. It's just up the hill from my kiosk at Hondoq Bay,' said Rosie.

'My main question is: do you think he had anything to do with Suzanne's murder?' I asked.

'Probably not, he definitely has links with the mafia but we think he's just their lookout man. We also think some people are after him. It could even be the mafia fighting amongst themselves, that's happened a lot in Malta, not so much here on Gozo but we do think there are other mafia members over here, even Maltese. They're not all immigrants like Stavola as most people believe. We have our own suspicions about who may have killed Suzanne, don't we Julie, it's just that we can't prove anything yet.'

'I think we need to look closer to home,' said Julie.

'What do you mean?' I asked rather tentatively.

'Stavola has made it far too obvious that he's been watching people. That's been done for a reason. I think his mafia bosses are looking to flush out somebody else. Perhaps Suzanne got in their way, but I don't think the mafia were directly involved in the car bomb, not this time anyway.'

'Nor do I,' Rosie added. 'Julie is right. It's not the mafia. It's more likely to be the UK government or one of their agents, a contract killer maybe. I don't think the mafia will want to be seen getting involved in any of this; it's not their business anymore.'

'But what about the kidnapping of Fiona Meredith, wasn't that the mafia?'

'Yes, but that was in 1997. Things have changed now,' said Julie.

'From what Rosie has told me previously, I'm buying into the belief Fiona is alive and that she's still being held captive, perhaps by the mafia, even here on Gozo. That was given more credibility when Danielle the hairdresser told me about an incident at her salon. I have a feeling the woman who was spirited away by the two men with a black Mercedes could be Fiona. I don't know. It's just a gut feeling.'

Rosie nodded.

'Yes, I know about that, Danielle was very upset and felt threatened at the time. The incident nearly caused her to give up the salon. She was so distressed, poor thing. Myself and some other customers talked her out of it. She's one of the best hairdressers on the island, I love her doing my perm,' said Julie.

'Remember what I told you on the phone, Frankie Fourfingers had given Suzanne some new information? I think that's why she may have been killed, just before she had a chance to publish a story, or call the police,' said Rosie.

'Yes, I know, I've been thinking along the same lines,' I said.

Rosie began to look quite agitated. 'Anyway, Jack, if you don't mind, your time is up, Julie and I have women's things to discuss. We're getting ready for the feast of Santa Lucija, it's only a couple of months away, and we have lots to sort out. How long are you in Gozo for this time?' she asked.

'It's open-ended at the moment but obviously as much as I would like to, I can't stay here forever, perhaps another week or two, three at most.'

'Okay,' said Rosie, 'I'll give you a ring if anything crops up, do you still have the same mobile telephone number?'

'Yes, thank you... oh and it was nice to meet you Julie, your blog post was very interesting by the way, even though it's had me worried. Sorry for intruding.'

'Good to meet you too, Jack. It wasn't an intrusion. It was nice to talk about my Edward. I need to find out the truth. Perhaps you will do that for me one day?'

'I'll do my best.'

'Just one more thing,' said Rosie handing me a business card, 'give this lady a ring, it's Hermione Grech, she's the current editor of the *Malta Telegraph*. Her brother is a good friend of mine. She'll be very interested in anything you have regarding Suzanne. They sort of knew each other. Perhaps she'll even publish your story!'

'Wow, thanks, that's very helpful. Thank you!'

The day was marching on and I had plenty of food for thought. Both Julie and Rosie seemed to know quite a lot but I wondered if they were telling me everything. I then looked at the business card Rosie had given me. Best not to phone at all, well at least not until I had written and finalised my story, I thought. I knew I now needed to give the whole scenario some careful consideration before proceeding with anything.

When I got back to the hotel I treated myself to a couple of glasses of red wine and spent some time on the patio overlooking the harbour. The sun was turning into an orange orb and the sky seemed to change quite quickly from blue into a magnificent indigo colour. There was some chatter coming from inside the foyer and disco music emanating from one of the bars down on the quayside. A ferry sounded its horn. I looked up at the sky again. I could see seagulls. About eight of them, their silhouettes swooping low until disappearing behind the imposing clock tower of the Church of our Lady of Lourdes on the other side of the road which leads up to the centre of Għajnsielem. Seagulls. So they do have seagulls on Gozo. I could feel myself smiling.

24

There was quite a commotion in the breakfast room at the hotel this morning. The head waiter was telling everyone that the Blue Lagoon and Comino had been placed out of bounds by the police. One woman said she'd seen a helicopter hovering overhead at first light.

'Two police vessels and a fishing boat went over just after the sun came up. The helicopter was hovering for nearly an hour. I could see it all going on from my window upstairs,' she said.

The waiter seemed to think a body had been found on the beach just down from the row of kiosks at the Blue Lagoon.

'Something serious must have happened. They don't normally close everything down if it's just a drowning. Usually, they just scoop the body up and take it to the morgue at Gozo General Hospital. It gets quite full in there this time of year,' he said.

'What, with people who have drowned?' I asked.

'No, not really, it's usually with elderly people. They suffer a lot with the heat.'

A conversation then went on between some people at the next table discussing mortuary staff at the Mater Dei Hospital on the mainland having sexual intercourse with bodies there. Apparently it happened a while ago, in 2010. 'I often wonder if that's still happening now,' I heard one of them say.

I shuddered at the thought. Just then, the head waiter joined their conversation.

'No, nothing was ever proven. I remember reading all about it. I think it was all just lies and rumours. The papers just wanted to make up a story. No, definitely not true,' he said quite adamantly.

Breakfast time had been quite interesting to say the least. As a reporter I felt my curious instincts kicking in, and decided to walk down to the harbour. I noticed a small military vessel had arrived with three soldiers on board. A crowd had gathered and the fishermen were making the most of it.

'Lampuki, denci, swordfish, all at a good price for you today,' I heard one of them shout.

I saw one of the chefs from the hotel handing over some money.

'Got a bargain, good bargain today,' he said.

It appeared the fishermen were all getting quite angry and frustrated because the police were preventing them from going back out to sea again while their investigations continued. All the pleasure boats had also been stopped and even the Gozo ferry had been prevented from sailing.

'This is no good,' I heard one fisherman say. 'This has never happened before. I've never seen such chaos.'

Tourists hoping to make their way back to the mainland and particularly the airport were becoming increasingly worried they may miss their flights home. Coaches were turning up from the resorts at Marsalforn and Xlendi. People were queuing outside the ferry terminal with all their baggage but nothing was leaving.

After a while, I decided to walk up to Horatio's bar, it had free Wi-Fi and was a good place to sit outside with a beer before the sun came round and it got too hot. Whilst there, the two fishermen who I had heard talking about Reno Stavola a few days ago walked past.

'Quick, let's get back up to the hotel,' I heard one of them say.

I had since found out that they both worked there, so assumed they had just popped down to the harbour to see what was going on.

After an hour or so, I was just about to move when I saw a private ambulance being driven slowly down the hill towards the quayside behind a No 303 bus. I decided to walk back down. When I got to the quayside the whole place had been cordoned off. The police had brought the body back from Comino covered in a blue tarpaulin. One of the police officers, a fisherman and the undertaker then lifted it from a trolley and into the awaiting ambulance. I could hear a woman crying and some people were crossing their hearts with their hands. Slowly, the ambulance moved away and the cordon was lifted. The horn sounded from the ferry and the long queue outside the terminal slowly began to shuffle forward. It was now mid-afternoon, some six or seven hours after the body was first discovered. I tried to listen to what the police officers were saying. They were in conversation with the soldiers on the boat, but unfortunately, they were all speaking in Maltese. I did hear one of them say, '*il-mejtin huwa persuna notorji,*' which I think means something to do with the body being a person of notoriety, but I wasn't too sure.

Later, I decided to spend the evening in Nadur. It's one of my favourite places on the island and a good place to mingle with the locals. Quite a few British expats live there and everyone seems to mix together quite well. Once again there was live music in the square, this time, outside the Gebuba wine bar. A young lady was sitting on a high stool with a guitar, singing folk songs. When I looked closer, I could see it was Danielle, the hairdresser from Victoria. She had such a beautiful voice. She glanced across at me and smiled and then played a few chords I immediately recognised...

'Suzanne takes you down to her place near the river
You can hear the boats go by, you can spend the night forever
And you know that she's half-crazy but that's why you want to be there...'

And the song went on.

When she finished singing, she told the audience, 'That's a song by Leonard Cohen, and that was for my poor friend, Suzanne Camilleri, and all those who knew and loved her.'

What she said sent a tingle down my spine. It was now three months since Suzanne had been killed. Just then someone put their hand on my shoulder from behind. It was Julie Etheridge.

'That was just beautiful, wasn't it?' she said.

'Yes, beautiful. I didn't know Danielle was a singer as well, she has a wonderful voice.'

'She certainly does. So Jack, I know you're staying at the Grand Hotel, what happened down in Mġarr today?'

'All I know is a body was found on the beach at Comino, it took quite a few hours for everything to get back to normal. They were stopping all the boats, including the ferry. It was mayhem down there for a while,' I said.

'Did you find out who it was?'

'No, I just heard a conversation between a policeman and a couple of soldiers. From what I could make out, it was a person of notoriety or someone famous.'

'That's interesting, there seems to be a lot of speculation, but nobody appears to know anything. Do you think it was suspicious, a murder maybe?'

'I do, but only because I was told that if it had been just a drowning, everything would have been back to normal a lot sooner. This took around six or seven hours, I guess it was something sinister for the police and forensics to take so long.'

'I agree. It will be interesting to find out who the victim is. Anyway, I must go and reunite myself with my brandy. Good to see you, Jack. If I find anything out, I'll stick it on the blog!'

'Can't you just email me, you know, keep it private?'

'No way, it's not the way I do things. If I think something or know something I stick it out there in the open so it's there for everyone to see. I owe it to Edward, surely you can understand that!'

'Yes, I think so. Anyway, take care, and enjoy your brandy.'

Julie unsettles me. It's been over twenty years since Edward died and yet she still talks about it all as if it happened only yesterday. Her blog post could be quite damaging and I've a gut feeling she still has a lot more to say. Perhaps I shouldn't be sharing information but as things stand, I'm getting a lot more from her than she's getting from me.

25

I had spent the rest of yesterday re-examining the last of Suzanne's files: SCPC?-06.19 was the very last. A short entry made the day before she was killed said, "Call from Frankie, Look out for Paul Cassar!" The entry was followed by ten question marks and then the "PC?" which I had seen endorsed against some of the entries in her other files.

I decided to do an online search for Paul Cassar in Malta, but quite a few came up, men and boys of various ages. No-one really stood out. There was one who used to be a government minister who lived on Gozo, but he had died in 2001 at the age of 81. I also scoured all the images of people with that name but there wasn't anybody I recognised, not from the papers or anyone I had met in person. After about two hours of looking I was really none the wiser and couldn't find any obvious connections, not to Suzanne anyway, so I reluctantly abandoned my search.

After yesterday's commotion down at the harbour everything was back to normal today. A large group of British tourists were down at reception checking in and the foyer was heavily obstructed by their suitcases.

'Hello, Jack, how are you?' shouted a female voice.

When I turned around I recognised the woman but had to think where from, and then it clicked. It was Helen Rickmeyer who works at the *Woking Tribune.*

'Oh hi, Helen, what are you doing here? Has Lisa sent you to spy on me?'

'Ha, ha, no not at all, this trip has been booked for months. We've come over for the LGBT festival.'

'That's a new one on me. I didn't know there was one.'

'That's because you're straight, your ignorance is getting the better of you,' she laughed.

'That's a bit harsh!'

'Anyway, this is my girlfriend, Caroline,' she said, introducing me to a rather large lady who was wearing a white baseball cap emblazoned with a small red Maltese Cross.

'Hello, Caroline, pleased to meet you, I hope you both enjoy your stay.'

'Thank you, I'm sure we will,' said Helen as she gave Caroline a kiss on the cheek.

Afterwards, I couldn't help thinking Helen was a very good looking woman. What a waste, I thought. But then, that's probably the very same ignorance she had just been accusing me of, albeit jokingly.

Just as I was leaving the hotel to walk down to one of the bars on the quayside, the head waiter came over.

'Morning, sir, how are you today?'

'Fine,' I said, 'all good, thank you.'

'Want a paper?' he said, almost forcing a rolled up copy of the *Malta Telegraph* into my hand.

'Err, alright, thanks.'

I didn't have much of an option. I was just about to throw it into a nearby bin when I noticed the photograph of a man on the front cover. It was Reno Stavola. Below the picture was a short article...

Comino Man Identified

A man found deceased on a beach near Lantern's Point, Comino, has been identified as fifty-eight year old Reno Stavola, from Qala, Gozo. The police have said in a statement that Mr Stavola had not died from drowning as first reported and are now treating his death as suspicious. Inspector Pierre Marcus Adonis stated, "We are appealing for witnesses. We have found marks on the body that suggest the victim suffered from trauma as a result of being struck from behind by some kind of blunt object before being asphyxiated. A short blue nylon rope was also found by the death scene. In particular, we would like to trace two fishermen who we believe may have been in the area at the time Mr Stavola died." Stavola made the headlines earlier this month, when he was arrested attempting to board a flight at London's Gatwick airport. He was later released without charge and flew back to Malta the following day.

I found all this to be quite shocking and thought about the two fishermen I kept seeing. I wondered if they were the same fishermen who were arrested just after Suzanne was killed. I thought about reporting what I knew to the police but was worried about getting involved. Fortunately, I overheard a conversation by a group of men who work on the pleasure boats down at the quayside. One said they had already reported the fishermen to the police.

I thought it could be Luis and Sam who work up at the hotel. From what I had seen before, they obviously hated Reno but they came down and spoke to the police of their own accord. One of the pleasure boat men mentioned them both to his friends and said he thought they were worried about being wrongly accused. Their conversation then changed to Maltese as another joined in so unfortunately I couldn't make out what they were saying anymore.

I decided to send Rick a text message to let him know what had happened. I know he had been very worried after Stavola had turned up at his mother's funeral, and again when he found out he was arrested at Gatwick.

Around 5pm, Helen and her friend Caroline emerged at the bar in the hotel.

'How was the festival?' I asked.

'Oh no, we haven't been yet. We've spent most of the day upstairs by the pool just sunning ourselves. We're off to the festival shortly. There's some live music and comedians and lots of other stuff going on. You should come too, you might enjoy it,' said Helen brandishing a Gay Pride Festival wrist band.

'No. Thank you for the offer, it's not my thing,' I said feeling quite embarrassed that I'd been asked.

'Oh by the way,' said Helen. 'Did you know Lisa was back with her husband?'

'What? Who? Which husband?' I said rather confused.

'The last one, what's his name? Oh, Jamie.'

'Jamie Arrowsmith?'

'Yes that's him.'

'Bloody hell.'

'So sorry, I thought you knew. She's been seeing him on and off for quite a while. She told me things weren't working out with you as well as she had hoped. He came back on the scene a couple of weeks ago. To be honest she did tell me she was hedging her bets. Lisa is quite an insecure woman, you know.'

'Well that just about sums everything up.'

'Jack, you must take a huge chunk of the blame yourself. She told me you were besotted with that dead woman. She didn't want to keep playing second fiddle to a ghost. She did give you every chance, you know.'

'I guess she did, but this is quite a shock. I didn't think Lisa was quite so shallow.'

'It's not about being shallow. It's about getting on with one's life. None of us are spring chickens anymore. We need to move on and get on with our lives. Lisa could see she had a second chance with Jamie and she's taken it.'

Eventually, Helen and Caroline left the hotel which gave me time to think. Once I had got over the initial shock I thought back to the last telephone conversation I had with Lisa. Her tone was different and although I didn't realise it too much at the time, I did get an impression she may have wanted to tell me something. Obviously, she decided not to, and I would never have guessed it would have been about her getting back with Jamie anyway. The whole thing, though, had really got me off the hook. I had my fling and I guessed, maybe, that's all she really wanted. An excuse to make her mind up about who and what was most important to her.

After watching the sunset fade behind the hill I decided to walk down to Horatio's. It was a busy evening. I noticed there were a lot of gay people at the bar, all hugging and kissing. It was all quite friendly and everyone was excited as they waited for a fleet of taxis to take them up to the belvedere in Nadur.

'Jack, Jack, are you sure you don't want to come with us?' It was Helen's friend, Caroline.

'Yes, sure; very sure. Have a good time. I'll see you guys later.'

'Okay. You don't know what you're missing!'

After they had all left there was a short period of silence as the mood changed. A young woman at the bar swapped the music over from the disco stuff which had been playing to something more 'middle of the road' as she put it.

'Another Cisk?' she asked.

'Of course, thank you.'

'Someone told me you're a newspaper reporter, is that right?'

'Yes, who told you that?'

'My aunt's friend, Rosie. We saw you getting on a bus in Victoria the other day and she pointed you out to me. She said you were trying to find out who killed Suzanne Camilleri.'

'Yes, that's right, do you know anything?'

'I only know what Rosie and my aunt know.'

'And that's about all I know,' I said. 'By the way, do you know anyone called Paul Cassar?'

'My aunt mentioned that name just after Suzanne was killed. Apparently that's who Suzanne thought was after her. Everyone has looked but he doesn't appear to exist. Even the police can't find him.'

'Yes, I've looked as well, you know on Google, but I couldn't find a match. There were a quite a few people with that name, but nothing obvious.'

'My aunt thought he may be Italian, but Paul is an English name and Cassar is definitely a traditional Maltese surname. We've all drawn blanks on that one,' she said.

'Sorry, what's your name? I know I should have asked sooner.'

'I'm Annie, Annie Etheridge.'

'Etheridge... are you related to Julie?'

'Yes, I told you already, that's my aunt, the one I've been talking about.'

'Well, that puts everything into perspective. It is a small world.'

'Yes, it is if you live on Gozo,' she laughed.

The evening had gone quite quickly and I thanked Annie for the conversation.

'No worries, it's been nice talking to you. I hope you enjoy the rest of your stay and find what you're looking for.'

After the news about Lisa earlier, this was just the tonic I needed. A little pick-me-up from a complete stranger, and a pretty one at that.

26

Helen and her girlfriend checked out of the hotel this morning before I'd had another chance to speak with them about Lisa. I saw them walking down to the terminal with their bags on a little trolley. I just wanted to ask Helen if she had told me everything. What she said had bothered me and I was feeling a mixture of anger and guilt. Deep down, I knew I probably only had myself to blame.

    I decided to take myself up to Nadur and walk along the belvedere to the Ta'Kenuna Tower and back. When I arrived, the street cleaners were still busy cleaning up the mess from last night's festival. Stray cats were scouring the rubbish for food. One, a tortoiseshell, decided to follow me part of the way before a discarded chicken leg from a barbeque drew its attention. I eventually reached the tower, an old semaphore point that had been overlooking the Gozo Channel for centuries. I was just about to sit down on a wall when I heard someone sobbing on a bench behind me. It was a woman with curly shoulder length black hair, in her late twenties or early thirties. I decided to leave her alone as I thought her problems obviously weren't any of my business. I then noticed the cat I had been stroking before was back and once again begging for my attention. The woman came over, knelt down and started stroking the cat as well.

    'Gorgeous, isn't she?' she said.

    'Yes, I saw her earlier, she was all over me until she found something to eat and now it seems she's followed me here.'

    'There are so many stray ones around, it's a shame. Many are born in the wild, down there in the farmland. I come here as much as I can to feed them, most are very friendly but you always find one that is quite vicious and always wants to give you a scratch.'

'Sorry, I noticed you earlier, you seemed quite upset,' I said.

'I'm sorry. Don't worry about me, I'm fine now,' she said as she wiped away a tear.

'Don't be sorry, it's none of my business, is it the cats?'

'No, no. My father has just died. I hardly knew him. He was estranged, didn't give a toss about his children even though we loved him, he was always in and out of prison and doing shady stuff. I'm not surprised he's ended up dead.'

'How? If you don't mind me asking.'

'He was strangled by a rope. They found him lying on the beach at Comino, just over there,' she said pointing to the island.

'Reno Stavola?' I said, feeling quite amazed by the situation I had just found myself in.

'Yes, how do you know?'

I decided not to mention the fact I was a reporter and that Reno had been following me around Woking just before I came to Gozo.

'I saw it all on the news,' I said.

'He's been in the news a lot. My brothers think someone had been trying to set him up. They think the police are even on it, which is why no-one has been caught for his murder. They wanted him dead and everyone knows it. People think Malta is squeaky clean and that there is no crime here but it has a dark underbelly, it's usually the Cosa Nostra.'

'Cosa Nostra?'

'Sicilian mafia. They do all their dirty work right here in Malta, everyone knows, even the politicians and they don't do anything about it. Everything is covered up by smiles and sunshine.'

'Are you Maltese? It's just that your accent sounds a little different.'

'I'm Sicilian. I came here with my mother when I was a seven-year-old girl. We left my father behind when he was put in an Italian jail for stealing a car. When he came out, he followed us here. My mother loved him, but she hated him as well, there was nothing in between. My mother hated the fact he was just a small time crook trying to play the big boy. She would never touch any of his money. "It has the devil's face on it" she used to say. Mama died quite a few years ago and I went to live with the Buttiġieġs down in Qala. They looked after me well but then I found out the whole family was involved in some really big stuff. Men from the mafia and the Government of Malta kept coming round. One day when I got home from work there was a police guard on the front door. I wasn't allowed in and no-one would tell me why. That's when I had to move out and came to live in Nadur.'

'It sounds like you've had a tough life.'

'Yes and no, really. I have good friends, but there are not too many of them. I don't trust many people. There are a lot of tongues wagging around here so I don't speak to many people. It's safer and easier that way and I don't get hurt anymore.'

'Well you're speaking to me.'

'I don't know you. You're from abroad. Sometimes it's easier to speak to a total stranger. I find you can have a more open and honest conversation with someone you don't actually know,' she said.

I was now beginning to feel guilty. She was pouring her heart out and telling me everything without knowing me. This was precisely the sort of information I had been looking for. It all felt very awkward and I was beginning to feel I should be truthful with her and formally introduce myself.

'I'm sorry, we've been chatting for a while and I haven't even introduced myself, I'm Jack.'

'Hello, Jack, I'm Lucette.'

'Lucette Stavola?'

'No, it's Lucette Buttiġieġ, I've never been called Stavola. My father and mother never tied the knot. I had my mum's name of Ciano until I married one of the Buttiġieġ family, it only lasted a year. My husband, Vincent, wanted a lot of children but I couldn't have any. We had a big fight. It happened the same day I found the policeman standing by the front door, it was the last straw. That's the day I left him. It was sad but I have been much happier ever since, I'm a free spirit now.'

'I've actually met a couple of the Buttiġieġ family when I was here on my last visit,' I said, wondering what the response would be.

'Which ones?'

'Rita, and her uncle.'

'Joseph?' she asked, looking rather surprised.

'Yes, that's right. I understand he's quite ill now.'

'I don't know. I don't speak to the family much anymore. Rita is a bitch. She's always had a thing for older men and put herself about a bit. In the end she got a job at the Grand Hotel. So, Mr Jack, what do you do?'

'I'm a freelance newspaper reporter. I'm over here investigating the murder of Suzanne Camilleri.'

'Oh God, you're a reporter. That happened a few months ago. It's still so fresh in my memory. Everyone on the island knew that poor lady but the Buttiġieġs were always wary of her for some reason. They were always whispering bad things about her.'

'Do you think they were involved?'

'No, not at all. The Buttiġieġs have always been rather strange but they are not a family of killers. One thing is for sure, though, they would have possibly known who was.'

'Do you think the police know?'

'The police? Yes, almost certainly but they have some very corrupt officers, particularly in the higher ranks. Some of them are being paid off by the mafia. If I know this, then everyone must know.'

We began walking back along the belvedere to the centre of Nadur. Lucette grabbed my hand, stopped, looked me in the eye and then gave me a kiss on the cheek.

'Thank you, thank you, it's been really nice talking to you, Jack. The day is still young, how would you like to buy me a drink?'

'Err yes, thank you, I would like that.'

The next thing I knew, we were hugging and kissing each other on the lips. She was running her fingers through my hair. Again, I really couldn't believe the situation I had just found myself in.

'Look, that's my house there,' she said as we passed, grabbing my hand.

I looked up and saw a small apartment with a balcony on top of a garage. There was a birdcage on the wall and some birds were chirping loudly.

'They're my two little angels,' she said.

When we got to the main square at Nadur, we found a quiet table outside the Rabokk pizzeria and continued our conversation. The more we talked, and the more I drank, the more I felt attracted to her. Her eyes were drawing me in, it was almost hypnotic but this was the daughter of the same man who had been scaring me shitless until he got himself killed. I looked further into her deep brown eyes. There was still one obvious question I needed to ask.

'Do you know why your father visited England just before he died?'

'He had a message for someone that was quite urgent, I don't know if it was ever delivered but he was arrested on his way back, that's all I know. It's something I found out from one of the fishermen down at the harbour. He came over to offer his condolences when I was down there yesterday.'

'Which fisherman?'

'His name is David. I've known him ever since I've lived here. He's one of the few people I can trust. He's a very old but trustworthy man. He helped me move in to my apartment here in Nadur. His wife is a lovely lady, never forgets by birthday and always brings me a home-baked cake. We've had some lovely evenings.'

I felt reassured it wasn't one of the fishermen from the hotel whom the police had questioned, and wondered if Reno's message was meant for me or Rick.

I was now beginning to wonder how the day would end. It was moving fast and I realised I had already spent nearly five hours in Lucettes's company. We made the short walk over the square to the Gebuba wine bar where the normal crowd was gathered. I noticed a couple were giving us funny looks and there was quite a lot of whispering going on.

'Oh, don't worry about them,' said Lucette, 'they're always talking about me, but they don't know anything. I just let them get on with it. Now, it's my turn to buy you a drink.'

It was a small statement, I had been paying for everything and Lucette was knocking back vodkas like nobody's business. I had also bought the pizzas, but didn't really mind, she was good company but I still had a bad feeling in my gut that everything was too good to be true. A man in his fifties being pulled by a woman so much younger just doesn't happen to me every day so I guess I was just playing along, waiting for the inevitable CRUNCH, and then it came...

'Would you like me to walk you back to your apartment?'

'No, no it's alright. Anyway I have a much better idea.'

'What's that?'

'How about I come and spend the night with you at the Grand Hotel?'

'What?'

'Yes, it would be great and I would be able to see what's behind that awesome hairy chest of yours.'

I smiled and felt myself hesitating.

'Come on, it will be fine, I will help you to relax and promise you a good time.'

I was just about to agree when she butted in.

'It will only cost you €200 for the whole night. I can get the bus back here before you go down for breakfast. It's simple.'

'Err, no thanks. I didn't think you were that kind of girl.'

'Well what did you think? You didn't think I actually fancied you, did you? How do you think I make my living? Why do you think all these imbeciles are whispering about me? Yes, I'm a good time girl and I like being paid to get fucked. That's who I am. So, Mr Big Boy, are you sure you don't want to have a good time with me?'

'Yes, very sure... thank you.'

She got up in a huff and went to speak to two men who were sitting in another part of the square. It was only then I realised she had been slowly ripping me off for food and drinks all through the afternoon and evening. I had obviously been drawn in and now felt somewhat ashamed of myself. On the plus side, Lucette had inadvertently given me some more information about the Buttiġieġ family.

27

I awoke this morning feeling quite confused. Reality had collided with a vivid dream and the surrealism of it all had quite affected me.

In the dream, moonlight was coming through a crack in the curtains in my hotel room. I could see a silhouette sitting on the chair in front of the mirror by the dressing table. I could make out a woman with long hair. She was moving slowly as if to speak. I sat up in the bed but remained silent. Everything seemed so real.

'So Jack, what shall I do with myself?' a voice said, 'tell me, how do I put myself back together? I need to be complete again. Jack, Jack, can you help me?'

I tried to slither back down inside the bed, but there were no covers. Almost hiding but with nowhere to go, almost frightened but not sure what to be frightened of.

'Jack, Jack,' said the voice again, 'help me, please, can you help me?'

By now, I was sure it was Suzanne.

'Suzanne, is that you?' I mumbled.

'Yes, Jack, of course it's me. Now help put me back together.'

'How do I do that?'

'I don't know. There are still some pieces missing,' she said.

'What pieces?'

'Well, most really, I don't know where to start.'

'You have an outline. I can see it, even now, in the dark.'

'Yes, this is my shadow.'

'Are you sure it's not your soul?'

'I don't know. What does a soul look like?'

'I don't know either.'

'Do you have my heart, Jack?'

'Yes, of course I have your heart. I've always had it. Ever since...'

'Ever since when, Jack?'

'Ever since, before it happened I suppose.'

'I knew that, Jack, I've always known that. Now give me my heart, I need it back. I need it to fight.'

'Fight what?'

'I need it to fight the enemy, I need to find retribution. I need it for revenge. The bastard must pay for this.'

'What enemy, what bastard, do you know who he is?'

'Yes of course I know. You know him too...'

Just then, there was a gust of wind at the window which caused the curtains to flap, allowing the first rays of early morning sunlight in. The silhouette faded although I could still see the outline in my mind's eye. It took quite a while for me to finally accept it was just a dream, but it felt so real.

'Suzanne, Suzanne,' I whispered, but now there was no answer.

After breakfast I went down to the quayside to give myself time to think. I had dreamt a lot about Suzanne since her death. I remembered the dream I had of her swimming in the sea at Dwejra even though we had never been there together. That was also a strange dream, but it was the one where she gave me a message. Was she trying to do it again? Was she trying to give me a name? She said in the dream that I know him too, but it ended without a real conclusion. Is the answer staring me in the face? Do I really know the person who killed her?

I was just about to get up and catch a bus to Victoria in the hope of finding Julie again when a tall thin man with slicked back silver hair came over and sat on the wall beside me.

'Hello, I'm Jim from Richmond in North Yorkshire, I'm seventy-three-years-old and I'm about to save your life,' he said as he reached out to shake my hand.

It was an odd introduction and I felt quite nervous at first as I was unsure of his motives.

'Don't worry, I just noticed your demeanour, I can see you're struggling both mentally and physically.'

'How do you mean?' I asked.

'I was drinking coffee at the kiosk over there. I saw you walk over to the wall about an hour ago, you were limping. I can recognise arthritis a mile off. Not only that, you've spent the whole hour just vacantly staring into space. I can see you're a man who needs to release his demons. You think too much. Am I right, lad?'

I smiled. It seemed strange being called 'lad' when I'm in my fifties. 'Yes, you're spot on, although I don't feel suicidal or anything. I managed to put those kind of issues well behind me when I was still in my twenties. My issues are more to do with handling grief right now. If you don't mind, I'd rather not say anymore.'

'That's fair enough, lad. I was where you are once. About fifteen years ago. I had to take a long hard look at myself to stop myself from doing something stupid, just after my wife died. I gave up the alcohol and smoking. I began to take brisk walks and do some mild exercises and now, I'm in the very best of health. Never felt better.'

'But what did you do about your mental health?' I asked.

'That put itself right by default. Because my body was cleansing itself, my mind became more positive. I became more confident and that helped me chase off the demons which had been banging about in my head for some time.'

'Perhaps then I should try something similar.'

'You should, trust me. I'm a retired osteopath. I should never have let myself get into that situation in the first place. In the end the remedy was quite simple.'

'What was that?'

'I started taking two teaspoons of apple cider vinegar a day. It took about three weeks to start working but when I started to benefit from the desired effects I threw all my prescribed medication away and have never looked back since.'

'Apple cider vinegar? Yuk! That must taste quite bitter?'

'On its own yes but I always take it with sugar or honey, or mask it in mint sauce. It takes the bitterness away. It's always worked for me. It's not any old apple cider vinegar mind, you need a top brand, Holland & Barrett do one called Braggs, it's a bit pricey but it does its job.' He paused. 'Well, I just wanted to share my story with you. You looked like you needed a gentle nudge in the right direction. Try it, believe me it works, and it might, just might, save your life.'

I smiled. 'Thank you. I'll look into it. Anyway, my bus has just turned up. I must dash. It's been a pleasure talking.'

'Take care, lad, remember, Braggs apple cider vinegar.'

I laughed and just about managed to catch the bus after fumbling around for my monthly travel pass. Talking to strangers is something I seem to have done a lot just lately.

Eventually, after what seemed an eternity stuck in traffic, the bus arrived at the terminus in Victoria. It had got quite cloudy and the elderly bus driver had been talking about the possibility of rain and even storms.

'It's nearly five months now since we had a proper drop of rain in Gozo,' he said, almost sadistically.

When I got to Luigi Vella Street, I walked straight over to the Maldonado restaurant. The same waiter who served us the other day was putting some crates outside.

'Good evening, sir, would you like a menu?'

'No thanks, just a beer, a pint of Cisk if that's okay?'

'Of course, a pint coming up - a large bottle, is that alright?'

'Yes, that's fine.'

'I see you're now a regular. You were here the other day, right?' he joked.

'Yes, I was hoping to find Julie again, you know, one of the ladies I was talking to, the one with the small pug dog.'

'Ah, Mrs Etheridge, her friend came in this morning when I was cleaning up, the other lady who was here with you. She was all excited.'

'That'll be Rosie,'

'She told me the police raided Mrs Etheridge's apartment yesterday and had taken her and some computers away. She said there was also a man giving out orders to the policemen and waving a gun around. It all happened quite quickly. If you look up the street there is still a piece of police tape hanging by her door. Both ladies had been in here only about an hour before.'

'So you didn't see anything?'

'No, we were very busy catering for a wedding. The street was full of people and parked cars. It would have been easy for all that to happen and no-one to notice. I hope Mrs Etheridge is alright. What do you think she might have done?'

'Err, I'm not sure, but I have my suspicions. I'll give her friend Rosie a ring and see what else I can find out.'

While the waiter went over to another table to serve a young couple I finished my beer and left. I found a quiet spot around the corner and called Rosie from my mobile.

'Rosie, it's Jack Compton. How are you?'

'I'm okay. I think I know what you're ringing me about.'

'Are you at the kiosk?'

'No, I didn't open today. I needed to be at home. You're going to ask me about Julie, aren't you?'

'Yes, I've just been to the Maldonado restaurant and the waiter told me what you had said to him about Julie.'

'Yes, she was released this morning, she's with me now.'

'Can I speak to her?'

'No, no. She's lying down and sleeping. She needs some rest.'

'So why was she arrested?'

'Wait a minute.'

I heard Rosie put the phone down, then a few footsteps and a door close.

'Right, Jack, I need to say this quietly,' she whispered.

'Julie had posted a new item on her blog page. It was all about the Government of Malta and that missing woman, Fiona Meredith, you have been asking about. Julie was thinking of taking it down but before she could, the police came and took her away. By her own admission, it was quite contentious. They've let her go now, but they've seized all her computers. She's been told that if they find anything else she will be charged and thrown in jail.'

'What for?'

'I don't know. We'll have to wait and see. I'm not sure what they can charge her with. Like in England, we're supposed to be allowed free speech here in Malta but our country's own interpretation of that often gets in the way. Free speech isn't really free.'

'Sorry, I don't fully understand.'

'Free speech is always challenged. I think our government is corrupt. Julie certainly does and obviously poor Suzanne and others before her did as well. She paid a heavy price for digging in too deep.'

'Look, Rosie, I must go now. Give Julie my regards. If she wants to phone me, please tell her she can. I've only got a few days left on the islands. It would be handy if I could see her again before I leave.'

'I'll try and persuade her to give you a ring. She's still in shock, so I'm not sure if she'll really want to, I'll see what I can do.'

'Okay, thank you.'

When I got back to the hotel I opened up my laptop and looked for Julie's blog. It had gone. There was just a message stating: 'Page HTTP 451: Unavailable due to legal reasons.' The police or the government must have taken it down.

I was now wondering why they had become so interested in Julie. Was there a connection between this and the murder of Reno Stavola? Rosie had mentioned Fiona. I was also thinking about the conversation I had with the prostitute in Nadur. Lucette had told me quite a lot. I was beginning to think there was just one piece missing from the jigsaw now. I kept thinking about the last file on Suzanne's USB stick. SCPC?-06.19. The missing link had to be something to do with Paul Cassar, but just how do I find him?

28

I had just returned to my room from breakfast when the bedside telephone rang.

'Good morning, sir, is that Mr Compton?'
'Yes, good morning.'
'This is Nina in reception. There's a lady here to see you.'
'Who?'
'She's given me her business card. It's the editor of the *Malta Telegraph*, Hermione Grech.'
'Oh, okay, thanks, I'll pop down to the foyer.'

On the way down in the lift I could feel my heart racing and was wondering why she had tracked me down. I remembered Rosie mentioning her the other day so I was bracing myself for the unexpected. When I got down to the foyer it was quite busy with people checking in and out. I could see a woman in her mid to late forties around the corner ordering a coffee at the bar. She had long blonde curly hair and was wearing a tight-fitting black pin-striped business suit. I couldn't help noticing the incredible length of her long blue varnished fingernails as she reached for her purse.

'Hello, Mrs Grech?'
'No, Miss Grech,' she said quite abruptly as she went to shake my hand.
'Ah, sorry,' I said, somewhat taken aback by her very husky voice.
'Don't be sorry, would you like a coffee?'
'Yes please, thanks.'
'Right, let's go and sit in the corner where it's a little quieter.'
'So how can I help you?'

'Well, Jack, I think we can help each other. My friend, Julie Etheridge, introduced me to Rosie. Her brother is a friend of mine. Rosie has been telling me what you know about the death of Suzanne Camilleri. I just thought we might be able to share some information and finally nail the case. As a journalist, I knew Suzanne fairly well so would like to find out what's gone on.'

'Nail the case? Sharing information with a rival reporter is not the usual way of doing things though, is it?'

'Ah, no, we won't be rivals. That's why I think we should work together on this.'

'I'm sorry, it's not really possible. I'm flying back to England in a couple of days. To be honest, I had hoped to have found out why she was murdered and who killed her by now. I believe there is just one important piece missing from the jigsaw. I know I'm close to finding it, I can almost smell it but I'm not prepared to divulge any more information, particularly with someone I don't know. I've probably done that enough already with Rosie and Julie which is probably why you're here.'

'It's true. But I have it on good authority that you're on top of it all and that you're a very good reporter. I sense you're very close, and yes, of course that's why I'm here.'

'Ha, ha, who's been telling you that?'

'Firstly, Rosie is convinced you're the only person capable of finding out who killed Suzanne. Secondly, we have a mutual acquaintance in Rick Storey. I worked with him until he had to go back to England to look after his mother. I phoned him last night to find out how he's been coping without her. He was feeling quite sore, you know, but sounds like he's getting his head around it all at last. Anyway, he still found time to sing your praises and suggested I get you on board.'

'That's really good of him, but it's difficult. Like I said, I'm flying back to England in a couple of days. I need to get back to the bread and butter stuff so I can pay my bills.'

'Well, Jack, I have a proposition. How about I pay for an extension to your stay here at the Grand Hotel? Let's say for around four weeks, and I'll also rearrange your flight home.'

'That's very kind, but I'm short on funds.'

'Not a problem, I'll pay you five hundred Euros a week to help keep you going. If you get me the story, I'll pay you a lump sum upon publication, how's that?'

'It all sounds very generous; I'm surprised you have faith in me.'

'It's not about faith. As I said, I knew Suzanne too. She was a very good journalist. Although we were employed by the same paper, we never really worked together but I do know that a few weeks before the end she was inadvertently pissing a few people off and drawing unwanted attention to herself, she was definitely onto something and I think that's what got her killed.'

'I'm assuming we're talking about what she may have found out regarding the Fiona Meredith missing person case?'

'Yes, I think Suzanne had found out who was behind the original kidnapping in 1997. She may have even found that elusive link behind what happened in Venice and the death of Diana. I'm not sure.'

'Do you think the mafia was involved?'

'Again, I don't know. Reno Stavola definitely had mafia connections. I think others on Gozo are just either sympathisers or go-betweens.'

'Do you think the mafia is operating on Gozo?'

'Well, I do have evidence that there is a mafia family active in Sampieri on the south coast of Sicily. Because of its close proximity to the Maltese islands, I think that's where they could be operating from. Suzanne had already reported they were using this country as a killing field.'

'That's very interesting!'

'Incidentally, Sampieri is where Reno Stavola was born, so read into it what you like,' she said, looking at her watch.

'Thank you, I will. So what shall I do now?'

'Just carry on as you are, give me regular updates and above all, keep yourself safe, we can't be too sure what we're really getting involved in. Suzanne was murdered for a reason and so was Reno Stavola, so be very careful.'

'Well that's reassuring, thank you. Just one question, what happens if I find all the answers and complete the story but for some reason you choose not to print it? I know the *Telegraph* has done that before. Rick told me once.'

'You don't get paid. Remember, things are different here. Malta is a small country. The paper doesn't have the money to splash around like the nationals in England. We're probably more on a par with the local press. What was the one you used to work for?'

'*The Woking Tribune.*'

'Well, Jack, you'll know that the internet and social media is what's driving the news these days and you don't need me to tell you that printed matter will soon be a thing of the past. It probably only has a few years left.'

'Okay, but I need to think about your offer.'

'Yes, do, but think quickly! I know you will say "yes" anyway.'

'That's very assertive!'

'I'm an assertive woman, Jack, and I don't stop until I get what I want.'

'I can see that. I suppose my answer has to be "yes". I can't really walk away from the investigation now everything seems to be coming together. I was wondering where to pitch the story when I had completed it anyway.'

'Jack, love, I have every confidence in you, more so, now we've met. Rosie seems to be a very good judge of character. Just do your best, and please don't let me down.'

'I won't.'

'Look, I must dash. I need to be on the next ferry. I have a meeting later in Valletta and I can't afford to be late. Remember, keep me up to speed and let me know as soon as you find anything. You can call me anytime.'

'Thanks.'

When Hermione left the hotel I could see her running quite awkwardly down the hill towards the ferry terminal. She paused, removed her high heels and then ran, more comfortably, barefoot. When she was out of sight I decided to give Rick a quick ring to find out what he thought about her.

'Rick, how are you doing?'

'Getting there I think, mate. Losing Mum hasn't been easy.'

'I guessed that. They say losing your mother or a child is always the hardest of all bereavements but I suppose they are all difficult in their own way.'

'That's very true, mate. I guess you're still grieving over Suzanne. Am I right?'

'Spot on. I'll tell you more about why when I see you for a pint one day. I've found out so much about her since she died. Her daughter, Lorca, told me quite a lot. It's probably my conversation with her which has made me even more determined to find the killer.'

'Are you close?'

'I think so, the name Paul Cassar keeps cropping up lately but nobody knows him. Suzanne once told me she felt she had an invisible nemesis. I think that could be Paul Cassar. If I can somehow make a connection, then I think I'll be close to finding the culprit.'

'I can't say I've heard of a Paul Cassar, but keep trying, mate. You know I'm with you all the way.'

'Thanks. Now, I've just had a visit from Hermione Grech, what can you tell me about her?'

'Christ, she didn't waste much time. I only spoke to her last night.'

'I know, she told me. She has only just left. I was watching her run down the hill in her heels to catch the ferry. I thought she was going to fall head over heels, if you pardon the pun. It was quite funny.'

'Ha, ha, we used to call her the stiletto queen when I worked with her. She always wore high heels and stockings. Jonah, the young kid who worked in the mail room was always drooling over her.'

'I think I can see why. So, what can you tell me about her?'

'Well, she's honest. She was my sub-editor for a while. We fell out time and time again mainly because she kept tearing my stories apart, reducing the word count which eventually cost me money.'

'I thought you were paid a salary...'

'I was. I got a very basic salary. Getting a story in the paper was like earning commission on top.'

'Well, Hermione has asked me to work for her on a freelance basis for the next four weeks. Hopefully by the end of that I will get a result and be able to complete some kind of story.'

'I told her to get in touch with you. She knew Suzanne was onto something but was never fully sure of what it was. It's only right you should be the reporter who gets the scoop.'

'Thanks, no pressure then.'

Rick laughed. 'Well I think you're definitely the man for the job.'

'Well let's see. Look, I'm off now. I'll give you a ring as soon as I'm back in England. That'll probably be around the end of October now.'

'Okay, mate. Take care, be good and all the usual bollocks.'

'Thanks.'

It was good to hear Rick sounding more like his normal self. My task now was to collate everything I know. Perhaps even to start writing the story. I was still confused about how much I would get paid once my piece was submitted. Working outside a contract is always risky. When I asked Rick about Hermione, the first word he used was "honest". Perhaps I should trust his instincts and, more importantly, trust her. To be fair, she did come across as someone I could work with.

This evening I decided to take a stroll down to the Gleneagles bar at the harbour. It's a place I had always bypassed but was always curious about. When I've been over to Gozo previously it had always been shut. This time, though, it's since had a lick of paint and I've seen people going in and out.

When I entered I was greeted by a fug of cigarette smoke. The owner here was certainly flouting the rules as there's a smoking ban in Malta as well. People were sitting in clusters. Everything looked shady. The place seemed to be housing all of the island's misfits, there was even a policeman in full uniform drinking and smoking at the end of the bar. I noticed his holster was open, so his pistol could not have been secured properly. I thought about saying something but decided to maintain my anonymous profile, choosing a table in the corner by the entrance. This was obviously once a fishermen's bar, crab and lobster nets were hanging from the ceiling with plenty of stuffed fish pinned sporadically on the walls between a series of old black and white photographs of fishermen displaying their catch around the harbour in the old days.

The music was quite loud, forties era, swing and jazz. After about ten minutes a group of four men came in and occupied the table next to me. All were clutching a glass of whiskey. I immediately recognised two as Luis Micallef and Sam Sultana from the hotel. They were the same two fishermen who had spoken to the police when Reno was found dead on Comino. The other two men, a bald guy, about forty, and a younger guy in his twenties, I hadn't seen before.

Eventually the music stopped and I could hear them talking but their conversation was all in Maltese. I heard Luis mention Reno and then I thought I heard one of the other men say "Suzanne". I decided to put my phone on record and discreetly placed it on the table next to my beer. Suzanne's name was mentioned repetitively and then the music started again. The bald guy kept banging his fist on the table. It sounded like he was swearing in Maltese, he looked quite angry. His young friend was trying to get him to calm down and make him shut up. Luis and Sam then got up and left after downing their whiskies quickly. A few minutes later the other two left.

After they'd gone I placed the phone to my ear to see if it had picked up anything. All I could hear was... *'Dak il-baqra Suzanne Camilleri kellha tmut. Hi kienet taf kollox. Reno kien jaf kollox. Hu kien jaf wisq. Huwa tkellem. Cassar min hu, hu ġibed il-kordi. Naħseb li r-Reno naqas minnu'*. None of it made much sense but I could also hear the name Cassar mentioned. I wondered if that was Paul Cassar.

When I got back to the hotel room I opened my laptop and tried to put what I had heard through Google translate. It took a few attempts because, like it is with most languages, the pronunciations didn't match the spellings. Fortunately, I had been to Malta enough times to get the gist of how the language worked and eventually got what I thought was an accurate enough translation. It wasn't very pleasant reading...

'That cow, Suzanne Camilleri, had to die. She knew everything. Reno also knew everything. He knew too much. He talked. Cassar, whoever he is, he pulled the strings. I think Reno failed him.'

It was clear from this all four men knew something. The bald guy who I hadn't seen before was clearly happy Suzanne was dead. It was also apparent they didn't know who Paul Cassar was either, which made the whole conversation even more intriguing. Again, I now had more questions than answers. These men, though, I believed, held the key to finding out who did kill Suzanne.

29

What I had overheard last night in the Gleneagles bar was not an easy pill to swallow. The fact someone was actually happy Suzanne was dead disgusted me. For the first time in a long time, I felt anger and anxiety, which is not a good mix. I needed to do something which would take my mind off things. I decided to finally make good use of my bus pass and visit an old friend from England who runs a bar down in Marsalforn. He was busy, but we still found time to chat about his usual subject, football, football, and even more football. The hours went by quite quickly and in the end I felt quite relaxed, which fortunately for me served its purpose.

When I got back to the hotel, it was already early evening and beginning to get dark. I decided to pop into the bar for a quick drink before going to my room. Something caught my eye on the TV. It was an item about a murdered Italian prosecutor. A photo popped up, but it was gone in a flash. As it was a rolling news item I decided to wait until the report came around again. After about twenty minutes a headline came up and I felt myself go cold. "Italian Prosecutor Murdered." The same photograph appeared. I now had time to look properly. It was Maria Allegranza. I felt myself go numb with shock. It was a similar feeling to the one I had experienced when Rick had left that message for me about Suzanne. The bar was quite noisy so I couldn't pick up on everything that was being said. I quickly downed my drink, went up to my room and opened the laptop. An article was already posted on the Euro News website...

Murder of Italian Prosecutor was a "Mafia Style Execution" According to Political Observers.

Maria Allegranza's body was found on Sunday as the sun was rising on the beach at the Sicilian resort of Pozzallo.

The 49-year-old victim, who had been involved in a recent investigation into alleged corruption between the Government of Malta and the mafia, died from a single shot to the back of the head, in what police believe was a "mafia honey trap of classical proportions".

Sources say Ms Allegranza travelled to the Sicilian resort of Sampieri for a short vacation from her home near Milan last Friday.

Pozzallo prosecutor, Marco Fernandez, said her hotel room, 12 kilometres away in Sampieri had also been ransacked and a number of items including her mobile phone, car keys, glasses and a distinctive leather jacket was missing.

The murder has shocked fellow prosecutors and those who hold senior ranks within the Italian police.

Ms Allegranza was known to have questioned members of the mafia concerning renewed interest in the disappearance of the British tourist, Fiona Meredith, in 1997. After a recent TV news report was aired, a leading mafia boss said that, "She (Ms Allegranza) was working outside her jurisdiction as a prosecutor and should stick to putting people behind bars. There will be very serious consequences if she carries on trying to turn stones when there is nothing for her underneath."

It was a bizarre and profound statement but one which has led police to believe the mafia is responsible for her murder.

Government officials and the police have reportedly said there was no evidence to suggest Ms Allegranza's murder was related to the death of Suzanne Camilleri, the Maltese journalist, in Gozo in June.

Mrs Camilleri died in a car bomb attack while driving from her home to a beach at Ramla Bay. It has, however, since been revealed both women once met briefly during the 1997 investigation into the British tourist who went missing in Venice when Ms Allegranza was an acting inspector in the police.

Prosecutor Fernandez said, "Both killings are very different. As yet, there is no evidence to suggest there is a direct connection although I do firmly believe it was the mafia who is responsible for the death of our dear colleague, Ms Allegranza."

A spokesman for the Prosecutor's department said on Euro News, "With great pain and insurmountable grief, our office is experiencing the loss of our beloved and talented colleague, Maria Allegranza, and we pray for sympathy to the sorrow of her relatives and colleagues."

Barbara Morvillo, from the Organisation for Security and Co-operation in Europe, tweeted: "Shocked by the horrific murder of Italian Prosecutor Mario Allegranza. I urgently call for a full and thorough investigation. Those responsible must be held to account."

Meanwhile, the committee to protect prosecutors in Italy said it was "shocked by this atrocious act of murder", adding: "The Government of Italy must employ all efforts and resources and put a mechanism in place to help prosecutors carry out an exhaustive inquiry to bring to justice those responsible."

Prosecutor Fernandez added, "A large amount of evidence was collected from the beach and Ms Allegranza's hotel room in Sampieri including DNA", and warned, "It is just a matter of time before the perpetrator is found".

Ms Allegranza's funeral is due to be held on Friday at the Island of San Michele Cemetery, in Venice.

Everything now made me feel quite poignant. I had only met with Maria once, that time a few months ago in London. She came across as a wonderful person, very genuine and of course, very passionate about her work. I noticed from the article she had been staying in Sampieri, the same place where Reno Stavola came from and where the mafia was supposed to have some kind of stronghold. It was too much of a co-incidence. Maria must have been onto something. Was she investigating the death of Suzanne? Was she close to finding out what had really happened to Fiona Meredith, or even her whereabouts? Or was there some other reason why Maria was killed?

I felt myself becoming quite emotional. I poured myself a whiskey from the mini bar and stepped out onto the balcony. I glanced up at the sky and looked at all the stars. I raised my glass, as if, in some kind of private ritual. It was the only way I knew how to cope. Quite strangely, the only way I could think of dealing with the death of someone, who after meeting only once, I had considered a friend.

30

Another night of hardly any sleep made it very difficult for me to concentrate on much else apart from the weather this morning. The news about the murder of Maria in Sicily had certainly taken its toll and somehow affected me a lot more than I thought it would. On top of what had happened to Suzanne, I suppose it was no big surprise.

The weather today was grim and for the first time in all my visits I have seen the Maltese weather at its worst, a shroud of grey sky, fast moving clouds with powerful streaks of lightning flashing fiercely through a peculiarly diagonal and lengthy presence of rain. For a spell there were hailstones the size of golf balls crashing on to the road outside. I had only really experienced short, sharp showers in Malta before, so this was all quite new to me.

From the breakfast room, I could see the main road down to the harbour had turned into a violent flood. It looked like a fast flowing river rather than the busy road I'd been walking down every day since I got here. All the ferries and tourist boats had been stopped. Small fishing vessels and yachts were bobbing about in the sea like toys and the fishermen were struggling with their catch on the quayside. People were coming into the front of the hotel to seek refuge. Both the foyer and bar was packed. Around the back of the hotel, water was building up as it gushed down from the hills behind. Members of hotel staff were kept busy with their buckets and brooms as they attempted to divert the water away from the rear entrance. Another man was laughing as he raised his arms to the heavens. 'We need this, beautiful rain, beautiful storm,' he kept shouting while doing nothing to help his colleagues.

After about three hours, the thunder and lightning stopped and the rain eased off. Eventually, some blue sky appeared in the distance and then some sunshine. After another hour, normality appeared to have been restored and the weather was nearly back to what I was used to. It didn't take long for the ground to dry so I decided to wander down to the harbour. The Gleneagles bar was shut so I went into the nearby Il-Luzzi bar for a pint instead. It's a small place right on the quayside and the owner was still mopping up after the rain.

'Enjoy the storm, did you?' he asked.

'Well, it was different. I've never been over here when it's happened that much before.'

He laughed, 'We're used to it. It's always good when it comes. It freshens up the place, you know, clears the air. This time of year, we get lots of storms. The biggest one I can remember was back in 2012. Someone died just over there, when a mast came down,' he said pointing to one of the fishermen's mooring posts.

The conversation went on for a while. I stayed for longer than I had anticipated and he introduced me to other members of his family, his wife and his two daughters as they arrived to help him.

'This is Jack, he's a newspaper reporter from England, he's staying up at the hotel,' he told them.

That comment came as a shock because I hadn't told him anything.

'How do you know that?' I asked.

'My friends, Luis and Sam, they pointed you out to me the other day. Don't worry, they're harmless, wouldn't hurt a fly,' he chuckled.

Now I became even more curious. I wasn't even aware they knew who I was. It was all becoming somewhat worrying. When they sat down at the table next to me with their two friends in the Gleneagles bar the other evening they must have recognised me. Perhaps that's why their conversation quickly turned from English to Maltese.

I noticed the weather looked like it was about to turn again so decided to make my way back up to the hotel.

'Good to see you. Hopefully see you again soon,' said the owner as I settled my bill.

'I'm Willie, by the way.'

'I'm Jack.'

'Yes I know,'

'Oh yes, of course you do.'

We both laughed. The bill came to eighteen Euros which equated to six pints. I didn't realise I had been there so long.

I had only been back at the hotel about twenty minutes when I received a call on my mobile from Rosie.

'Hello, Jack, it's Rosie speaking. I have some news for you.'

'Hello, Rosie. Who's dead this time?' I half joked.

'Not dead, but nearly. It's Joseph Buttiġieġ, he's in intensive care at the Mater Dei.'

'Oh yes, I knew he was ill. Lung cancer, I believe. I remember being told he was only diagnosed with it quite recently.'

'Yes, that's right, but that's not all. A friend of mine, Ailina, went to visit her husband, this is how I know. She saw a police guard on Joseph's room. She asked a member of hospital staff what was going on and they told her Joseph was being questioned by Inspector Azzopardi "as a matter of urgent priority". Ailina seemed quite flustered by it all when she came round to my house this morning.'

'Inspector Azzopardi? I remember that name. He was the one whose name cropped up when Suzanne was killed. Do you think it has anything to do with that?'

'Possibly, but it could be to do with any number of things. You know, Reno's murder, mafia dealings, anything.'

'Well, thanks for telling me.'

'That's not all.'

'What do you mean?'

'Julie has decided to leave Malta. She said there is nothing here for her anymore. She's fed up with all the hassle and needs to get away as soon as possible. There's no-one for her in England so she's going to stay with a cousin in Texas.'

'Texas, America?'

'Well, what other Texas is there? Houston, Texas to be precise. She has a cousin who's married to a young local girl out there. He's already agreed to let her stay for as long as she needs to. She had to go to Valletta today to sort her visa out.'

'Do you think she's running away from something?'

'I don't think so. Anyway, she's my friend and I wouldn't tell you if she was.'

I laughed.

'Why are you laughing? We are very good friends. That's why I've let her stay at my house. I don't think she really has anyone else to turn to.'

'Sorry, I didn't mean to laugh. What about her son, Michael?'

'She doesn't know where he is. He went off backpacking around the world with his little gay friend and hasn't been seen since, although Julie does seem to think he may be in America which could be why she's chosen to fly out there.'

After the phone call had finished I was left to ponder. I was wondering if Nina, the new girl downstairs in reception, might know anything. If she knew Rita, which was possible, I might be able to find out why Joseph Buttiġieġ was being questioned. I knew I had to be careful. Luis and Sam, who work in the hotel's kitchen, could be involved. It was all beginning to feel rather tricky!

I decided to go down to the reception area and speak with Nina but there was a guy working who I hadn't seen before.

'Can I help you, sir?'

'Sorry, I was looking for Nina. She was working here a little earlier.'

'Nina? Yes, sorry, she left early. She's gone to visit her uncle at the Mater Dei.'

'That wouldn't be Joseph Buttiġieġ, would it?'

'Yes, he's very ill. Do you know him?'

'Yes, sort of, we've met before a couple of times.'

'Is Nina related to Rita who used to work here by any chance?'

'Yes, they're cousins. More like sisters, really, but just cousins.'

'Okay, thank you. You've inadvertently answered my question.'

'How do you mean?'

'I just wanted to know if Nina knew Rita. You've told me they're cousins, which is obviously more than I expected.'

'You didn't pick up on the family resemblance then?'

'No, they look nothing alike. They're completely different.'

'Look closely at their eyes, the whole family has what we call in Malta "a thousand yard stare", they all have it. You will definitely see a similarity.'

'We use that saying in England too. I think it's another one which came over from America.'

'Not at all... it's been used by the members of the mafia in these parts for years. The Americans just borrowed it. Anyway, may I ask why you were enquiring about the Buttiġieġ family?'

'I'm a journalist. I'm just doing my job. It's all linked to the death of Suzanne Camilleri a few months ago.'

'Ah yes, I heard there was a reporter staying here, you've visited us a couple of times now, haven't you?'

'Yes, three or four times now including twice since Suzanne was killed.'

'That was a bad day for the island, a bad day for the whole of Malta, in fact. There have been so many murders over the last ten or twenty years, I don't like it. It puts shame on our country.'

'Do you think the mafia are to blame?'

'I don't know, ask the Buttiġieġs. They are not members of the mafia but everyone knows they have close ties with Sicily. I think they are the go-betweens, but listen, I didn't tell you that.'

'I understand what you mean. Your secret's safe. I've been thinking exactly the same.'

'Listen, I heard once that even the Government of Malta had hired a hitman to take out their opponents on more than one occasion. There is a lot of corruption going on in this country, it's been happening for years. I've even known our local councillors to take backhanders. Hush money, I think you call it in England.'

'If you don't mind me asking, are you English?'

'My father was English. My mother is Maltese. We lived in the north in a little place called Broughton Moor. It's up near Workington and Carlisle. My parents ran a pub there called the Miner's Arms. They had owned it since the early nineteen-eighties. When my father died last year we came back to Gozo to live. I've been working here, mostly nights, for a few months now.'

'That may explain why I've never seen you before. I'm usually up in my room by ten at night.'

'No doubt after a few drinks in the bar!'

'How did you guess?'

'Not a guess. You're English. You're on your own in a foreign country and listen; it's exactly what I would do.'

I laughed. 'You're right there.'

'Look, I hope you find what you're looking for in Gozo but tread carefully. Trust me, not everything is as pleasant as it seems.'

'Thank you, I found that out the other evening in the Gleneagles bar.'

'The Gleneagles bar? My advice would be to leave that place well alone. I've known some very hardened Maltese people who have refused to go in there. The clientele are very territorial, even the British and Irish expats who frequent the place.'

'Well, I don't think I'll be going back in there now anyway. Once is enough, even though I would have gone in there again earlier today if it had been open.'

'Listen, have a good night, it's Jack, isn't it?'

'Yes.'

'I'm Gareth. Perhaps we'll speak again.'

'I know. That's what it says on your name badge.'

'How observant of you, remember, just watch your back, okay?'

'Thank you, I will.'

Gareth seemed to be quite up to speed with everything that's been going on even though he'd only recently returned from England. His mere tone seemed to suggest, like Rosie, he knew more than he was letting on. He looked uneasy and seemed to backtrack, particularly each time the Buttiġieġ family was mentioned. It could have been because Nina was his work colleague but I sensed there was something he wasn't telling me. To be fair, I suppose I had only just met him so he wasn't really obliged to tell me anything. On the face of it, no-one is.

I had thought about going to the Mater Dei to see if I would be allowed to visit Joseph on his death bed but today's bad weather thwarted that idea, and perhaps it probably wasn't the right thing to do anyway. I was now thinking about taking a walk up to Qala in the morning to see if I could find out a little more about the Buttiġieġs and their activities. 'Catch them with their trousers down,' as my poor old editor Nancy at the *Woking Tribune* used to say.

31

I knew I was getting closer to finding some real answers but was aware Hermione would want something more concrete. I noticed yesterday that the *Telegraph* had already run a small piece on Maria's killing in Sicily - just six lines, it wasn't much.

I wasn't sure if Hermione actually knew there was an historical connection between Maria and Suzanne. I decided to bring her up to speed with all the latest developments - not that there were too many, so far as my investigation was going. Each time I attempted to ring, though, her phone cut out without even going to voicemail. After a couple of hours trying I was beginning to get concerned. I rang Rosie but she said she hadn't heard sight or sound of Hermione for over a week. I managed to get a landline number off the internet for the paper and gave it a ring...

'Hello, could I speak to Miss Grech please?'

'Hermione Grech?'

'Yes, yes please.'

'Wait!' the male voice said quite abruptly.

Eventually another man came on to the phone. 'How can I help you?'

'I would like to speak to Hermione Grech if possible.'

'You can't, she's not with us anymore.'

'What do you mean?'

'She left us last week. She's gone.'

'Gone? Gone where?'

'I don't know. Anyway, who am I speaking to?'

'Sorry, I'm Jack Compton, I'm one of your freelance journalists.'

'I have never heard of you. We have no-one working for us with that name.'

'Hermione came to Gozo a couple of weeks ago and signed me up to provide a story on the Suzanne Camilleri killing.'

'What do you mean, signed you up? Did you actually sign anything?'

'No, but we had a long conversation. We shook on it.'

'Then you're not a freelance journalist with the *Malta Telegraph* then, are you?'

'She agreed to pay for my extended stay in Gozo, rearrange my flight and everything, that's why I'm still here.'

'Then you're stupid, aren't you!' he shouted.

'Anyway, who are you?'

'I'm Terry Mancini, I own the paper and I'm the person who is editing it now. I already have a journalist working on the Camilleri killing, he's close to bringing in a story. Sorry Mr Compton, I don't need your services. I bid you goodbye.'

Shit, fuck, bollocks. I could feel myself shaking with anger. I grabbed a miniature whiskey from the mini bar and sat out on the balcony. I had to decide whether this was all worth it. My funds were at rock bottom and I was relying on everything Hermione had promised me. Now, I was well and truly in the mire.

It took a couple of hours and a few more whiskies to calm myself down. Even the hotel maid asked me if I was okay. She looked rather concerned by all the empty bottles left on the side and advised me to go to the supermarket and get one big bottle because it would work out cheaper. The fact of the matter is I'm not even a great lover of whiskey.

I felt I needed to phone Rick to see if he knew what was going on with Hermione. He said he trusted her but now I felt very let down. He needed to know about the shit I've been left in...

'Rick it's Jack.'

'Hi, mate, what's up?'

'It appears Hermione has left the *Telegraph*. I haven't been able to get her on her mobile and ended up speaking to the paper's owner. I was wondering if you knew anything.'

'Not really, I saw something she had posted on her Facebook page the other day. I couldn't make much sense of it but now you're telling me this, it's starting to fall into place.'

'What?'

'She'd clearly had a problem with someone but didn't say who it was. It looks like they'd been harassing her. She put up a few expletives and had a right old rant. I guessed it might be Mancini but I haven't seen anything since.'

'When I phoned the newspaper office, some other guy answered first. He was quite abrupt. I sensed he felt very awkward when I asked to speak to Hermione. That's when he got Mancini to come to the phone.'

'I don't know what to say, mate. Did you say you couldn't get hold of Hermione?'

'That's right. I couldn't.'

'That's probably because you have her work number. They've probably taken her work phone off her. Look, I have her personal number somewhere. I'll ring her on that to see what's going on. I'll get her to phone you.'

'That would be great, thanks.'

I now had to decide very quickly what I needed to do. Should I cut my losses and abort everything and head back to England or should I stay and dip into the last of my savings and get myself into debt? I really wasn't sure what to do.

After about an hour on my laptop I managed to manipulate my online savings account and transfer some money, enough to pay for another two weeks here and arrange a flight home. If I don't get the answers I'm looking for during these two weeks, then everything will have been in vain.

I was just about to take a shower when there was a knock on the door. It was the hotel maid.

'Sorry, sir, I've just come to replenish the fridge.'

She replaced six miniatures, two wines and four whiskies.

'There you are sir, enjoy. Remember what I said.'

'What?'

'Go to the supermarket, it's cheaper!'

'Thank you.'

She gave me a polite smile and then left. Just then the bedside telephone rang.

'Hello, is that Mr Compton?'

'Yes, who's that?'

'It's Nina down in reception. Can I come up and talk to you please?'

'Yes of course.'

After about ten minutes I answered the door. It was Nina, a quite pretty young lady, petite, long dark curly hair with beautiful green eyes and distinctive pencilled eyebrows.

'Hello, Mr Compton. I understand you've been asking questions about my family.'

'The Buttiġieġs?'

'Yes, of course, the Buttiġieġs. I'm Nina Buttiġieġ. I know you have already met my cousin Rita and my Uncle Joseph. My other cousin, Phillip, works in the kitchen. He told me you met in the hallway downstairs when you were talking about the photographs on the wall.'

'Oh yes, I remember, but he never told me his name.'

'He is good friends with Luis and Sam, they always go fishing together.'

'So how can I help you?'

'As you know, my Uncle Joseph is a very sick man. I don't want any big upset with my family. The police are doing a very good job upsetting us anyway. I want to tell you we are a very good family. We care about people. Some people think we are the mafia but we are not the mafia. Yes, we have been guilty of helping them in the past but that has always been for the greater good. We are not monsters. My Uncle Joseph will help anybody. My stepsister Lucette will help anyone too.'

'Oh yes, I met Lucette up in Nadur a couple of weeks ago.'

'I know. Did she ask you for money?'

'Eventually, but nothing happened. I was just taken in by her. I didn't realise she was a prostitute.'

'She's not a proper prostitute, just an embarrassment to the family. We don't talk to each other very much these days, mainly because of what she chooses to do for a living. I worry, though, that one day she may get hurt. So what are you going to write about us?'

'Nothing at the moment, my story has kind of run aground and I'm not being paid. All I wanted to do was find out who killed my friend, Suzanne Camilleri, and write something on that.'

'Well it wasn't the Buttiġieġs.'

'I've guessed that already. Was it Reno Stavola?'

'No.'

'Do you who know it was then?'

'No, but I think I know who does.'

'Who?'

'Can't say.'

'Why not?'

'Look, I still have my family to protect. When the time is right, you will find out, but now is not the right time. There is some unfinished business to be completed. When that is done, everyone will know.'

'What business? And why are you telling me this?'

'Like I said, the Buttiġieġs are not the mafia. More like just winged messengers now.'

'Can you tell me anymore?'

'No, not yet. Stay here where I can find you. You will get what you want.'

After Nina left the room I felt quite stunned. It was an unusual conversation and one that made me believe the Buttiġieġs hold the key to everything. Everything must be hinging on Joseph's condition in the hospital. I was now wondering if he had sent Nina to speak with me.

The evening was getting on and I was thinking about getting ready for an early night when there was another knock on the door. I thought it was Nina again, so I quickly made myself decent. When I answered, it was Hermione.

'Hello, Jack, sorry to bother you so late. I remember you telling me your room number last time I was here so I took a chance you might be in. I've checked in myself for the night, I'm a few doors along the hallway.'

'Bloody hell, you were the last person I expected to see today, what's going on?'

'Let me in and I'll tell you everything.'

I sat Hermione on the balcony and fetched some wine. She was fumbling in her bag for her cigarettes but then she realised she had left them in her room.

'I owe you an explanation, Jack. It's not been an easy few days for me and I've left the *Telegraph*.'

'Yes, I know, I only spoke to someone called Terry Mancini around lunchtime. He's the owner, I believe?'

'He is, and he's the reason for all my problems. Everything I've done or tried to do lately, he's criticised. It ended up in a big row and then the bastard sacked me. I was going to leave anyway, as I've been setting up my own online paid news service. I think he found out what I was up to and decided to give me a hard time.'

'What do you mean by "paid news service"?'

'It's essentially a blog which people subscribe to. It's in part funded by advertisers and it's already paying for itself. Leaving the *Telegraph* is no big deal. I think it's on its way out anyway.'

'Well, to be honest, I've been calling you every name under the sun today. I've felt well and truly stitched up. Today has not been a good day.'

'Who've you been mouthing off to about me then?'

'No-one just myself, I suppose.'

Hermione laughed. 'Ah, that's alright then.'

'So why are you here in Gozo?'

'I needed a break and I've been staying with friends in Xlendi for a few days. I need to be on an early ferry in the morning. That's why I've checked in here for the night.'

'That's good. So what about the story and my expenses you were going to sort out?'

'That's why I'm here, Jack. I still want the story. I want you to write it for my new blog.'

'That's great, thank you, and I must say, a great relief. I've been moping around all day feeling like I'd been stitched up like a kipper.'

'What do mean, kipper?'

'Don't worry. It's a saying we have back in England.'

Hermione paused and rifled through her bag again, eventually producing a large white envelope.

'Right, sign that. It's a contract.'

When I opened the envelope, there was a two-page contract and a bundle of Euros.

'That will cover your expenses for the next week or two. I haven't rearranged a flight yet as I want you to complete the story first. I know you're close and I don't think you need any unnecessary worries, like money for instance.'

'Thank you. I must admit, I had feared the worst.'

'I'm an honest woman, Jack, trust me. Now, I must go and get some shut eye. Here's my new card with all my contact details. Phone or message me as soon as you get anything.'

'Thank you, I will. By the way, did you speak to Rick today? He was going to call you.'

'He may have tried, but I've changed all my numbers. I just don't want that bastard Mancini phoning me, at least not until I've got all the legal stuff sorted.'

'Okay, I understand that. Anyway, thanks for coming to see me. It means a lot.'

'It was top of my list of priorities and we need to carry on with your friend Suzanne's great work.'

'I appreciate that.'

Hermione clutched my arm, pouted her lips and gave me a peck on the cheek and then left the room. When I counted the money, it came to a thousand Euros. It sort of confirmed that she meant business and I felt I could trust her again, although I did wonder about her blog. I quickly opened my laptop and did a quick search by entering her name. True enough, her blog was there. It was called *The Commentator* and was essentially a running commentary of current affairs. Everything was topical and it all had a controversial edge. I noticed it sailed close to being political without a firm affiliation to any particular party. I began to understand why she wanted my story. I also worked out from the number of adverts and the fees she was charging that she must be making around ten-thousand Euros a month already. In social media terms, that's fucking good money. The day had ended better than I'd expected.

32

An unexpected visitor at the hotel this morning was Rosie. She'd been down to the ferry terminal to drop off a friend and phoned me to see if we could meet for a chat before she went to open the kiosk. We grabbed a couple of coffees and went out on to the patio.

'This is a pleasant surprise, Rosie.'

'Well as people always say, I was just passing. I thought I'd stop by to see how everything was going.'

I told her about what had happened with Hermione and about my conversations with Gareth and Nina. Then asked her about all the other stuff Suzanne might have been into.

'As you know, Suzanne was besotted with the missing woman case and the death of Princess Diana. It took up nearly all her time. She knew about all the corruption here in Malta, but other journalists were taking up the mantle. It was like a crusade. People were getting killed. One journalist was blown up in a car bomb attack near her home on the mainland back in 2017. Suzanne's death was very similar and many people have been asking if the same people were responsible.'

'What do you think?'

'Personally, I don't think so. Suzanne was on a different course. Yes, it was known that towards the end she had ruffled a few feathers with her style of reporting but like I said, she had left all the stories of corruption within the Government of Malta and even the police to others. Those stories were becoming "old hat" as you say and just didn't interest her anymore.'

'It's hard to believe there's so much corruption going on in such a beautiful place. I always thought Malta was almost crime free.'

'Jack, you couldn't be further from the truth. Reality speaks for itself.'

'What do you mean?'

'Look, it's quite complex. Malta is perceived to be one of the most corrupt countries in Western Europe. The corruption is practically on an even keel with Italy. Other countries like Greece, Romania and Slovakia, are equally as bad.'

'How do you know all this?'

'I live here. I listen, I read. That's how I know. It's not difficult. Everybody knows but most of us live in denial. We like to think it's not happening. The tourist board for instance would like you to believe everything is perfect. It's not.'

'I keep hearing the word "corruption", but what kind of corruption is it?'

'In layman's terms, it's money laundering. There are very stringent rules but they are not being adhered to. It's all very complicated. A lot of it has to do with offshore business accounts, you know, tax avoidance and that kind of thing. The other thing which is corrupt is the passport system. Anyone can get a Maltese passport. There's an American who rents a garage up in Nadur. He used the address of his garage to get residency. Loads of people are doing it. It's got him a roam free passport to the whole of Europe. Malta is a soft touch and this is what got Valerie killed.'

'Valerie?'

'Valerie Farrugia. She's the journalist I was telling you about who died in the car bomb attack on the mainland in 2017.'

'Oh yes, I seem to remember that. I think I've seen some tributes and banners when I've been to Valletta.'

'Yes, you most definitely would have. Suzanne admired her a lot. She was always talking to me about Valerie. You know, Valerie wrote this, Valerie wrote that. Suzanne, and now I think even Hermione, have been inspired by her. I must warn Hermione to be careful, very careful.'

'I was thinking that as well. I've seen the blog she's just started up, it's very controversial.'

'She sent me a text message with her new number last night. I'll speak to her but, like Suzanne, she's a hard-headed woman so probably won't listen to me anyway. Look, Jack, I must go. I need to open the kiosk. It's a lovely warm day, so I'm expecting to be quite busy.'

'Okay, thanks for stopping by.'

'You're welcome. Anyway, take care and I hope you get to finish your story soon. Oh, and if you find out who killed Suzanne, I want to be the first to know, right?'

'Yes, right,' I said with an air of reservation.

This afternoon, I decided to walk along the cliffs from Mġarr Harbour to Hondoq Bay and then take the road up to Qala. It's the same walk I had done on my last visit albeit by a slightly different route. The sun was bright and there was hardly a cloud in the sky. I noticed some of the original footpath had fallen into the sea so part of the route I had intended to walk had become impassable. On the way, I had to hold on to some branches to help keep my balance as a few stones tumbled down from a ledge just above from where I was walking. When I looked down towards my feet, one of the stones was actually a fossil of a seashell. Part of the shell was still attached. It must have been prehistoric as the ground I was walking on was some 400 feet above sea level.

When I got to Hondoq I went over to the kiosk and asked for Rosie. Her assistant, Sylvia, a slim black girl with unusually bright blue eyes, was working.

'Sorry, is Rosie about?'

'No, she had a phone call and had to go, she's given me the key so I don't think she'll be back today,' she said in broken English.

'Ah, okay. It's not important. I only saw her at the hotel this morning. I'm just passing through on my way up to Qala.'

'Passing through from where?'

'From Mġarr, I took the route along the clifftops.'

'You must be thirsty. Do you want a drink?'

'Of course, thank you.'

Sylvia had seen me before and immediately brought over a large bottle of Cisk and refused payment which was very kind. Although I did think, what if she's doing that with everyone each time Rosie's back is turned? Rosie would be losing money hand over fist.

After about an hour sitting and people watching, I decided to make my way up the steep hill to Qala. It's quite an energy sapping walk but it's the views which are quite breathtaking. When I reached Qala I thought I'd get another drink but both the usual bars I visit, Zeppy's and the Kupita, were shut. The whole village was like a ghost town. Everything felt quite eerie. There was no-one about. I had been there a few times in the past and it was always quite vibrant with the locals and expats mixing well together in the street, even at siesta time.

I was just about to begin my walk along the main road back to the hotel in Għajnsielem when the church bell started ringing. It was a slow toll... DONG... DONG... DONG... still no-one was about. I guessed it was a death knell. I walked closer to the church and then suddenly, an old woman appeared, fell to her knees at the steps and crossed her heart.

'Joseph, Joseph,' she kept mumbling.

The church is St Joseph's, the parish church of Qala. Gradually, a few more people appeared with some going straight inside. A very old gentleman with a full head of white hair and a distinctive tanned and wrinkly face came and stood beside me, crossed his heart and then put his hand on my shoulder.

'You don't understand, do you?' he said in perfect English.

'I think someone must have passed away,' I replied.

'Yes. Joseph, our good friend and servant, Joseph. May the good lord bless him and long may he rest in peace. He was named after this church.'

I was surprised that I hadn't already worked it out. Joseph Buttiġieġ must have died. I told the man I had met Joseph and knew other members of his family.

'He was a good man. We got a call from Fifi just now. He died at ten o'clock this morning. All his family were with him. His funeral will be here at dusk tomorrow,'

'Who's Fifi?'

'If you don't know, you're not supposed to know,' he snapped.

Eventually the old man made his way into the church with two young girls at his side. I made my way back along the road to the hotel knowing that tomorrow I would be attending a funeral. It was all very sad, but I knew it was an excellent opportunity to perhaps find some, if not all, of the answers I had been looking for.

Back at the hotel, the bar was quite busy. There was a steady stream of people arriving and then going out onto the patio with their drinks.

After about five minutes I saw Nina come in, she looked away at first but then came over when she saw me looking in her direction.

'It's Uncle Joseph,' she said.

'I know, I heard a little earlier. I'm sorry.'

'We went to the Mater Dei last night when we heard he was given the last rites by the hospital priest yesterday evening. He died this morning. It was peaceful but he had a smile. I will never forget that. We all loved him and we will miss him.'

'Are all these people part of your family?'

'Some, not all, many are just friends who have come to meet us here to pay their respects and find out the funeral details.'

'Ah yes, I understand that's in Qala, tomorrow.'

'How do you know that already?'

'I was in Qala earlier. The church bell started ringing and an old man spoke to me. He had two little girls with him. After a while they joined some others and went into the church.'

'That sounds like Isaac. He is a good friend of our family. He's also Rita's godfather. He lives down on the road to Hondoq near the deep sea diving shop. I've known him all my life. He's not a person you would want to upset even though he's mellowed in recent years as he's got older.'

'He mentioned someone called Fifi, do you know her?'

'We all do, but we are not allowed to say anything. She's a recluse and doesn't like being spoken about. She is very well respected by our family. She is like a Madonna to us. We all love her and protect her. I cannot say any more than that.'

'Do you mind if I come to Joseph's funeral tomorrow?'

'Anyone can come to the funeral.'

Just then we were joined by Rita and Lucette.

'Hello, Mr Compton, how are you?' asked Rita.

'Fine, I see congratulations are in order,' I said looking down at her belly.

'Yes, three months to go. It's very hot carrying this thing around inside me. I've seen a scan. I think it's going to be a boy. I'm going to call him Joseph.'

'And how are you?' I asked Lucette.

'How do you think I am, I'm in mourning, you crazy man!'

I sort of wished I hadn't asked, so made my excuses and went back to the bar as the three women mingled with others out on the patio.

I was now becoming more intrigued about who Fifi was. Could it be Fiona Meredith? I used to know a Fiona at school and some people called her Fi or Fifi. I thought back to my conversation with Danielle at the hairdressers in Victoria. I was now almost convinced that it was Fifi who was whisked away by the men in the black Mercedes the day all the traffic got held up. Things were slowly beginning to come together. I just had to hope I wasn't veering off in the wrong direction.

33

I knew today wasn't going to be easy. I had no appropriate attire to wear to a funeral and couldn't really afford to go out and buy a black suit and shoes for the occasion, so I resigned myself to looking on from the sidelines.

I stood in the main square by the church railings as people were mingling and waiting for the hearse and all the Buttiġieġs to arrive. My main reason for attending was to catch sight of Fifi, the woman Nina and the old man I met yesterday had referred to. If I could see anyone who remotely resembled how Princess Diana might look like now, I felt I could be on to something.

One by one, the mourners arrived; pausing on the steps outside the church as the bell unsubtly announced there was a funeral going on with its solemn intrusion. More and more people were arriving, the men in black suits and walking canes. Women, somehow more elegant with their faces covered with veils or sunglasses to conceal their emotions.

As the hearse arrived I felt a poke in my back. It was Nina.

'You're not dressed for a funeral,' she whispered.

'Neither are you!' I said, observing she was only wearing a burgundy off- the-shoulder dress and nothing on her feet.

'I've been up all night preparing Uncle Joseph's body for today. You know, making him look handsome again. He'd lost a lot of weight in his last few weeks, I hardly recognised him but it was rather comforting seeing him at peace at last and without all the recent pain.'

'So why aren't you attending his funeral?'

'I am,' she said adamantly, 'I'm here, aren't I? It's just that I gave up on God a few years ago. I will never walk into a church again. My family are angry about it but I am not a hypocrite. They all know I loved my uncle, he was my life, he guided me through so much, just like he has with many of us but he had been let down by God. I don't believe there is a God anymore. He carried on believing and I have to respect that.'

'I don't believe in God either, is that why you did what you did last night, you know, get him ready for today?'

'Yes, of course, but it's tradition.'

'Tradition?'

'Yes, in a way we celebrate the life of a person rather than mourn their passing. Of course everyone is in tears. We wanted to bury Joseph in his favourite brown suit but he had lost so much weight he didn't look right. I've covered him with a simple shroud the funeral director gave me instead. I hope he likes it.'

'I think I'd be too squeamish to do what you have done. In many ways, when someone dies in England, we are protected from the body unless we choose otherwise. Death is still a very taboo subject back home, although in Victorian times people even used to pose with the dead for a photograph with the rest of the family before burial. I don't really know why so much has changed since that era.'

'Here in Malta, nothing has changed, tradition is very important to us. Some outsiders are trying to influence change but I can't see that happening. There's even been talk of cremations here, something all Catholics are strongly against. That will never happen, although it would make sense as there is a huge shortage of burial places and that is a big problem in Malta.'

Just then, Nina paused as the coffin was slowly removed from the back of the hearse by four pallbearers. After steadying themselves, they slowly walked with the coffin on their shoulders, up the steps and into the church with a procession of family members, including Rita and Lucette, behind. I was looking for someone who could be Fifi but all the women were dressed the same, although one woman with cropped hair, and the only person to arrive by car, attracted a lot of attention as she entered the church flanked by what looked like a couple of bodyguards.

'Is that someone famous?' I asked.

Nina paused. 'No not really, just an old family friend. Anyway, they'll all be in there for about three hours, a requiem mass takes a long time. I'm going to the bar to find my sandals and then I'm walking ahead to the cemetery, it's on the way to Hondoq if you want to join me.'

Nina took me across the street to the small Ite ad Joseph Bar which had one of its big green doors partially closed probably out of respect for those attending the funeral. Inside everything was hushed. A young boy about fourteen-years-old was serving.

'No beer, no beer,' whispered Nina as I reached for my wallet.

Instead, the boy produced a large carafe of red wine.

'It's a special day, help me drink this. It's good wine. It's been produced by friends of us Buttiġieġs for years and years, you'll love it,' she said excitedly.

I found Nina very accommodating and wondered if there was any ulterior motive behind her taking me to the bar.

'So what are we doing here? Everything feels quite surreal.'

'Don't worry. But hey, thank you for not denouncing my uncle in the papers before he died.'

After a couple of hours the bell started to toll again with its DONG... DONG... DONG...

'Come on, let's get down to the cemetery, it's not too far.'

'Yes, I know, I've passed it a few times before.'

We both sat on a pile of bricks opposite the main gate and admired the early signs of a beautiful sunset. Nina unapologetically lit a cigarette as we waited for the cortege to arrive.

'Are you going to the graveside?'

'No, of course not, I'll come back tomorrow on my own. I have to go back to the house soon and help prepare the feast, we have a couple of waiters from the hotel helping us out and I need to be there to make sure they're doing everything right. There can be no mistakes today.'

As she was speaking the cortege came into sight. The hearse was followed by the black Mercedes I had seen arrive at the church earlier. Around sixty people were following on foot. The hearse stopped outside the main gate and again, the pallbearers carefully removed the coffin, hoisting it onto their shoulders before slowly walking around the small chapel to a plot overlooking the countryside.

'Okay, I've got to go now. Thank you for talking to me this afternoon and thanks again for not reporting anything about Uncle Joseph. Oh, and by the way, I like you.'

'Like I said, I wouldn't have, and oh, thank you for the wine. It was the best I've ever tasted. I like you too by the way.'

'Good, see you again soon maybe.'

'I hope so.'

Nina dashed off as the last of the mourners were still arriving. Just as I was about to leave and make my way back to the hotel, I noticed the woman with cropped hair being helped from the back of her car. She briefly lowered her sunglasses and looked in my direction before being shuffled into the cemetery by the chauffeur and the two men who seemed to be minding her. By now I was convinced she was Fiona.

When I got back to the hotel I decided to give Hermione a quick courtesy call to update her on the latest events. She had heard Joseph had passed away but seemed surprised I didn't get booted and suited to attend the funeral ceremony properly.

'Why not?'

'Because I wasn't prepared to purchase clothes I would only probably wear for a few hours. I couldn't really afford it and besides, because I don't believe in God, I always feel uncomfortable going into a church where everybody celebrates his existence.'

'Okay, anyway you should have let me know, I would have paid for a suit. You could have charged it to my account.'

'Thanks, it's a little late now, I'll remember next time.'

She laughed. 'What next time? Do you know who's going to die next?'

'No, obviously not.'

'So, did you find out anything new?'

'Let's just say for now, things are heating up and I think I'm getting very close. The Buttiġieġs are not saying very much and I'm certain they know more than they're letting on. I spoke to Nina earlier, Joseph's niece. I think she's frightened. I'm sure she wanted to tell me more, if not everything she knows. I think she's the key to finding out what's really been going on.'

Hermione paused before answering which gave me time to decide not to say anything about Fiona or Fifi as she's now known. I still didn't trust Hermione enough with that kind of information in case she decided to hijack the story for herself.

'Well, you keep chipping away at Nina and see what else you can find out,' she said.

'I will, don't worry.'

After the call had finished I went out on the balcony. The sky was lit up with the brightness of stars and I could hear loud reggae music emanating from the Gleneagles bar. I thought about taking a stroll down to see if any of the Buttiġieġs or their associates might be there, but as it was getting late I decided against it.

My next plan was to work out when to speak to Nina again. In an odd sort of way I was warming to her and felt a mutual kind of respect, although I didn't really know what she was after. I also had to remember how old I was getting and she's still quite young. The mirror doesn't lie and sometimes I find the reflection quite depressing. I'm not that youthful handsome looking bastard in the sharp grey suit anymore.

34

I noticed Nina wasn't at the reception desk this morning so decided to enquire. Gareth was working overtime until 11am and said she should be in by then to finally relieve him from his night shift. It was something to do with her being up very late after yesterday's funeral. Whilst we were talking, a short stocky man in a tatty blue suit and white open-necked shirt walked up to the reception desk.

'Good morning, I'm here to see one of your visitors, a Mr Jack Compton. I believe he's been staying here for a while.'

Gareth looked at me with an air of concern.

'This is Mr Compton right here,' he stuttered.

The gentleman turned and reached out to shake my hand.

'Hello, I'm Inspector Azzopardi of the Pulizija, I need a quiet word, my friend.'

Gareth turned around and said we could use the manager's office behind the reception desk. The manager was on his morning rounds and Gareth said he would let him know what was going on by using the internal two-way radio system. Myself and Inspector Azzopardi stepped into the office and closed the door.

'I suppose you're wondering what all this is about. I'm Allen Azzopardi and I've been investigating the terrible murder of Mrs Camilleri.'

'Yes, I recognise your name,' I said nervously.

'I've heard from one of my contacts you were good friends with the poor lady.'

'Yes, we were very good friends. We used to work together at the *Sunday Herald* in London over twenty years ago and stayed in touch ever since. I've been over here to Gozo to visit her several times. I've also met her husband, Peter, and their two children.'

'Yes I know. The boy is still very angry about what happened to his mother. I hear from him constantly. He was always begging for answers but not so much recently. I think he's moved to Valletta.'

'So why do you want to speak to me and how did you know I was here?'

'Firstly, we had to question a lady called Julie Etheridge a few weeks ago. She was inadvertently interfering with our investigation. I'm here to ask you to make sure you don't do the same. We arrested Mrs Etheridge but later released her without charge. That is when your name came up and she told me what you were doing.'

'I see. So how can I help?'

'I want you to stop going around the island asking questions. I am confident of apprehending your friend's killer very soon. We are in the final stages of securing the evidence we need before making an arrest.'

'I thought you had already made some arrests a while ago.'

'I did but it was none of those. They were all found innocent and I had to let them go. It was all to do with the elimination process.'

'So who is it?'

'You don't expect me to tell you that at this stage, do you? What do you think I am? Do you think I'm stupid?'

'No, of course not. I suppose I was just thinking out loud. It was an obvious question for me to ask.'

'Well, my friend, it's my job to ask all the questions, especially with this matter. It's absorbing a lot of time and resources and I don't want to see all my good work compromised or ruined by a foreign newspaper reporter.'

'I understand that but can I just ask, is there any connection between Suzanne's death and the murder of Reno Stavola on Comino?'

'Mrs Camilleri and Mr Stavola? There is nothing to suggest a connection. The murder of Reno Stavola is being investigated separately by my colleagues and so far there has been no common ground to link the two incidents. That is all I am prepared to say.'

'So what shall I do now?'

'I want you do nothing at all, unless you want to fly back to England. I could arrange a flight for you. If you must stay, I want you to say nothing. I don't want you to ask any more questions. If you do, I might have to arrest you for interfering with my investigation like Mrs Etheridge, is that clear?'

'Yes, very clear.'

'When an arrest is made you will know fairly quickly. It is in the public interest for us to find the killer. When we finally have that person in handcuffs everyone will know virtually straightaway. People have been baying for my blood because the hunt for the killer or killers has gone on so long. They expect to see results and I have been constantly criticised by the public and even my superiors from day one. I want to see an end to this case with the right result, you know, justice for your friend.'

'Thank you. Justice is what her family wants.'

The inspector looked at me oddly. 'Yes, justice is what they will get.'

We shook hands and walked out to the reception area. Nina had just arrived and was taking over the shift from Gareth who was looking rather tired. Inspector Azzopardi walked out of the hotel and got into a car which had been parked outside before driving off up the hill in the direction of Nadur. I decided to grab a quick beer from the bar and get my head around the conversation I had just had. How close was the inspector to making an arrest, and who was it, I kept thinking? I was then joined by Gareth who insisted he bought me a beer.

'Sorry about that, I didn't realise the police were looking for you.'

'Well, they're not really. He just wanted me to stay out of the way. He seems to think I could be interfering with his investigation into Suzanne's murder. He's advised me to back off and not go round asking any more questions.'

'Suitable advice then.'

'For him maybe, but I suppose if he catches the killer then it's worth it. It will just be more difficult for me to get a scoop on the story because he will announce it to the whole damn fucking world as soon as he has someone in handcuffs. Everyone will know at the same time and any story I write will be next to worthless. I think I still need to do some more digging and find out who the killer is before a formal arrest is made.'

'How will you do that?'

'I'm not sure but people must know. I'm sure the Buttiġieġs must know something, even if they're not involved.'

'Believe me, they're definitely not involved, it's not their kind of thing. Nina and Rita, for instance, would be mortified if you think they are.'

'It's just that the Buttiġieġs seem to be central to everything I've been looking into so far, especially Reno Stavola, and now a person called Fifi.'

'Ah, Fifi. I would leave her well alone if I was you. That would set the Buttiġieġs off and rub them up the wrong way. They are very protective of her. She has some kind of hold on them. No-one ever speaks of her very openly and I suggest you don't either.'

I gulped on my drink. In a way Gareth was telling me everything without saying too much. The very fact he was so guarded about Fifi's existence only served to confirm all my suspicions. I didn't really need convincing anymore. I knew Fifi was Fiona Meredith, I just needed her to tell me herself. I couldn't help thinking Nina could be the person to help me.

'So how is Nina after yesterday, is she okay?' I asked.

'She seems fine but like me, she's very tired. She's working until nine tonight and that's when I'll be coming back on duty to relieve her.'

'I don't envy you that one.'

'Don't, we're used to working hard in Malta. It's no big deal. One thing I must say before I go, I do know Nina has a little light shining for you. I don't know why but she seemed pleased to see you walk across the foyer just now. Please, though, don't ask any more questions about her family. It will only piss her off. She's had enough on her plate lately. She's been very upset and worried about her family's reputation.'

'I know. She's already asked me to back off. She was worried I might write some kind of story about Joseph. I hope I've put her mind at rest on that.'

'Okay, good. Just be careful with her. You have been warned.'

Gareth downed the rest of his drink and left. I felt quite numb. Got at, really, but quite flattered someone so young like Nina was interested in me.

I decided to go back up to my hotel room and draft an article on what I know so far. The sun was too bright for me to work on the balcony so I went back into the room and worked from my laptop on the writing desk next to the bed. Each time I tapped in a few words, I seemed to freeze and then delete the words. I knew what to write, but just couldn't. It was a kind of writer's block I hadn't really experienced before.

In the end I chose to walk down to the harbour for a drink at the Il-Luzzi bar. It seemed a safe place to go, although I had met the owner before and he knew who I was, he didn't know too much about what I'd been doing so I felt comfortable going there. I was conscious Inspector Azzopardi may have arranged for someone to follow me and knowing how the police work in Malta, that could be a strong possibility. When I got to the bar, the owner wasn't there but a big guy called Luke, who I recognised from one of my previous visits, was serving.

'Oh hello, Jack, I remember you. I've been told you were back again.'

'Hi, yes, I've been back a few weeks now, although I'm probably going back to England soon.'

'I hear you've been investigating the death of that lady reporter. Any joy yet?'

'Some but I'm just going to let the police do their job and see what happens.'

'There's been a lot of police over from the mainland this morning. They came across on the nine o'clock ferry.'

'I know. I was visited by one of them.'

'Who?'

'Inspector Azzopardi, he's leading the murder enquiry.'

'Christ, forgive me. He is as bent as hell. Everyone knows he's on the take but yet he still he keeps his job.'

'He told me he's close to making an arrest.'

'Well let's hope so. He doesn't do anything without some kind of reward from one of the criminal gangs, though. There's a lot of blood money on the islands and the gangs use it to pay him off when clearing up after their enemies.'

'You seem to know a lot.'

'A few years ago, my brother Chris was a gang member. Things got too hot for him and he fled to New Zealand. He's living near Christchurch now on the south island but still fears for his life. That's how bad it can get and Azzopardi was one of the main reasons why he left.'

'Was he going to arrest your brother?'

'No, Azzopardi threatened to have him killed. Some people in the police were on the take from one of the Sicilian gangs. My brother somehow got caught up in it all. Things calmed down in the end and the gangsters eventually left the island.'

'Was it anything to do with the Buttiġieġs?'

'No, not this time. Anyway, the Buttiġieġs have been quite dormant since the late nineties. There's an air of respectability around the family now, ever since that Fifi woman took charge.'

'Fifi?'

'Yes, she seemed to come from nowhere. The whole family immediately appeared to lay down their arms. It was quite strange. They were linked to Reno Stavola, you know, the man who was murdered in Comino? She had something to do with him but it all went rather strange. No-one really knows what happened or what Fifi looks like, she's a recluse and refuses to socialise. Her face is always hidden.'

'Yes, I noticed that at Joseph Buttiġieġ's funeral yesterday.'

'I was there too. I thought I saw you talking to one of the Buttiġieġ girls outside the church.'

'Yes, I was. I was talking to Nina. She's working up at the hotel at the moment.'

'Do you know Rita, her cousin?'

'Yes quite well. I've noticed quite recently that she's pregnant.'

'Oh yes, with the reporter's baby. Not you, though!' he laughed.

'Which reporter?'

'That Frankie Fletcher bloke. Everyone is always talking about him. I think he got himself arrested and was taken back to England a while back. He was a tosspot. He and Rita had a fling a few months ago and she got herself in the family way. It's definitely his baby.'

'Fucking hell, he's been putting it about a bit over here. He's got to be in his seventies as well. I already know he's fathered a son over here called Michael. I've only ever spoken to Frankie once and that was on the phone. Nothing really surprises me with him anymore. He sounds like a loose cannon.'

'That, he most certainly is.'

'Anyway, Luke, I need to get on. Thanks for the beers, I really have to get back to the hotel and do some work on my computer while I'm still partially sober. It's been a weird old day and I'm still not sure how it might end.'

'Okay, I'm working here tomorrow and then I'm off for a few days, but I hope to see you again soon.'

'You will and thanks very much for the chat, it's been really useful.'

Luke laughed. 'Anything to get at Azzopardi is always good. I hate that bastard.'

Walking back up to the hill towards the hotel I decided I would need to speak to Nina at some point. I remembered Gareth had told me she was due to finish her shift at nine.

In all the excitement, I realised I had been without my mobile ever since I put it on charge before breakfast this morning. When I picked it up there were three missed calls from the *Woking Tribune's* landline which was unusual. If Lisa wanted me for any reason she would have called me from her mobile. I felt curiosity getting the better of me and decided to ring back. After a couple of minutes, a woman answered. It was Helen Rickmeyer.

'Hello, sorry, this is Jack Compton, has someone been trying to get hold of me?'

'Yes, I have,' said Helen quite hurriedly.

I sensed she had something important to tell me so wasn't quite sure what was going to happen next.

'Has something happened?'

'Sort of, well, not really but it's all to do with Lisa.'

'What's to do with her?'

'She called in yesterday and told us the paper will be closing down the week before Christmas. It has come as a complete shock. It's an absolute bolt out of the blue.'

'What's the reason?'

'The big wigs over at the *Infinity Group* in Reading have blamed our poor circulation figures and recent drop in advertising sales. Our numbers have been plummeting over the last few months to be honest.

Perhaps we all should have seen this coming. The newspaper's been going since 1894 but has, if I'm really honest, been in decline for a few years. They're shutting down a total of six out of ten of their rural titles as they look to streamline the business. I think they're opting for a new online social media based model to keep up with all the modern trends.'

'It's a real shame but I do understand, it's starting to happen here in Malta as well. Is this the reason you've been trying to contact me?'

'Not completely. The main reason I've contacted you is to see if there's any newspaper admin jobs out there. Do you have any contacts? I'm thinking of moving to Gozo with Caroline. We both absolutely love the place and are thinking about renting an apartment in Marsalforn.'

'That's a brave move. The only real contact I have is the *Malta Telegraph* but everything is going very much downhill with them as well so I wouldn't hold out much hope. Their contact number is available on their website. Anyway, you said Lisa "called in". What does she have to say about all this, I thought she might have contacted me herself?'

'She's not at work at the moment. She's been off with stress for the last week or so.'

'Stress?'

'You know I told you she was back with Jamie? Well, it didn't last very long. He had a massive chip on his shoulder about everything and he beat the living daylights out of her as they were leaving The Sovereigns the other Friday night. He was arrested later in town and as soon as he was released, he disappeared. No-one has seen him since.'

'Blimey. Poor Lisa, perhaps I should give her a ring.'

'Perhaps you shouldn't!'

'Why?'

'Well if things had worked out between you and her, none of this would have happened. She confided in me when you both came back from your dirty little weekend in Paris. She thought you two would have a future together. Obviously that was not the case.'

'Okay, I'll lay low for now, but if you see her, please ask her to ring me.'

'I will. Oh, and by the way, when are you planning on coming back to England?'

'Probably in a couple of weeks once I've finished working on my story. You know, the Suzanne Camilleri murder.'

'Oh yes, well good luck. Please give me a shout, though, if you hear of any jobs or cheap apartments going over there.'

'I will and thanks for letting me know what's been going on.'

'Desperate times, desperate measures,' Helen said just as she put the phone down.

I couldn't help thinking how rude and abrupt she sounded. When I first met Helen in the *Tribune* office a few months ago, she seemed quite polite. I now had to decide whether to contact Lisa to see if she was okay or just simply let bygones be bygones and put it all down to experience. Too much had been happening lately and I still had some very strong feelings for Suzanne. Somehow her spirit seemed to have a firm hold over me. In a way, it was strangely comforting and perhaps my own subconscious way of dealing with her death.

When it reached 9pm I decided to pop down to the hotel bar. I hoped Nina would be free for a chat. As I walked past the reception desk it looked like they were just handing over. Nina looked drawn and slightly upset but still acknowledged me as I went through to the bar. I ordered my normal pint and found myself a spot in the corner by the window. Eventually, Nina walked into the room, turned and smiled and then gestured as if asking if I would like another drink. I nodded and she smiled again.

'I get the impression you're a bit of a heavy drinker,' she said as she plonked herself down beside me.

'I don't know, maybe. I'm just a single man abroad and I need to do something with my downtime.'

'Downtime?'

'Well, quality thinking time as I call it.'

'It's just whenever I see you, you always have a drink in your hand. When we talk, you always mention bars and pubs. I'm sure you must be an alcoholic!'

'Not true.'

'Then, dear Jack, you're in denial.'

'Not really. I do take the odd day off, just to prove to myself that my body is not alcohol dependent.'

She laughed. 'Okay, okay, I believe you.'

'Good, thanks. So does that mean I can now breathe easy?'

She laughed again, 'Of course not. Just be aware I can read your state of mind. I promise I will never mention it ever again. Just be careful. That is all.'

'Thank you.'

The rest of the evening seemed to pass very quickly and I noticed the waiter and the bar staff hurriedly clearing the bar and wiping the tables.

'Time to go,' said Nina.

'Go where?'

'Your room of course, it's too late for me to travel back home to Qala now and trying to get a cab this time of the night will be next to useless.'

'Sorry, I thought you had a room here?'

'No, I haven't. Rita did but after she fell pregnant the other month with Frankie Fletcher's baby, Uncle Joseph insisted I should still live at home when I started working here. He didn't want the same thing to happen to me.'

'Okay, that seems quite wise, so what do you want to do now?'

'Wait!'

Nina walked over to bar and whispered to the barmaid who was just about to leave. She came back gleefully brandishing a bottle of Victoria Heights.

'Look, I've got this. I know it's your favourite red wine. It will stop you wasting money on the mini bar.'

It was now obvious Nina was expecting to spend the night in the hotel room with me and by now I was feeling quite apprehensive.

'Don't worry,' she said as we entered the lift. 'I won't bite, I promise,' she added with a smile.

We ended up sitting on the balcony. Everything was very still and quiet except for the clatter of cars disembarking from one of the late night ferries down at the harbour.

'Tell me, have you ever been in love?'

'That's a difficult question.'

'Difficult. Why?'

'Well let's just say, if you'd asked me about politics or religion I would be able to give you plenty of honest answers and perhaps a few dishonest ones too. When it comes to love, I feel stuck. It's awkward and really is a subject I prefer not to talk about too much.'

'Okay, but do you know what love is?'

'Love has many permutations. People interpret it differently. They have their own personal take on what love could be, well, at least that's how I see it.'

'So, tell me, Jack. Have you ever been married?

'Yes, a very long time ago. She's dead now. Her name was Karen but for some reason she always decided to call herself Kazkia.'

'Did you love her?'

'Yes, at first, but after a while I realised that I wasn't really in love with her.'

'Have you ever been in love with anyone else?'

'Yes, some time ago I met a very beautiful lady. She was quite a bit younger than me, a lot like you actually, she seemed to come out of nowhere. Unfortunately it didn't last and after about eighteen months she was gone as quickly as she came.'

'Do you hate her for that?'

'No, I try not to hate anyone. You know, good karma and all that. I still love her as much today as I did then. You can't always help who you fall in love with.'

'Did it hurt when you split?'

'Yes, of course it did, it still does, very much.'

'What was her name?'

'I'm not saying, not yet anyway, but I will say, though, her name looks beautiful every time I see it written down, just beautiful.'

'That really does sound like true love but what about Suzanne?'

'Suzanne was just a work colleague who I got on well with and admired a lot. As you know, she was married, so as much as I wanted it to, nothing was ever going to happen. Not romantically or sexually. I suppose I respected her and her husband too much for that.'

'I've never been in love, well, not really,' Nina whispered.

'I'm sorry.'

'Don't be. Jack, you sound like a very good man. Now, can I ask you a delicate question?'

'What?'

'Will you take me to bed?'

The question came completely out of the blue as Nina walked from the balcony and into the bathroom suite. I could then hear the shower running. She was in there for about five minutes before she emerged wrapped in one of the hotel's large white bathroom towels with her hair still wet. By then I had sat down on the end of the bed and was pondering what to do next. Should I, will I, can I, I kept thinking as she kissed the back of my neck and then spread-eagled and seductively sprawled herself on the bed beside me?

'Don't worry I'll keep the towel over me until you're ready. You don't have to make love to me if you don't want to. I'll understand,' she uttered almost sympathetically.

The whole scenario reminded me of when I was in Paris with Lisa. I decided to walk back out onto the balcony to finish the last remnants of wine from my glass. After about ten minutes I stepped back into the room. Nina was fast asleep and snoring sweetly. I sat down in the armchair next to the bed. I couldn't help thinking what a beautiful young lady she was, but also how vulnerable she was in her moment of grief, sort of complex and complicated at the same time. I wasn't prepared to take advantage of that. I would not attempt to make love to her, not at least until the time was right. I needed to let her rest, and once again take stock of everything that had been happening. Today had been a long and funny kind of day and it had all been a lot to take in.

35

When I awoke this morning, Nina had already gone down to reception to start her shift. I felt quite glad nothing had happened between us other than a couple of kisses. As I opened the curtains I found she had left me a note on the bedside table... 'Thank you for a beautiful evening. I am in love with your mind, excuse me, but I am not in love with your body.' The note made me smile and I detected a sense of humour in her which had not been evident before. I was just about to take a shower when there was a quiet knock at the door. It was one of the young waitresses from the bar downstairs.

'Sorry Mr Compton, Nina asked me to fetch this up to you. She thinks there's an article in the paper that may interest you,' she said, handing me a copy of the *Malta Telegraph*.

'Okay, thanks.'

I closed the door and hastily fumbled through the first few pages, and then found a lengthy article about Suzanne...

Suzanne Camilleri and the Wild Goose

Did an unnecessary wild goose chase lure Telegraph reporter to her death?

Mystery surrounding the death of the Malta Telegraph journalist, Suzanne Camilleri, deepened this week when it emerged she had been interviewed as part of a BBC documentary for its weekly Panorama programme. The interview was never broadcast because producers felt they had no real evidence to substantiate a conspiracy theory that

Camilleri had been investigating since she worked for the Milan News Agency in 1997.

Journalists don't get blown up in car bomb attacks for no reason. So what, exactly was she on to?

Just a week before her murder, the journalist describes in the interview, several vile graffiti attacks on her home, attempts to cut off her income, the freezing of her assets and a number of vicious posts on various online platforms by internet trolls describing her as a "witch".

Rather poignantly, the journalist posted on her own website about the danger she felt she was in just five days before she was blown up in her white Toyota Starlet on her way for her routine morning cup of coffee at a beach café in Ramla Bay.

"I got rather used to it all, you know, and once quite wrongly blamed my own son. Paranoia was taking over my life. It was like a wound that would never heal," she says during the recording.

The BBC interview in 2018 concentrated on an investigation into a number of alleged UK government conspiracies and cover-ups believed to have been carried out in the late 1990s.

Mrs Camilleri is heard answering questions in blunt detail of years of harassment and threats to her life. She said it was because she had been investigating events surrounding the death of Princess of Diana in 1997 but her findings were never published. "I am very close to finding out the truth and will soon be in a position to expose the Government of Malta's involvement as well as the UK government and their security agencies. Even the mafia are involved." She went on, "I am in a situation where some people who can't even read English, and cannot understand anything I've written, still decide to have a pop, they are aware of who I am but are unaware of what I'm really all about. I am not another Valerie Farrugia," she said, referring to a fellow journalist who was murdered in similar circumstances in 2017. "They fix their bias on hearsay and rumour and come to hate me as if I am that witch some people say I am. I'm very passionate about what I do, but always fair, I believe I'm honest and I just want to share the *truth," she says quite emotionally. "I do not want to be that person who ordinary people in the street love to hate."*

Mrs Camilleri had been well-known in Malta since her mid-20s, firstly working for the Times of Malta as a receptionist and trainee journalist before working for an international news agency in Milan. This is where she grew her reputation and where she was working when Diana, Princess of Wales was killed in that fateful car crash in Paris on 31st August 1997. She then went on to work as an investigative journalist for the Sunday Herald in London until July 2011 and became one of many reporters who found themselves out of work following the now infamous phone-hacking scandal which saw the paper cease publication. After a brief sabbatical she returned to her native Malta and became a senior investigative journalist with the Malta Telegraph. Indeed, a very much loved and respected member of our staff.

While a car bomb may have silenced Camilleri, her investigation into the alleged 1997 conspiracy lives on but without much fruition. Hermione Grech, a former colleague says, "My friend, Suzanne Camilleri, was very close to unravelling what she described as possibly the biggest cover-up involving the Maltese and UK governments and the Sicilian mafia in modern history. This led to even more intrusive scrutiny of her in Malta and placed an enormous strain on her personal and family life. She even once accused her own son of trying to harm her. She later revoked the accusation and for a while suffered from bouts of severe depression."

In the BBC recording, Mrs Camilleri describes how members of the public were encouraged to film and photograph her and post the results on social media. Many of the pictures appeared on a blog run by public relations professionals working for the Government of Malta. The blog contained hundreds of pieces about Camilleri describing her as, "useless, delusional, a liability to Malta's national security and a witch." In the documentary she says, "In one year alone, there were 250 posts openly insulting me on the internet. I'd be down at the café at Ramla Bay having a cup of coffee and people would jump out of the sand and take photos of me. Within minutes those photos would appear on the government's own blog site with an inappropriate caption. It was just plain harassment and I don't think I have a proper life anymore."

Asked by the BBC to respond to the criticisms Suzanne Camilleri had made of the Government of Malta, a spokesman who did not wish to be identified said, *"There was a feeling between ministers that Camilleri should be given a taste of her own medicine to deter her. She was an interfering gossipmonger who made wild accusations and who had no place in our society."*

"So did the Government of Malta order her killing?" the interviewer asks. *"Of course not, that is not in our constitution. Perhaps she should have been tried in a court of law for treason but she was clever, always operating just inside the legal boundaries. Anyway, we do not have a suitable statutory law for such an offence. Perhaps in this case, we should. The UK government did nothing. They just laughed off her accusations. If they had reacted differently then we too would have taken Mrs Camilleri more seriously. It was felt she was just a foolhardy woman on a wild goose chase with no proof about anything."*

The Government of Malta stated at the time of Suzanne Camilleri's murder that they had played no part in the journalist's death. This was an odd statement at the time because at that stage, no-one had actually stood up and accused the government. *"We have never advocated any violence against Mrs Camilleri or her family, or any other Maltese citizen,"* said the spokesman, adding, *"Malta had a very lively social media, which was often wrongly very critical of government."*

Suzanne Camilleri married her own second cousin, Peter, in 1992 and went on to have two children, Adam and Lorca, who are now both grown up. She was hired to work for the Malta Telegraph in January 2012 following the collapse of the Sunday Herald in London the previous year. Her remains were left to the University of Malta following an instruction and signed documents attached to her Will.

We can now reveal there were some attempts to silence Camilleri much earlier on. Some diaries, discovered in a drawer in the Telegraph's office, state that in 2013 after reporting on the activity of a drug trafficker, the Camilleri's family's cat had its throat slit and its body left on the doorstep of their home. A year later, a number of rubbish bags were set on fire at the front of their house in the middle of the night. Later that same year, graffiti was daubed on the front door... 'Die Witch. DING DONG Die, Camilleri' it said. In 2016, whilst in Victoria, a hate-fuelled mob of schoolchildren egged on by a local homeless man followed her through the streets, insulting her and chanting slogans until she sought refuge in a convent. The nuns bolted the door and called the police.

Camilleri never really understood why there was so much hatred against her. "It can only be the Diana thing. People loved that woman and for some reason, some people think I'm trying to undermine the wonderful life she had, particularly in her final years with Dodi Al Fayed. I never set out to insult the Princess's memory like some people have suggested," she says in the BBC interview. "I have never done anything to attract such a level of harassment and certainly don't deserve it." However, she openly admits to pointing an imposing finger of accusation towards the dark forces everyone knows are at work within the Government of Malta and many observers feel Camilleri's death was indeed, their retaliation.

Camilleri feared for her family. Her husband, Peter, an invalid, claimed his state benefits had been cut in half and their son, Adam, was expelled from the University of Malta, allegedly for dealing in Class A drugs. An accusation the family has always vehemently denied.

When pressed about the death of Suzanne Camilleri and what had been happening to her family members, Joseph Muscat, the Prime Minister, said in an email via his spokesperson he did not involve himself in individual matters, and he had been assured by his fellow ministers nothing irregular had occurred. "All proper and correct procedures had been followed," he insisted.

Suzanne Camilleri's biggest fear was that her reporting style might discourage others, women in particular, from speaking out. She remembered other journalists around the globe being killed simply for unveiling the truth. "Here in Malta it's no exception," she said whilst commenting on the murder of fellow journalist, Valerie Farrugia, on the mainland in 2017, also in a car bomb attack. She described a "continuing climate of fear" saying, "all journalists in Malta must know they are operating under the goodwill of those they write about. Provided we only write the truth, there is no real reason to stop."

Before Camilleri was killed she felt she was close to exposing what she described as one of the biggest multi-national cover-ups in modern history, an alleged conspiracy involving a missing British woman who was said to resemble the late Princess of Wales and who was apparently abducted in Venice in 1997. Other reporters are thought to be following up the story since Camilleri's death but so far, while the hunt for the killer or killers goes on, there is as yet, no real evidence any kind of conspiracy had ever occurred.

Someone, though, wanted her dead and the police are continuing with their enquiries.

I had to read the article a couple of times to make sure I had taken everything in. I noticed Hermione's name was mentioned which was quite unsettling, if not annoying. The article had been written by the paper's owner and editor, Terry Mancini. The whole thing seemed disrespectful and appeared to show Suzanne in a bad light. I decided to give Hermione a call.

'Hermione, it's Jack.'

'Hi, Jack, I was expecting to hear from you today. I assume you've seen the *Telegraph*.'

'Yes, I bloody well have. What's going on?'

'Not a lot really.'

'Mancini put that piece together before I left, I knew it was on the back burner but didn't think he was actually going to publish it.'

'Well I'm far from happy he's published it. Basically the whole article undermines and makes a mockery of what Suzanne was all about.'

'I thought that at first, but what about when you get the answers Suzanne was looking for? You'll leave him with egg on his face.'

'As far as I see it, he's not in the equation. I didn't think you knew Suzanne that well anyway.'

'I didn't, he's just misquoted me from an old conversation we had, that's all. Anyway, have you got any more info for me yet?'

'Well I'm getting close. I hope to have something concrete for you over the next few days. I want to put all this to bed soon and start living a normal life again.'

'Normal life? I've forgotten what one of those is like, dear.'

'That's you and me both then.'

The conversation didn't really go anywhere but I needed to get the article off my chest. I thought it could act as some kind of springboard if I did find something, and like Hermione said, it could leave Mancini embarrassed if I was able to prove Suzanne was right about a conspiracy all along.

I decided to catch a bus to Victoria but not before I had thanked Nina for her little note.

'You're very welcome,' she said as she rushed from behind the desk to give me a quick hug and kiss.

At the bus station I had to think why I had travelled to Victoria. The days were becoming cooler so I suppose it was the attraction of visiting the market and sitting in St George's Square drinking coffee. I was just about to get up when I saw Rosie approaching with some chap I hadn't seen before.

'Hello, Jack, this is my friend, Ronald. He's just helped me carry some supplies to the car. The kiosk needs replenishing and I needed a strong pair of hands. Ronald used to be a journalist, didn't you Ron?'

'Hi, Ron, Ronald, sorry, what do you prefer?'

'Ron will do. So you're Jack. Rosie's told me all about you, more than once.'

I couldn't help noticing Ron had a big red jolly face and no hair, just a jagged scar about three inches long across the top of his head. I was rather taken aback by his immense size and the fact he was wearing an Arbroath football shirt.

'Are you from Scotland?'

'No, never been there in my life.'

'Why the Arbroath football shirt?'

'I bought it here in a car boot sale. It was the only shirt I could find which actually fitted me,' he laughed.

'So how long have you known Rosie?'

'Not long, a couple of years, maybe. I hear you know another acquaintance of mine.'

'Who?'

'Hermione.'

'Hermione Grech?'

'Well there can only be one Hermione.'

I laughed. 'Yes, I know her. I'm working for her at the moment. She's just started a new news style blog since leaving the *Telegraph*.'

'Yes, I've heard but you can't be making any money out of that, can you?'

'She's paid me a little so far to cover my expenses. It's allowed me to stay in Gozo for a few weeks longer. If I get the scoop I'm hoping for then she's promised to pay me much more.'

'Well I wouldn't hold out much hope on that. Have you done your maths?'

'I know how much she's taking in advertising revenue so that's given me a pointer.'

'But what about if you do get that big scoop you're talking about? How much are you expecting her to pay you?'

'Thousands, I hope.'

'Nonsense, she hasn't got that kind of cash to pay anyone. If I know Hermione, she's been leading you up the garden path. She only has to flutter those big false eyelashes of hers to get what she wants. You've obviously fallen into the same trap.'

'Yes, she is like that I'm afraid,' said Rosie as she joined the conversation.

'Well, thanks, that's made me a feel a whole lot better about myself.'

'Think of it like this: it's better to know now than be disappointed when you deliver your story and then find out you'll only get paid in peanuts,' said Ron.

'It's like this, Jack. You know I want you to finish your story and I will help if you can. My advice would be to tout the nationals. As you know, we have three here in Malta including the *Telegraph*. Swallow your pride. You won't make any money sucking up to Hermione and she will only use you to make more money for herself no matter how generous she appears to be at the moment. She's simply speculating to accumulate and if you're not careful, you'll be another one of her victims. I think Terry Mancini at the *Telegraph* must have seen straight through her and that's the real reason she lost her job,' said Rosie quite assertively.

'Look, I know Terry Mancini pretty well. Yeah, okay he can be an ass but once you get to know him, he's fine,' said Ron.

'I remember speaking to him on the phone when I was trying to get hold of Hermione. You're right, he did sound like an asshole.'

'Well, Jack, my advice is to do this: once you have your story, keep it close to your chest. Visit the *Telegraph* office in Valletta and ask to speak to Mancini in person. Rosie has told me all about your friend Suzanne and how you've been tracking something she was investigating. If you get what you're looking for, I guess it would be worth a four-figure pay out. Don't succumb to Hermione for just a packet of peanuts.'

'Thanks, Ron, that's quite sound advice. I'll bear it in mind.'

'Mind you do. Now, we had better get off our backsides and take Rosie's stuff down to the kiosk. Good to meet you.'

'Good to meet you too, hopefully see you again sometime.'

'That'd be good.'

Rosie had already walked halfway across the square and waved back at me when Ron caught her up. A lot of what he said made sense and I felt like an idiot for not thinking about what Hermione was getting me into. He was right. Her mere appearance can be off-putting, even though I don't find her at all attractive. She wears too much war paint and sticky on bits; nails, eyelashes, hair extensions. Not my cup of tea at all.

Thinking about my next move I was more than aware that it was Hermione who was bank-rolling my extended stay in Gozo. Now, it was all about my loyalty to her or what had to be right for me. I knew I had to tread very, very carefully.

When I got back to the hotel, Nina had already finished her shift and someone else was manning the reception desk. As I reached my room, I noticed the door was ajar, which was slightly unnerving. I hesitated before entering but was relieved to find it was Nina. She was sat out on the balcony reading a magazine.

'Sorry, Jack. I took the liberty of using the master key card to get in. I wanted to see you before I went home. I didn't realise you'd be so long when I saw you go out this morning so I decided to wait here until you got back. I hope you don't mind.'

'No, it's okay. I was just slightly worried when I saw the door was open. There's been so much going on lately what with the police coming to see me and all the other things.'

'Other things?'

'The things I'm here to investigate.'

'Oh yes, sorry I didn't think.'

'Don't apologise. Anyway, it's nice to see you here. A pleasant surprise really.'

'I just wanted to thank you again for looking after me last night. I felt weird but you were lovely to me. I only really needed a cuddle and you were there for me, so thank you.'

'I must admit I watched over you for a while. The moon was shining through the window. You look very pretty when you're asleep.'

'Thank you. I took the liberty of pouring a glass of wine, want one?'

'Why not? Waste not, want not.'

'Ha, ha, there's no way you would waste it, I know all about your drinking habits, remember?'

'You're right. Anyway, since you're here, do you mind if I ask you a couple of questions?'

'What questions?'

'Frankie Fletcher for one. I still haven't got my head around the fact your cousin is pregnant with his baby.'

'Oh, Rita, they had been flirting on and off each time he visited over the last couple of years. He's stayed here a few times and that's how they met. She was infatuated by him but as soon as he found out she was expecting, he told her to fuck off and accused her of trying to trap him. He had a go at her for not taking contraceptives. Uncle Joseph and the rest of the family wouldn't allow her to have an abortion and now she's ended up carrying a baby no-one wants.'

'That's a shame. Will she have it adopted?'

'No, the nuns in Victoria will help her. She's agreed to do some work at the convent. They will also help her learn to love the baby even though she's fallen out with Frankie.'

'He does have a reputation with the women, I know of at least one other who has fallen pregnant by him but that was over twenty years ago. Who knows? There may be more!'

'He has a certain charm, apparently, even at his age, although I just can't see it myself. I've always considered him to be a big fat slimy individual who always reeks of tobacco.'

'Well at least I don't reek of tobacco.'

'Don't worry, you're not slimy either. I like you.'

'Thanks. And according to that note you left this morning. You don't like my body.'

'Hee, hee, the note was just a joke. Okay you're not perfect but you're my favourite old man. I love your mind and the way you talk. Your body is something that I'll just have to get used to.'

'But you're so much younger than me.'

'Age is only numbers. Okay, you're fifty-something and I'm only just the wrong side of thirty, so what?'

'Anyway, let's take it steady and see what happens. You're a very nice young lady. I have to go back to England soon and I'm not in the business of breaking hearts.'

'I'm already dreading that day. I sometimes miss our little conversations. I still can't thank you enough for not writing about Uncle Joseph. That Frankie bastard would have done.'

'Fortunately, I'm not him. But I would like to ask one more question.'

'What?'

'Fifi, why does no-one want to talk about her?'

'It's not that they don't want to, it's because Uncle Joseph and all the other family elders demanded we didn't. She's been around ever since I can remember, I think I was seven or eight-years-old when I first saw her properly. She's always been mysterious.'

'Is she English?'

'She speaks with an Italian accent but I do know she speaks English very well.'

'Okay, that's very helpful. Did you know that I've been trying to trace an English woman who went missing in Venice in 1997?'

'I have heard. So do you think it could be her?'

'To be honest, I'm certain. I just need to speak to the lady.'

'That would be very difficult, even I've never really done that, just a few nods and smiles but that is all. She always has those two dopey mongrels watching over her every time she goes out somewhere.'

'You mean the two men she was with at your Uncle Joseph's funeral?'

'Yes, I know the chauffeur, though. He's a Stavola, a cousin of Reno's. Everyone has a lot of cousins in Malta.'

'Do you have any brothers or sisters?'

'I have a little step-sister, Paula, but she's mentally unstable. She's being looked after in an institution on the mainland. She's twenty-three but I don't see her anymore, it's too upsetting. Since she was put away in 2002, I have always treated Rita like a sister.'

'Well, apart from your eyes, you and Rita don't look alike.'

'Good, thank you, you certainly know how to compliment a girl.'

'I try. Anyway, how do you think I will get to talk to Fifi? Could the chauffeur help?'

'His name is Anthony. I'll tell him there's a reporter here in Gozo who would like to talk to her. I'll ask him to pass on a message with your details. I daren't do any more.'

'That's more than I could ask for. Thank you.'

'Look, Jack, I have to go now. I have the next few days off. Maybe we can go for a drink and a bite to eat on one of those days, what do you think?'

'Yes, I'd like that, thank you.'

'Okay, here's my mobile number. Give me a ring when it suits.'

'Don't worry, I will.'

There was something about Nina I was finding quite unique, special even. Something about her which definitely made me want to see her again.

36

After a couple of days without any real results, I was beginning to think I was coming up against far too many barriers and concerned I may have got as I far as I could with my investigation. I was hoping to have heard something back about Fifi by now but, as yet, nothing. I was also thinking about the dilemma I was facing with Hermione and how to withdraw my services. I had made up my mind to follow Ron's advice if I ever managed to secure the story, and go immediately to Terry Mancini at the *Telegraph*.

I was just about to leave the hotel for a walk when I felt my phone vibrate. It was a text message from Rick...

'Hey, mate, have you heard the news? Frankie Fletcher has been shot dead. Have I got anything to worry about?'

The news was shocking, and once again Rick was the person breaking it. I went back up into the hotel room, opened my laptop and did a quick Google search. There wasn't much until I found an article by the *South London Journal* on their website, dated last Saturday. Today was Tuesday so I was quite surprised I hadn't heard anything already...

Man Shot Dead in Southwark Pub

A man believed to be in his early seventies is dead after a shooting at a pub in Southwark, South East London on Friday evening.

The incident happened at around 5.30pm inside the Union Jack pub in Union Street in front of horrified office workers enjoying a drink to celebrate the start of their weekend.

Police later confirmed the victim had been identified as Francis Fletcher, a high-profile investigative journalist who had recently been assisting the British security and intelligence services with their enquiries. It is thought Mr Fletcher, commonly known as Frankie, was living in a safe house near the pub and had been electronically tagged "for his own protection". No arrests have been made at this point and no suspect descriptions have been released.

A Metropolitan Police spokesperson later told the SLJ that, "MI6 has immediately taken over the investigation itself, insisting it is a matter of national security." The spokesperson declined to give any further details, only adding that, "Right now our officers are questioning pub-goers who may have captured camera phone footage relating to the incident and local residents in the area, just to see if they had heard anything. We are also speaking to nearby businesses in case they may have picked up anything unusual on CCTV. Anything of relevance will be passed on to our MI6 colleagues."

Through undisclosed sources, the SLJ understands the killing may be linked to an historic cold case going back over twenty years. Frankie Fletcher was widely known throughout the media world and had worked as a freelance reporter for newspapers in Europe and the United States. Up until recently he was working in Malta before being brought back to the UK by agents connected with the British security services. It is still not known why Mr Fletcher had effectively been placed under house arrest, or indeed what he may have been investigating on the Mediterranean island, which had so concerned those responsible for bringing him back to London.

Part of Union Street was cordoned off while forensic officers examined the scene looking for evidence as part of the investigation. They were expected to remain on site for "for some time".

Rory Greenslade, 33, who had been working in the pub at the time of the shooting, told the SLJ, "We had been pretty quiet all afternoon but the bar was starting to fill up with people who had just finished work for the weekend. Most of them work in the office block just around the corner. I noticed an old guy who

I had earlier served rum and coke to, go outside for a smoke. I had seen him in here a few times but only quite recently, I remembered him because the thumb was missing from one of his hands. He was outside for about twenty minutes before coming back in to use the loo. I was just about to serve a woman when someone dashed in from nowhere and went straight into the gents' toilet. I heard a loud thud and then I saw a man rush out again, he was so quick, I didn't really get a good look at him. I went into the toilet to see what had happened and there was the old guy I had served earlier slumped on the floor with his face down in the middle urinal, he had been shot in the back of the head. There was blood everywhere, it was horrible."

On Saturday morning, the police cordon and evidence markers were still visible. Three surveillance cameras could also be seen near the entrance, though it is not immediately clear whether they may have captured the incident itself. Police are believed to be closely examining CCTV footage taken from within the pub.

The cordon erected by the police has affected a number of nearby business outlets, with some shops and restaurants remaining closed.

One man, who did not want to be named, told the SLJ he arrived at the pub with his girlfriend just a few minutes after the shooting. He said some drinkers had rushed out into the street screaming when news filtered through that a man had been shot dead in the toilet. "Police told us to stand back, so we couldn't see much, everyone was terrified."

"It's all rather scary because we visit the Union Jack quite often, it's our local," said an elderly gentleman who lives in nearby Nelson Square. He added, "I come to the pub to play crib or to watch the football on the telly with friends two or three times a week, so when you hear of something like this, it sort of scares you. There's quite a lot of gun and knife crime going on around here lately. I don't think the police are doing enough to stop it."

I decided to phone Hermione and tell her about what had happened. I was also aware Julie Etheridge was the mother of Frankie's son, Michael. There was also Rita to consider. The news was not only shocking but delicate as well. Telling Hermione first, which I should do anyway, means she will probably contact Julie as a matter of course. That is something I would find no pleasure in.

I was just about to reach for my phone when it rang.

'Jack, hello, it's Rosie. Good to see you the other day. Did you know Frankie Fletcher has been killed?'

'I've only just found out. I received a text message from a former colleague. I've just been reading about it on the internet.'

'I've spoken to Julie by phone, she's still in America. Of course she's very upset. She was told about the shooting only this morning and is now wondering if there's a connection between the murder and the police raid on her apartment. She really doesn't know what to think.'

'I have to say, it's feasible. Do you think it could be linked to Suzanne's murder?'

'Possibly, they were both investigating the same thing. Frankie was the person who Suzanne had been getting her most recent information from. There has to be a connection.'

'So you don't think this is all merely a coincidence?'

'No not at all.'

'If you don't mind me asking, who told you Frankie had been murdered?'

'The police, I was being nosy. I saw a policeman enter Julie's old apartment just as I was walking by with Ron at first light this morning, so I went over and spoke to him. The policeman didn't know Julie had moved away.'

'Okay, I think I need to pass this news on to Hermione.'

'Well, that's good, but Hermione already knows. Julie and Hermione have already spoken on the phone. Julie phoned me back to tell me what was said.'

'That's interesting. I was about to phone Hermione anyway. I hope we can speak again soon.'

Everything seemed to be getting rather complicated and now I knew Hermione had already been told, I felt I was lagging one step behind with everything. I needed to be careful when I phoned her.

'Hi, Hermione, it's Jack.'

'Jack, Jack, I've heard, what are your thoughts?'

'Rosie told me Julie thinks there may be a connection between Frankie's murder and the raid on her apartment a while ago, I think I will need to follow that up asap.'

'How will you do that?'

'I think her recent blog posts may be the main reason.'

'Me too, I've somehow gone into panic mode and deleted a couple of items from my blog, mainly for my own peace of mind. You can't be too careful. Okay, look, keep me posted. As soon as you get anything please, please tell me.'

'Yes, I will. Thanks.'

For some reason, Hermione seemed to be sniffling down the phone and sounded quite upset. I knew I had to tread quite carefully in all directions now until my jigsaw was complete.

I decided to give Rick a courtesy call.

'Hi, Rick, thanks for your message earlier, more bad news then!'

'Yeah, mate, sorry about that. I was watching the TV this morning and it was on the main news. I messaged you as soon as I saw it. So, do we have anything to worry about, bearing in mind there appears to be a killer on the loose who doesn't like journalists?'

'Obviously we need to be careful but I don't think we're anybody's targets. Frankie Fletcher had been given some form of protection and that was for a reason. Whoever killed him may have killed Suzanne. There is a link but something still isn't sitting right.'

'What about Reno Stavola?'

'I'm not sure, I think it's linked but not directly. He was probably killed for other reasons. He was known to be closely linked to most mafia activities on Gozo and mainland Malta. I think it could have even been the mafia who ordered his murder.'

'Does Hermione know yet?'

'Why are you asking?'

'She has a daughter, Tabatha, she must be around thirteen-years-old now, Frankie was the father.'

'What?'

'Yes, it was the worse kept secret ever. You've met Hermione now, you will have seen how well scrubbed up she is. Frankie was her bit of rough. She never admitted he was the father, but we all had an abacus and could do our sums. No other chap was in sight so it had to be him.'

'Fucking hell, I'm shocked. That may explain why she sounded more upset than I expected when I spoke to her on the phone just now. I've recently found out he's got another kid coming. Rita Buttiġieġ, who used to work here at the hotel, she's very young and had a fling with Frankie and got herself pregnant when he was on Gozo a few months ago.'

'Well he was putting it about a lot for an old geezer, that's the world of journalism for you. Nothing should surprise us anymore.'

'You're dead right there. I suppose if it's all a big secret I shouldn't say anything to Hermione.'

'She's not stupid, if she rates you as a reporter, she'll know you would have found that out by now.'

'Ah right, so thanks for telling me then.'

'A pleasure, mate, just phone me when you get something. I'm getting pissed off looking over my shoulder every time I go out. It's a psychological thing, paranoia. It's ever since that Reno Stavola guy turned up at Mum's funeral.'

'You sound like me,' I joked.

'No joke, it's weird that Stavola is the one who should end up dead, and now Frankie Fletcher. I'm always thinking worst case scenario. It's like being back in the school playground, you know, "Bang, bang, pop, pop, you're dead, I'm not". It's not a game anymore and to be honest, I'm scared shitless, mate.'

'I think I know where you're coming from. I feel the same. Look, Rick, I have to go now. As soon as I hear anything, I'll let you know.'

'Cheers, mate, be safe.'

'I will. Thanks.'

I couldn't help thinking Rick was worrying unnecessarily. It's usually me who overthinks things. I guess he may be feeling insecure since his mum died. He's never spoken about his father. Perhaps I should ask. Now I was thinking about Hermione. Maybe it's because she's the mother of Frankie's daughter she wanted to know so much. What surprises me most is she's friends with Julie Etheridge, the mother of Frankie's son, Michael. Something must have happened to bring them together. They must obviously share a common bond but that's probably something to do with their children.

Another big question: was Frankie's murder carried out by the same person who killed Maria Allegranza in Sicily? The shootings certainly do bear all the hallmarks. Rick said, "be safe", but it's important I don't let the paranoia he was talking about get the better of me too.

I needed to phone Nina. She must have heard about Frankie's killing and I was wondering about Rita's reaction to it all.

'Nina, hello, it's Jack.'

'Hello, Jack, I was just about to ring you. Where are you?'

'In the hotel room.'

'Well, come down, I'm here to collect my wages. We can have that drink now if you like.'

When I got down to the foyer there was the usual early afternoon ritual of people checking out with new guests arriving. I went through to the bar and Nina was sitting in the corner.

'I've got you a Cisk, just ask at the bar, my lovely friend Olivia, the lady with the blue streaks in her hair will pour it for you,' she shouted.

'Thanks.'

Olivia was quite busy so it took what seemed like an age before I could get served and join Nina at the table... 'So, dear Jack, you've probably heard about what's happened to Frankie by now.'

'Yes, I had a message from a friend this morning. I've since read about it all on the internet. How's Rita coping?'

'She doesn't need to cope. In fact she's quite ecstatic. She seems quite happy he's dead.'

'I suppose people handle grief in many different ways.'

'What I didn't tell you was although she was infatuated by him, it was all about his money. He was always flashing the cash and walking around with that big gormless grin of his. Yes, they were flirting but he effectively groomed her and then somehow she got pregnant. There's simply no way that she would have consented to having sex with him. She must have been drunk or something.'

'Why didn't Rita go to the police?'

'Uncle Joseph said he would sort it out but before he could do anything, he got ill. It all happened just before Frankie was arrested and taken to England. The police wouldn't have done anything anyway. I don't think they like our family much.'

'So what's Rita going to do now?'

'Like I said, the nuns will help her. If she bonds with the baby, fine. Otherwise there will have to be an adoption.'

'Okay. By the way, did you manage to speak to Fifi's chauffeur?'

'Anthony? Oh yes, I gave him a note with your room number and mobile telephone details. He told me Fifi knows you're on the island and has been asking questions. She saw you with me outside the cemetery at the funeral.'

'I thought she did. She appeared to look over her sunglasses at me.'

'Yes, I noticed that.'

'Anthony's confident she will agree to speak to you but on her terms. That's all he would say.'

'Thanks for everything. I suppose I will just have to wait and see what happens.'

'Please don't ask me any more. It was difficult enough approaching Anthony. I don't want to bring any unwanted attention to myself even though I don't think I'm really doing anything wrong.'

'I respect that.'

Nina and I then sat almost in silence at the bar for a good ten minutes making seriously pleasant eye contact with each other. I felt like a teenager on his first date but at the same time, quite awkward.

'Come on, dinner,' I said, deciding to break the silence.

'Where?'

'I don't know, anywhere.'

Nina laughed. 'Come with me, I'll show you where.'

She took me by the hand and we walked out of the hotel and down to the harbour. We came to a restaurant called the Veranda.

'This is a good place, good fish; good local rabbit. In fact it's always very nice food here. The owner's a grumpy old so and so and he drinks too much wine but his wife Natalie, she's lovely. I've known her all my life.'

We were just sitting down when Nina's mobile phone rang.

'Sorry, I need to take this.'

Nina walked a few yards away towards Horatio's and then appeared to walk in circles before walking back again after about four or five minutes.

'That was a nurse from the hospital. Rita's been taken in. She's had a miscarriage. It must have been all the excitement. Look, I have to go. Stay here if you want. I'll get a taxi up to Victoria and be back as soon as I can. I just need to make sure she's alright.'

'Would you like me to come with you?'

'No, just stay here but let me know if you decide to wander back up to the hotel.'

'Okay, I will. See you soon.'

Just as Nina had left, the owner, a tall skinny man with swept back grey hair and a handlebar moustache came out to take the order.

'Sorry, my friend has had to dash off. Can I just order a drink for now?'

'Yes, but you will have to sit over the other side if we get busy.'

'Okay, that's fair enough.'

'What do you want to drink?'

'A glass of Victoria Heights please.'

'We only sell it by the bottle.'

'Okay, I'll have a whole bottle then, I've got plenty of time.'

'Red, white or rosé?'

'Err, red, thank you.'

'Are you paying by card or cash?'

'Card if that's okay?'

'I'm not taking cards today, our machine is broken.'

'Okay, cash it will have to be then.'

'Do you want to pay now or later?'

'I'll pay at the end if you don't mind.'

'Okay.'

All I wanted was a drink. I could see what Nina meant by 'grumpy', and he was... fucking grumpy. About an hour had gone by before Nina phoned.

'Look I'm staying at the hospital. They're going to let Rita out first thing in the morning. She needs some company and the nurses are going to let me stay with her.'

'Of course, that's fine.'

'I'm sorry. I was really looking forward to eating a meal with you.'

'Never mind, we can pick up the pieces tomorrow.'

'Yes, I would like that.'

After the call had finished the owner came out again.

'Another bottle?'

'I don't think so. I haven't finished this one yet.'

'Don't you like it?'

'Yes, I love it, that's why I ordered it.'

'My father, he used to work in the Delicatè vineyard you know. He used to tread the grapes before they had machinery.'

'Pardon?'

'Have you found a corn plaster in your wine yet?' he laughed.

'So you do have a sense of humour!'

'Yes, of course, it's just that no-one understands me, particularly the younger folk.'

'I'm sorry I wasn't able to stay for a meal. My friend had to rush off. Her cousin was taken to hospital.'

'Ah, Nina. Yes, I saw you with her. She's the best of the bunch. Look after her. She will give you a good life.'

I'm not sure what the restaurant owner was thinking so just put his comment down to polite conversation. I eventually made my way back up to the hotel. The day was finally starting to take its toll.

37

The two men I had seen guarding the woman I believed to be Fiona Meredith at Joseph's funeral were down at the reception desk just after breakfast this morning. One of them was talking to Nina and the hotel manager. I walked over quite cagily to introduce myself.

'Hi, I'm Jack.'

'We know,' said the taller man.

'Sorry, this is Marco and Danny. They work for Fifi,' said Nina.

Marco was the taller of the two, while Danny sounded quite effeminate.

'We've come to take you to see our boss. You must be honoured. She doesn't usually want to speak to anyone.'

'Go on,' Nina said. 'There's a car waiting outside. They're going to take you to Qala so you can talk to Fifi.'

'Okay, thanks.'

'Don't worry. We'll go for that meal when you get back.'

'If I get back,' I said quite nervously.

She laughed.

The car, a black Mercedes, drove up the hill quite slowly and turned right onto the main road to Qala. Everything was quite hushed. Eventually we came to a secluded house called Fluke's Cradle on the hillside just outside the village. It had tall electronically controlled iron gates and overlooked the countryside and sea towards Comino. Once inside I was taken to the kitchen area and was asked to sit at the end of a long wooden table. Sunlight was streaking through the half-closed plantation shutters and the tree blowing in the breeze outside gave the effect that the shadows were dancing on the wall next to where I was sitting. Eventually the door opened and a silhouette of quite a short woman appeared. She opened the shutters fully and then walked around, almost shuffling to the chair at the other end of the table. When she sat down I could see her properly.

'So you are Jack Compton the English reporter. I am Fifi Paganini.'

'You speak very good English.'

'I should. I am English. I believe I am the woman that people have been looking for lately. I used to be known as Fiona.'

'Fiona Meredith?'

'Yes.'

'So why have you agreed to see me?'

'My work is done. Over twenty years of living this life has hurt me.'

'If you don't mind me saying, you seem to have survived pretty well,' I interrupted.

'It has not been easy.'

'So how did you get here?'

'That's why I've sent for you. I want you to record my story, report the truth. I will tell you everything provided that you do not distort a word I'm saying. Understand?'

'Yes, of course, so where shall I start?'

'I suppose from the beginning, the very beginning.'

The woman in front of me came across as rather nervous, which I didn't expect. As she removed her sunglasses I immediately looked for some kind of resemblance to Princess Diana, but there was none. Her grey hair was cropped and her eyes kept flickering each time she spoke. She removed her cardigan and I noticed a number of tattoos; a warrior and serpent design down her left arm and a scorpion on the right side of her neck. She also had an anchor on her right forearm with lots of hieroglyphic markings which obviously meant something to her.

'So, who is Fiona Meredith?'

'I was born in the Royal Hampshire County Hospital in Winchester on the 15th July 1961 and brought up on my parent's manor estate in Oakley, near Basingstoke. I heard both my parents died from separate ailments just three days apart in March 2004. I hadn't seen them since I was lost in Venice in 1997.'

'Lost?'

'We'll come to that.'

'My first school was the primary school in Oakley opposite the village church. I then went to a girl's grammar school and finished my education at Durham University where I studied classical music, with the violin being my specialism. My first job was at an art gallery in Salisbury. I then found jobs with a couple of music publishing houses in London where I fell in love with Nicolo Paganini, hence my *non de plume*. It was whilst researching his music in Venice in 1997 that my whole life changed.'

'What happened?'

'The year before, I was earning some extra cash because I could impersonate Diana, you know, the Princess. I was good at it and my picture was on the television and in lots of papers. Soon after I arrived in Venice on my own, I sensed I was being followed. The moment I stepped into the Hotel Kette, I didn't feel safe. A man kept appearing in the small bar in the foyer and again at breakfast. His name was Reno. I was stupid enough to accept an invitation to dinner from him and everything went on from there.'

'When was this?'

'It was the first week in August. It was very wet, raining very hard and I remember San Marco Square being completely flooded. Everyone was wearing those polythene boots they sell to stop their feet from getting wet. We had a drink in Harry's Bar near the waterside. It was very expensive so we left. The next thing I knew we were down an alley. Three other men came from the shadows and put a bag over my head. I remember the outboard motor of a boat being started and then I was dragged aboard. Everything happened so quickly.'

'That must have been very harrowing.'

'It was. The next morning I found myself tied up and gagged on the floor of a stable. God, it was awful. My hair was caked in horse shit and straw.'

'And then what?'

'Reno and one of the other men came in and they had a discussion about Diana. There was a big argument and they were hitting each other on the chest. "Stupido, stupido," I remember Reno shouting. I was kept in that hole for weeks, systematically raped, sodomised and tortured. I lost all my teeth when they placed a specially-made horseshoe in my mouth to shut me up. They would persistently masturbate and urinate, even defecate all over my face, it was disgusting. I felt degraded.'

'But you survived, how?'

'After a while they got bored. One of the men wanted to kill me, cut my body up and dispose of it down a drain. Reno shot him.'

'What? Shot him dead?'

'Yes, of course, dead. He then shot the two other men. The area outside of where I was being held was quite secluded. Reno burnt their bodies and buried the leftovers under a trough. It wasn't a very pleasant experience. Reno, though, never touched me and even though he was the man who instigated my abduction, I accidently began to fall in love with him.'

'So why do you think you were kidnapped?'

'I know why.'

'Why?'

'There was supposedly a British operation to remove Dodi Al Fayed, you know, assassinate him. It was a wild plan. It originated from MI6. Someone wanted to make sure Princess Diana was kept safe but for some reason, they needed a decoy. I think the actual plan was to kidnap her and kill me. Use my body for the funeral, you know, but it would never have worked.'

'It sounds very far-fetched.'

'I was three inches shorter than the Princess, and at the time, I had no children. The whole thing was flawed from the very start. Anyway, the car crash that killed the Princess happened in Paris a week before all this was supposed to happen so everything went flat. That, though, for me, was just the start.'

'Are you sure the Paris crash had nothing to do with these plans?'

'It was just fate, a pure coincidence. The crash happened a week before Reno and his mafia friends planned to kidnap the Princess and kill Dodi on behalf of the UK government. They wanted Dodi out of the equation. Someone within MI6 was foolish enough to engage members of the Sicilian mafia in my kidnap and then hired someone within the Government of Malta to help cover it all up. It was all a bad mistake and if I wasn't the victim in all this, it would all be quite laughable.'

'So what happened next?'

'Reno was completely out of his league. He was only really ever a small time crook. He laid low for a while, he had to. The relatives of the men he killed were looking for answers. As far as I know the remains were never discovered. In the end the mafia came looking. We eventually fled here to Gozo exactly a year after my abduction. Everything stayed quiet for a while until one day Reno met a couple of his old friends down at the harbour. They were fishermen and were known to have ties with the mafia in Sicily. By now, Reno was really out of his depth, we weren't an item anymore, but I decided to help him.'

'How?'

'I agreed to become the head of the so-called mafia here on Gozo. It was a sort of liaison role and was all a sham. We were really just a mouthpiece for those operating from Sicily. Reno couldn't and wouldn't do it and because of what had happened to me, I saw it as my best way to retaliate. Joseph stepped in to make sure I remained safe, and of course, anonymous. I wasn't supposed to have been kept alive. A man called Paul Cassar who worked for the Government of Malta was the go-between. He later went into hiding and was never heard of again.'

'So who killed Reno?'

'The Sicilian mafia. By deduction and elimination, they calculated that he must have killed his three accomplices. They hadn't been seen since 1997. They knew he was still alive but his friends weren't. The son of one of his victims had grown up. He's called Drago and is now feared very much, even by some of the older mafia gangs in and around Sampieri.'

'That's near where the Italian prosecutor, Maria Allegranza, was murdered, isn't it?'

'Yes. Did you know her?'

'We recently met in London. She seemed very pleasant and was really helpful. Do you know who might have killed her?'

'Anyone could have. She was a prosecutor and before that a senior policewoman. She was always putting members of the mafia behind bars. Her death had all the hallmarks of a contract killing.'

'Do you think the murder of Frankie Fletcher in London the other day was also a contract killing?'

'Almost certainly, it could even be the same man who carried it out. Governments or their agencies quite often hire members of the mafia or other gangs to do their dirty work. It's not a big secret anymore. Most governments are corrupt these days and when that corruption is exposed, people start getting killed. Anyway, I'm glad that man Fletcher is dead, he was a pig.'

'Did you know him?'

'I knew of him. Joseph despised him but because he was such a good man he never said a bad word about anyone. I knew deep down he wanted to see Fletcher dead, though. I wouldn't be surprised if he had arranged something from his deathbed.'

'Do you think that's why the police were at the hospital, just before Joseph died?'

'Oh yes, almost certainly.'

'So what's going to happen with Rita?'

'Be careful here. Rita and your friend, Nina, are very dear to me and it's only because of Nina, I have agreed to speak with you.'

'Why?'

'They don't know yet but I am about to tell them.'

'Know what?'

'It's complicated, but I knew their mother, Georgina. She was a strange woman and had rejected them since birth, partly through some kind of mental illness. She died just a few months after I arrived here in Gozo. At that time, the girls were around nine and ten. I adopted them by default after developing a relationship with Joseph in the wake of her death. I am, I suppose, their secret stepmother.'

'So, am I right in thinking Joseph was actually their father?'

'Yes, of course although you wouldn't think it. Uncle Joseph to them, but yes, he is, or rather was their biological father but they never knew. Joseph already had three grown up sons from a previous marriage but they never got on with Georgina. It's their families though who have helped look after the girls. Rita and Nina didn't even know they were sisters, they still don't. They were always kept on the periphery even though Joseph doted on them. Because of who I was, he couldn't really let them get to know me either.'

'You're right. It is all very complicated. I heard there was another daughter, Paula.'

'Joseph had her with another woman in one of his weaker moments. She also went mad and was being cared for in an institution somewhere near Valletta the last I heard.'

'I must say, it's quite an experience for me to meet you at last. The primary reason I'm here in Gozo is to find out who killed my former colleague, Suzanne Camilleri. I know she was investigating your disappearance at the time of her death. Do you think that she may have stumbled on something?'

'I think Fletcher had rumbled that I was living here in Qala and had probably told her. Over recent years, my security had become less of a priority because no-one was showing too much interest anymore. I knew that at some point, word would get out that I was living here. For some reason no-one, not even my original family in England, ever accepted that I was really dead. I think your friend was in possession of that kind of information. She was a respected journalist over here. I liked her, always enjoyed reading her articles and columns, and just in case you're thinking it, I don't know who's behind her murder.'

'I had a visit from Inspector Azzopardi a few days ago. He told me to stop asking questions about you, and about Suzanne's murder. He said that he felt I was interfering with his investigation.'

'Ah, Azzopardi. Don't worry too much about him. Although to be fair, he does get results. I've managed to get him to shut down a couple of contentious blogsites. People were guessing things too much. Writing stuff about me they know nothing about, it was all based on foolish conjecture. I have that abomination of a man wrapped around my little finger. When I shout, he hops, if you know what I mean.'

'I think so. One last question. Before Reno was killed, he came to England for a few days. He separately followed me and a former colleague around. What was he after?'

'I sent him. I needed to be sure whatever you were going to report wasn't going to compromise my position here in Gozo. When it became obvious your main intent was simply to find out who killed Mrs Camilleri, I pulled him off the assignment. Then the idiot somehow got himself arrested at the airport. I think that's what probably unsettled his mafia friends.'

'So what happens now?'

'Write your story. Call me when it's finished and I will get Anthony to pick you up and bring you here so I can read it. I will then decide if you can publish it.'

'That's rather controlling!'

'Jack Compton, my sweet, who do you think controls this island?'

'Okay, thanks, I get the message.'

'Look, go now but not a word to Nina or Rita. I'll send for them this afternoon and speak to them, I'll tell them everything. It's time they both got to know the truth.'

'Sorry, did you know about Rita losing the baby?'

'Yes, I know. God works in mysterious ways. Now go. Anthony will take you back to the hotel.'

When I got back to the hotel, it was just after 3pm and Nina and Rita were standing outside. I thanked Anthony for the lift as they approached the car.

Nina gave me a quick hug before telling me Fifi had just been in touch and had asked to see the pair of them immediately.

'You've just been to see her, Jack, what did she say?'

'Quite a lot, in fact, nearly everything I wanted to know.'

'So what does she want to see me and Rita for?'

'I can't really say, it's best if you hear it from her, she has something very important to tell you both.'

'Is it something we should be afraid of?'

'Not afraid. Anyway, like I said, it's best if you hear it from her.'

At that point Anthony called both women over to the car. Nina at first, and then Rita. Both appeared reluctant to get in. I gave them a quick wave as the car sped off but neither looked back.

38

Nina was back busy behind the reception desk this morning and immediately called me over just as I was going in for breakfast.

'Jack, we have a problem.'

'Fifi?'

'No, not her, I'll tell you all about that later.'

'What then?'

'Your hotel bill, it hasn't been paid as expected. The card number we were given has been declined.'

'That was Hermione's card. She was supposed to be paying.'

'I know.'

'Okay, okay, I'll sort it. I'll transfer some more savings into my current account to cover it.'

'Sorry!'

'Don't be, it's not your fault.'

'There must be a simple explanation.'

'I have a hunch, anyway, here's my own card details. Give me about thirty minutes and I'll ring down so you can take the payment.'

'Okay, how long are you going to stay for, so I know how much to charge?'

'Good point, take it up to the end of next week. My funds are very low, so I won't be able to stay too much longer.'

Nina's facial expression changed. 'Stay longer, if you can.'

'I'll see.'

She turned away looking quite disappointed. When I got back to my room I opened the laptop and there was an email waiting for me which hadn't come through on my phone.

'Sorry Jack, Hermione,' is all it said.

I went to open her blog but it came up with an HTTP 451 message, the same as Julie's blog a few weeks ago. I then remembered something Fifi had said. She must have persuaded Inspector Azzopardi to shut Hermione's site down as well. I then tried to call her but the phone went unanswered, not even taking me through to voicemail. On the plus side, all this did solve my dilemma about submitting my story direct to the *Telegraph* instead of to Hermione, as Rosie's friend Ron had suggested. Having met Fifi yesterday, though, everything had been thrown into even more doubt.

I eventually met up with Nina again just after 7pm and found myself walking hand in hand with her down towards the harbour. A couple of her friends drove by beeping their horns. I wasn't sure if they were just being friendly or making fun of her because she was with me. This time we decided to go to the Tmun restaurant. I had been there once before on a previous visit and remembered they had a great choice of fish on their menu. It was very busy so we asked for a table near the back. It was quite secluded and somewhere we felt we could have a conversation away from all the other diners.

'Thanks for helping me to sort out the problem with the hotel bill this morning.'

'Don't worry, that's my job.'

'So, how's Rita after all her trauma?'

'She's very sore but things will heal. She's sad that she's lost the baby but I don't think it will have a lasting effect on her.'

'Is that because it was Frankie's?'

'Yes.'

'So, how did you get on with Fifi yesterday?'

'It was quite weird. On the way there, we were talking in the back of the car. When we were girls we saw Fifi once and pretended she was our mummy. There must have been something in our genes that connected us to her. I'm just over a year older than Rita and we shared different things. This was the only time we really felt anything together and properly bonded, it was really strange.'

'How did you react when she told you she was your stepmother?'

'For a couple of minutes, there was just stunned silence and then Rita started sobbing. Fifi got up and walked round the table and gave her a hug.'

'What did you do?'

'I got up as well and held Rita's hand. In the end we were all in tears and just hugged and kissed each other for what seemed like an eternity. That was the nice part.'

'What do you mean?'

'I then had to ask who our father was. What Fifi told us had thrown everything into disarray. And then she confessed.'

'Joseph?'

'Yes, obviously she told you. We had always known him as Uncle Joseph. When Fifi told us he was actually our dad I was both angry and happy at the same time. We paused for a glass of wine and then Fifi announced all the other Buttiġieġs were coming over for supper. She explained the whole family knew everything and it was a secret they had all vowed to keep from us until such time Fifi decided to tell us the truth herself. We were told our mothers had died when we were both young. We never knew we had the same mum. As you know, we thought we were just cousins. Neither of us knew who our father was and I guess we were always too frightened to ask.'

'It must have been quite a surreal moment.'

'It was. Fifi told us all about her kidnap in Venice and that her original name was Fiona Meredith. She told us about Reno Stavola, how she fell in love with him and how she thought that he almost certainly saved her from being killed. She told us about all his activities and how she came to be with Joseph. For some reason, Reno was starting to turn against her and Joseph stepped in, threatening to expose Reno's links with the mafia to the police. In the end, Reno became nothing more than a servant to Fifi and Joseph. He ran their errands and acted as a middle man between Fifi and the mafia in Sicily. Fifi told us Joseph had mellowed in his old age and wanted all the violence to stop. For a while it did, but as you know, just recently three or four people have been killed. She was adamant though, your friend Suzanne's murder was not part of "this messy business" as she put it.'

'So what now, are you going to see Fifi again?'

'She suggested we see her regularly, about once a month. She still has some business to attend to. She told us about you and the story you are going to write about her. Once all that's been done, she's hoping to lead a normal life, well as much as she can after everything she's been through.'

'Oh, the article, yes, she wants to vet it first before I submit it for publication.'

'Yes, she told me. She also asked me if you and I were lovers.'

'What?'

'It's true, she did.'

'What did you say?'

'I didn't say anything, I just smiled.'

Just then the waitress came over and took our order. The break in the conversation gave me a chance to quickly go to the loo. Whilst giving my face and hands a quick wash, I looked hard in the mirror. What do I want from all this, I kept thinking? I knew Nina was going to ask me some questions, perhaps about a possible future together. When I got back to the table, Nina decided it was her turn to 'powder her nose' as she put it. After about an hour of waiting, the food finally came. Nina had ordered sea bass and I had opted for swordfish, by which time we were already on our second bottle of wine.

'Do you think you will actually go back to England at the end of next week?' Nina asked.

'It's probably a case of having to, mainly due to funds, or rather a lack of them. Hermione has stitched me right up.'

'She probably didn't mean to, though.'

'Well it's happened now. I'll just have to deal with it.'

'You'll get paid for your story, though, won't you?'

'Ah, the story I haven't written yet. I started writing it but things kept changing so I deleted what I'd done. I've decided to wait until I have all the facts and answers before I start again.'

'I thought you had all the answers. You got those from Fifi yesterday, didn't you?'

'I got some answers and they are very valuable, but, I still don't know who killed Suzanne and that's why I came here in the first place.'

'Sorry.'

'It's okay. Anyway, how's your food?'

'Wonderful, thank you, the best sea bass ever, how's the swordfish?'

'The swordfish is excellent, not quite enough of it, but excellent, thank you.'

Nina insisted she should settle the bill. We then went for a walk. It was a beautiful moonlit night and the sea was very calm compared to recent days. Again we found ourselves holding hands. We found a bench on the edge of the harbour and watched the last of the day's fishing boats return.

'You know we spoke about love the other night. I do love your mind. You do have a wonderful way of saying things.'

'I've never been told that before and it's certainly something I've never picked up on myself, thank you. But according to your cryptic little note, you're not in love with my body, though.'

'Like I said, that was a joke. You only need to tone your body a little bit. You know, exercise more, change your diet and cut down on that bloody drinking!'

'Ha, ha, sadly you're very right, I have no excuses.'

'Do you love me?'

'I like you a lot. I love the time we spend together but like I've said before, I'm very conscious of the age difference. I'm old enough to be your dad.'

'Don't worry about that, old man. Age is just numbers, and, like I've said before, you're my favourite old man.'

We both laughed and decided to walk back up to the hotel.

'Look I have a cab booked. I have my usual early start in the morning so I'll see you sometime tomorrow.'

We parted company on the steps of the hotel with a final hug and a kiss.

'Thank you for tonight,' said Nina.

'No, thank you. It's been beautiful, really beautiful.'

'I love you!'

'Err, I love you too.' I said, without thinking.

I sometimes wonder if I say too much, which is how I often get myself into awkward situations. That was something I certainly did with Lisa. This, though, seemed quite different, natural even.

39

It was difficult to sleep again last night. A few days had gone by since I met up with Fifi and I was getting restless as nothing much had happened since. My flight back home to England was booked for a couple of days' time and time itself was running out... and fast. Was I ever going to find out who murdered Suzanne?

My unexpected relationship with Nina was pleasant and becoming stronger by the day but at the same time I felt things had become complicated, more so since my departure from Gozo had been arranged. Rightly or wrongly, I was becoming very fond of her and loving every moment we had been spending together so I knew it was going to be difficult when the time eventually came to say goodbye. Just as I was thinking of her, I received a text message...

'Good morning Jack. Inspector Azzopardi was here at the hotel just now. Can you give him a ring when you wake up? He said he has something to tell you in confidence.'

Being told by Nina that he wanted to tell me something made me feel more than a little apprehensive. I decided to have a quick shower and a cup of coffee before I made the call.

'Inspector?'

'Azzopardi, yes.'

'Sorry. This is Jack Compton. I've been given a message to ring you.'

'Yes, good. Can you come to the police station in Nadur Square? I have something to tell you.'

'Is it important?'

'Yes, of course it's important.'

'What is it?'

'I'll tell you when you get here. It's something I need to tell you face to face and in person.'

'Okay, what time?'

'Midday will do.'

'Okay, I'll see you then.'

I decided to walk up to Nadur from the hotel. I thought it would give me some necessary thinking time and a chance to psyche myself up for whatever Azzopardi was going to tell me. When I got to the police station the door was wide open. A uniformed officer was sitting just inside.

'Hello, I've come to see Inspector Azzopardi.'

Just then Azzopardi appeared and waved me through to an office at the back of the building.

'Thank you for coming to see me. Please understand I am about to give you some privileged information which for now I would like you to keep to yourself. Later today, however, what I have told you will be in the public domain. Do you understand what I'm saying?'

'Yes I think so.'

'I wanted to tell you in person that we swooped on an address here in Gozo in the early hours of this morning and arrested a man in connection with the murder of your friend, Mrs Suzanne Irene Camilleri. He's been taken to our headquarters in Floriana for further questioning where he will also be visited by Europol and FBI officers, after which I expect him to be formally charged with the killing.'

I was stunned and felt myself fall into an awkward silence.

'Are you alright, Mr Compton?'

'Err, yes, thank you. Obvious question, who is it?'

'This is why I wanted to speak you personally. He's known as Paul Cassar.'

'Paul Cassar, the Maltese government agent who disappeared off the face of the earth?'

'Yes.'

'So where's he been?'

'I'm afraid to say, right under our noses, moving amongst us all the time and even pretending to help us with our enquiries.'

'Fucking hell, pardon my French, are you looking for anyone else?'

'No.'

'So how did you get him?'

'We had to get some international help. Malta's policing resources do not enable us to investigate murder on such a scale. We drafted in Europol who helped us with the murder investigation itself. The FBI provided a team of forensic and IT experts who told us how the car bomb was made and how it was detonated.'

'How?'

'That's all above my head, I'm afraid, but I can tell you a laptop was seized from the suspect's address. Do you remember your friend, Mrs Camilleri, was concerned there was an online hate campaign against her?'

'Yes, she had a list of around 250 names of people who had been posting threats on her blog and Twitter and elsewhere.'

'What then, my friend, if I told you all those names were invented by and belonged to just one person?'

'Excuse me?'

'This is how we eventually nailed our suspect. Our FBI colleagues traced his internet activities back to the same IP address and to the various accounts he had been logging into and then were able to link it back to his Wi-Fi account. I believe you know how it works. Apparently, unravelling it all is quite a simple process but complicated by too much red tape. FBI officers were somehow able to cut through all that and give us a name, that of Paul Cassar.'

'How come he has been able to lie low for so long?'

'Again, this is why I wanted to speak you in person. Paul Cassar is only an alias.'

'Alias?'

'Yes, you know he worked for the Government of Malta.'

'Yes, I discovered that whilst making my own enquiries.'

'I thought you did. I have to tell you my friend that his real name is Peter Camilleri.'

'What, Suzanne's husband?'

'Yes, my friend. We now have all the evidence.'

'I don't believe it. But why would he want to kill her?'

'He knew she was close to uncovering the so-called corruption that took place concerning the disappearance and subsequent relocation of our mutual acquaintance, Fifi Paganini.'

'Fiona Meredith?'

'Yes. Mrs Camilleri had found out a man called Paul Cassar was involved in an alleged government conspiracy to conceal Miss Meredith's identity and place her in a mafia stronghold here in Gozo, following her kidnap in Venice all those years ago. It never occurred to her that in reality, she was hunting down her own husband. I think she was killed because she was very close to stumbling on all the facts and he knew that.'

'Fucking hell, excuse me, I can't get my head around this.'

'My fault, I wasn't sure how you would react to this news, it's something I wasn't expecting myself, well not until Reno Stavola was killed.'

'Is there a connection?'

'Not exactly, but he was also in possession of the same information, he'd obviously known all along because of his involvement at the outset.'

'Did Fifi have anything to do with his death?'

'Potentially, she could have, but I know she recently told you herself, the son of one of his accomplices who Stavola shot dead whilst holding Miss Meredith after her kidnap, came knocking. He's obviously a grown man now and has become a senior member of the feared Cosa Nostra family based in Sampieri, Sicily. We have reasonable belief he ordered and possibly took part in Stavola's killing. I think it's just a coincidence that it happened during our investigation into Mrs Camilleri's murder.'

'Have you arrested him?'

'No. He's back in Sicily now, out of my jurisdiction, and he can stay there so far as I'm concerned.'

After about thirty minutes we took a break from the conversation and both went out into the square to allow Inspector Azzopardi to have a smoke. I was just happy for some fresh air whilst I tried to get my head around everything and put it all into perspective. A small crowd had gathered outside and was starting to ask questions. Azzopardi was quite clever, telling them to watch the evening news bulletins on television.

'A formal statement will be made from Valletta by my superiors later this afternoon,' he said.

When we got back into the police office the conversation continued...

'How did the car bomb work?' I asked.

'Like I told you, I don't know. Not the technicalities of it anyway. What I do know is the FBI officers eventually discovered it was detonated from Peter Camilleri's own cell phone, they traced the moment of detonation back to a sim card. His number was traced from a signal picked up by a mobile network phone mast. It triggered a component which was attached to a circuit board connected to the bomb. The bomb was packed with nails and TNT which he had carefully placed under the driver's side of his wife's car. They later found a note hidden in an encrypted file on his laptop which set out the timings of her daily trip down to Ramla Bay. Mr Camilleri had calculated that her journey time from Imnarja Street down to the bay took just thirteen minutes. By deduction, if he activated the sim card nine minutes after she left the house, she would be safely away from any built up areas and halfway down the hill to Ramla. Of course, as you know, this was where the bomb exploded.'

'Do you think he made the bomb himself?'

'Yes. Remember, he's a former government agent. He would have access to bomb-making instructions and was probably once trained on how to assemble one. He would have almost certainly been trained on how to diffuse a bomb. Don't forget, if you wanted to make a bomb to kill someone, instructions are readily available on the internet if you know where to look.'

'Do you think it's the same kind of bomb which has been used to kill other people in Malta before?'

'Yes. My personal view is that I think it was a copycat style killing. The bomb, I've been told, consisted of all the same components as the one used to kill another journalist, Valerie Farrugia, in Malta in 2017. He, I think, has to a certain extent, mimicked that crime.'

'Bloody hell. I still can't believe all this.'

'Nor can I, my friend. Nor can I.'

'I understand the Government of Malta and the UK government as well as the mafia were all involved at the outset in the plot which led to the kidnap of Fiona Meredith and ultimately, Suzanne's murder. What do you think will happen there?'

'In my experience nothing will happen. We have just arrested Peter Camilleri, a former government agent. He was quickly taken off our hands by Europol, probably on the orders of our government. Your

British Prime Minister will deny any wrongdoing as usual and will almost certainly blame the press for stoking up hysteria. The mafia members, who we now know were involved, as far as I'm aware, are all dead.'

'So what now?'

'Watch the television, my friend, it'll all be on the news. My work is done.'

'And what about Suzanne's two children?'

'We haven't seen the boy. There's been no recent contact. The girl, Lorca, is being looked after by friends. She was in the house when her father was arrested this morning.'

'What will happen with Fiona Meredith?'

'What about her? She's a free woman, she has done nothing wrong. Despite recent events, her presence here in Gozo has helped us keep the island relatively safe and free of crime for the last twenty years or so. She was able to tame the Buttiġieġs and at the same time keep any mafia activities on the island to a minimum. My predecessors in the police couldn't do that and even I've found it difficult. Let sleeping dogs lie, I say. Let them sleep. Remember, Miss Meredith, as you call her, is the original victim in all this. Now go, my friend, go, and good luck. I have given you information other reporters won't have, so use it wisely and please make sure you quote anything I've told you, accurately.'

'Thanks, I will.'

When I left the police station, I went to the nearby Rabokk pizzeria which was chock-a-block with locals. It seemed unusual but then I realised word had been getting around there had been an arrest in connection with Suzanne's murder. I remembered what Azzopardi had said, so I still needed to keep schtum. There seemed to be a lot of speculation.

'Who do you think it is?' I heard one person ask another.

'I don't know but I saw Lorca being led away by a policewoman this morning. The poor girl was in tears,' was the reply.

I decided to drink up quickly and make my way back down to the hotel. When I arrived Nina was just finishing her shift.

'Come on, let's go for a walk,' she said reaching out to grab my hand.

'So what did Inspector Azzopardi want you for?'

'They've arrested a man for Suzanne's murder. He's expected to be formerly charged this afternoon. Azzopardi tipped me off there was going to be a special press release on television later on the evening bulletin.'

'Did he tell you who it was?'

'Yes, but I have promised Azzopardi I won't say anything until I know a formal charge against the suspect is made. I think it's just in case something goes wrong at the last minute.'

'So you're not even going to tell me. Don't you trust me?'

'Of course I do. Look, why don't we watch the news together later, that'll solve the issue and help me keep my word to Azzopardi.'

'God, you're so typically English, stiff upper lip and all that.'

'Sorry, I thought I was completely the opposite.'

'Well you're not.'

'Thanks.'

After we had spent a couple of hours chatting outside Horatio's we walked back up to the hotel and sat by the television in the lounge area of the bar to watch the latest news.

'Isn't that Peter Camilleri?'

'Yes.'

'Poor man, I can't imagine how he must be feeling now they've got someone for his wife's murder.'

'Keep listening.'

Eventually a headline came up: 'Suspect Charged over Journalist Car Bomb Killing.'

'Who is it then?'

'Listen?'

It seemed to take an age until the newsreader eventually said who it was.

'Peter Camilleri,' whispered Nina.

'Yes.'

'Oh my God... What an evil bastard. I don't believe it!'

'Nor did I, but that's what Azzopardi wanted to tell me. He knew I was friends with Suzanne. Until today I thought I was friends with Peter as well. Not anymore, you're right, he is an evil bastard. I so wish Malta had the death penalty.'

'I don't. Anyway, I think I can understand why you're feeling so bitter.'

'Bitter is an understatement. To be quite honest, I'm very fucking angry.'

'So what's happening now? Are you going to write your story?'

'Everything's already on the news so anything I write is not going to be an exclusive anymore.'

'You mean a scoop.'

'Yes. Azzopardi though has given me some inside information which other reporters won't have. I've decided that I might write my story as a feature article, probably for the *Telegraph's* Sunday supplement. If Terry Mancini agrees, it should sit there quite nicely.'

'Terry Mancini?'

'He's the owner of the paper.'

'Oh, okay. Do you think he'll publish it?'

'To be honest, I'm not sure. I haven't even met him yet. The Maltese press is screaming out for stories and Mancini would be foolish to turn it down. Suzanne's murder is hot news. I also promised to show it to Fifi when it's finished but time is running out and I probably won't be able to complete it until after I'm back in England. She wants to read it before anything is published.'

'So how will she see it?'

'I'll send her a draft as an email attachment.'

'Have you got a headline for it yet?'

'Yes.'

'What?'

'It'll probably be something like, Journalist Murdered by Her Invisible Nemesis.'

'Wow, how did you come by that?'

'Suzanne once described her tormentor as an invisible nemesis. I thought it could be Paul Cassar but he was untraceable. In the end it turned out I was right, Peter Camilleri was Paul Cassar. I was so close all the time without knowing it. To be honest, that's eating into me. I really can't believe I didn't see it.'

'That's crazy.'

'Yes, but like I said, that's the way it's turned out.'

'Okay, so now, changing the subject completely... What about us?'

'Us?'

'Yes, you and me!'

'Ah. I've been thinking about that.'

'Thinking what?'

'Maybe you could come to England for a holiday, stay at mine perhaps.'

'Not good enough.'

'What do you mean?'

'I want more. I want you all the time, forever.'

'I don't think that's possible. You live here and I live in England.'

'Well, I also have some news. Rita and I are moving to England in a few weeks' time. Fifi, has arranged it.'

'You mean your stepmother,' I joked.

'Oh yes, well, she phoned me last night. She told me she has inherited the family mansion from her parents many years ago. It's near Basingstoke. The house has always been kept a secret. The main building has been let out but there is an annexe. Fifi... I mean, my new mum, wants me and Rita to start a new life. We're going to live there, at least for a while, so you see, you're not going to get rid of me that easily.'

'So did Fifi's parents know she was being held in Gozo and was still alive all this time?'

'No, never, they knew nothing but someone in the UK government did and for some reason they and the security services ensured via a firm of lawyers the house stayed within the family. It must have been very awkward for the UK government because they had originally planned to have Fifi, I mean my stepmother killed.'

'Blimey.'

'And that means I can now be with you in England. You can come and live with us if you want!'

'Err, that is good news, well, in a way, but why would you want a long-term relationship with me anyway?'

'I don't know. You're old and your cologne always reminds me of wet grass, you also drink too much. For some unexplainable reason I've fallen in love with you and I think you love me too, am I right?'

'Perhaps.'

'Perhaps? What do you mean perhaps?'

'Look, everything is happening so fast. We've only known each other for a few short weeks. Yes, I like you a lot but there are things to consider such as our age difference for a start. What will you do for work? Can I continue as a journalist? Should I move out of my flat? Rita will also be with us.'

'Yes, you're right, things have been moving quite quickly, but Rita and I have discussed all this. We're still getting used to the fact we're actually sisters, and that in itself feels quite strange by the way.'

'I bet it does.'

'Fifi explained that all she wants now is to make amends and for us both to be happy. Rita has always wanted to run a bistro in England and I can help her.'

'But you don't have to move to England just to be happy.'

'No, we don't but it's a new opportunity. We can always come back here to Malta if it doesn't work out.'

'It sounds like Fifi has already made your mind up for you.'

'In a way she has.'

Nina stood up, walked a few steps and then came back over to where I was still sitting. She glared at me for a second and then pressed herself down firmly in my lap and then kissed me on the forehead.

'Just one more thing, Jack.'

'What?'

'Let go of Suzanne.'

'I'm sorry, that's easier said than done.'

'No, it's not. I can feel your pain. You need to untie that knot of grief you have inside you. Be free. Suzanne would not want you to be hurting like this.'

'But you didn't know her.'

'I'm a woman, Jack. Everything you've told me about her says that she was a good person. She would almost certainly want you to get over her and carry on with your life and be happy.'

'You're probably right.'

'I know I'm right. Look, whatever they are, you will always have the memories. I've already learnt in life that memories are all part of the healing process. Remember what I've told you before. Celebrate her life. Don't mourn it, otherwise it will just eat into you forever.'

Everything Nina was saying was beginning to make sense and I couldn't help but look straight into her eyes. There was a sparkle and a look I had never seen in a woman before.

'You're beautiful,' I said.

'I know,' she joked.

We both laughed and hugged. Perhaps I did feel that I might be in love but I wasn't quite ready to tell her yet. There was still one thing I had to do...

40

...Nina was right. I somehow needed to find some kind of closure. My feelings for Suzanne were still getting in the way. I needed to walk where she once walked. Somehow feel her spirit. Somehow find that perfect moment when the sun breaks cloud and the angels come, one last moment, to bring it on myself to finally accept the inevitable and kiss her ghost goodbye.

ABOUT THE AUTHOR

Born in Farnham, Surrey in 1956, Mal Foster produced his successful debut novel 'The Asylum Soul' in 2015. His second book, 'Fly Back and Purify,' a paranormal drama was published in 2017. Also an established poet, his work has appeared worldwide in a number of anthologies, newspapers, magazines and across the internet. A former local journalist, he is an avid fan of progressive rock music but turns to the late Canadian singer/songwriter and poet Leonard Cohen when pressed about who and what inspires him.